WILDLIFE

Joe Stretch was born in 1982 and brought up in Lancashire. He moved to Manchester at the age of 18 to study politics at Manchester University. His band, Performance, in which he is the lead singer and lyricist, released their debut album in 2007. His first novel, *Friction*, was published in 2008.

ALSO BY JOE STRETCH

Friction

JOE STRETCH

Wildlife

VINTAGE BOOKS
London

Published by Vintage 2009

2 4 6 8 10 9 7 5 3 1

First published in Great Britain in 2009 by
Vintage

Random House, 20 Vauxhall Bridge Road,
London SW1V 2SA

www.vintage-books.co.uk

Addresses for companies within The Random House Group Limited
can be found at: www.randomhouse.co.uk/offices.htm

The Random House Group Limited Reg. No. 954009

A CIP catalogue record for this book
is available from the British Library

ISBN 9780099532071

The Random House Group Limited supports The Forest Stewardship
Council (FSC), the leading international forest certification organisation.
All our titles that are printed on Greenpeace approved FSC certified paper
carry the FSC logo. Our paper procurement policy can be found at
http://www.rbooks.co.uk/environment

Printed in the UK by CPI Bookmarque, Croydon, CR0 4TD

For Pia

'We are not free. And the sky can still fall on our heads.'
Antonin Artaud, *The Theatre and its Double*

THE COMPUTER WAS sleeping. Liv Moberg only had to disturb the mouse to wake it and bring its screen to life. She bit her bottom lip and placed her fingers on the keys.

She began by watching videos because she liked to keep up to date with the world of entertainment. But when Liv began to watch videos online like this, watching one would invariably lead to her watching another and she would soon find herself whiling away two or three hours.

Because the videos came constantly. Events came quickly. It was like watching blood run from a cut: wars, erections, shocking interviews, embarrassing accidents – all recorded with shaking hands and camera phones by psychos, soldiers, funny fuckers, brimming tosspots. It often happened that Liv Moberg, once she started to watch these things, couldn't tear her eyes away.

And even when she had told herself sternly that she had been at the computer for long enough, she would still find one or two other things to do. She would check her emails.

She would tinker a little with her profile on whichever social networking site she was enjoying at the time. There were always things that needed her attention.

On this occasion, Liv decided she would edit her 'Interests'. She decided it was high time that she listed the things that genuinely interested her on her online profile. This way the world would know for certain what Liv Moberg liked and there would be no embarrassing confusion. She held her breath and stared at the ceiling in thought. And just a few minutes later she walked away from the computer with a satisfied spring in her step. Under 'Interests' she had listed three things. She listed: Fun, Sex and Events.

I AM A young man and I know my bollocks off by heart. The past is in my head and it's moulding like a slice of birthday cake, and although I'm not desperate to remember, I can. I can remember everything and can even write it down.

I remember people were amazed by each other. They met. They were astonished. They said, dear me, you look incredible, fuck me, you *are* fantastic, you've got genuine guts and your soul's elastic. You are. Suddenly. Speaking as a human. It's unreal to finally meet you.

I remember there was talking. More than anything else, people talked about the Wild World. You couldn't go down the shops or flush a toilet without being reminded that something called the Wild World was coming soon. Are you ready to get excited? Apparently we were. We always are. We start talking. The Wild World this. The Wild World that. No more piss and hardly any crap. No more struggle or huge disappointment. None of that! The idea of the Wild World was everywhere. It stretched above us like a new sky.

You should know, I'm calm. It makes me nervous I'm so

3

calm. You could tell me that aliens are tentacle-fucking in the White House and I would only turn my head to one side and breathe. I would only think of home, of birds and fishes, of rain, of love. The Wild World meant nothing to me. I like wildlife and that's what's so sad.

It would be quicker to just spew it all out like this, in one go. I could just hack it all up over your shoes. But you would only sip from some drink and hiss 'As if' and that would piss me off, make me groan, make me rattle like the skeleton of my broken year. What am I saying?

I'm saying this: I could spit this story at your feet. But I won't. Because I don't. I can't. Because you and me, we need, let me whisper it: *Fun*. And, of course, the truth is simple. I see that now. The truth is desperate and just because girls like Liv Moberg love fun and love sex and love events, it doesn't mean life's going to be one long goal celebration. It might just be a bit of a joke.

Knock knock.

Scratch.

The living are haunting the living.

Knock knock.

Scratch.

I

The Wild World

'A Wild World will come. And with it the end of our days. Finally, armed with our future, a Dickhead will rise.'

Extract from a press release issued by
Wild World UK

1

JOE ASPEN SPENT New Year's Eve staring into his toilet. Rather than going out and going absolutely mental, Joe just stared into his toilet for hours and then listened as, around midnight, his heart croaked like a Coke can.

It's New Year's Day and Joe's lying in bed. New Year's Day arrives looking weatherless. Fresh light and air so still you'd have to breathe to know it's there.

On the chest of drawers above the bed two stuffed puffins are kissing each other. I could fall in love with a puffin, thinks Joe, opening his eyes. I could be a puffin and peck the beak of my puffin lover. I could build a nest in a cliff. I could do all that so easily.

Above the puffins, hanging on the wall, is a calendar. It has hung here since Christmas Day, waiting patiently for the new year to begin. January is a blank grid, untouched by pencil or pen. Above January is a photograph of a leopard, its body wound and tightened, ready to pounce down on its prey.

Joe Aspen gets out of bed and shuffles with socked feet

in the direction of the window. It's there, he thinks, peering out. The world, he means. Or, more precisely, Rusholme, Manchester, the junction where Platt Lane meets Wilmslow Road. The traffic lights flick through their cycle for their own amusement, in the absence of cars. Both roads are New Year's Day dead. Colourful lights changing in a cold light. Joe turns away from the window because it is time to piss in the sink.

Joe's been pissing in his sink for a week. There is already a very yellow stain around the plughole. The reason for pissing in the sink is simple. A week ago Joe's girlfriend left him to work in London. She wanted a better life. Wanted to pursue a career in events management and get away from Joe. She took everything with her apart from the wildlife calendar and a small crumb of shit which she left clinging to the grey porcelain of Joe's toilet. Joe knows, like all men know, that were he to piss in his toilet he would be compelled by God to piss this morsel of shit away. He would, as a man, simply have to fire it off the porcelain with a forceful jet of urine. This can't happen. This piece of shit is all he has left of the girl he adored.

Taking a crap is out of the question, too, because of the inevitable flushing. The little crumb would never survive. It must be given enough time to dry and grow hard, to tighten its grip on the toilet bowl. It's true that the day she left, Christmas Day, the little crumb had survived two flushes. But Joe knew that it wouldn't survive many more. It would eventually disappear, leaving, at best, a stain. It was as he ate a nut cutlet alone on Boxing Day that Joe decided that, from now on, he'd have to do his poos publicly.

After pissing, Joe runs both taps simultaneously. He rinses his fingers and stares at his reflection in the mirror.

He has made one New Year's resolution: to stop dyeing his hair black. He's been dyeing his hair black throughout the five years he has spent in Manchester. At the age of twenty-four, he feels it's time to stop. New year. New ideas. No more dyeing.

Joe leans in towards the mirror and pulls two clumps of hair apart to get a close look at his roots. So far nothing. Still black. He can't actually remember what his natural colour is but he suspects it is a mousy brown.

Joe's girlfriend came from the Faroe Islands and was called Life. Her real name was Liv, pronounced *Looeeve*. Only no one in England pronounced it like that and she disliked the imperative bluntness of Liv. She decided to translate her name. In Faroese, Liv means Life. Not surprisingly, everyone enjoyed the opportunity to call a beautiful young girl Life. Though some called her Lie for short.

Joe returns to his bedroom to where the puffins are still kissing. I want to be a puffin, thinks Joe, instead of a human. They eat puffins in the Faroe Islands. Joe has seen it for himself. He'd visited the previous Christmas and Life's grandmother had slaughtered seventeen birds for a feast.

The beauty of Life cannot be done justice. She is five foot ten, has golden hair and large human breasts. Her face is slightly generic, as if, with its blue eyes and full red lips, Life is staking a claim to possessing the definitive female face, the only face that matters. Her perfection goes on. In millions of years, metal robots will discover the remains of Life's backside and ejaculate instantly into their silk underpants because Life is the next generation, the next type of human. Life is so successful socially that she demands a new form of reality, where it rains vodka and coke and where wankers are punctured at birth. Life is funny.

For such a beautiful girl, she's caring. She's a shit cook. She can take her booze. She bleeds honour. Life likes being spanked on her naked arse. She makes this fun and liberating. Life likes sex in public places. Her favourite film director is Nicolas Roeg and, in truth, Joe Aspen was lucky to have ever known her.

Christmas Day was dead to begin with. Joe woke up with his face held against Life's arse. This was normal. He did this every single night. He would stir at some blue-lit hour to discover that Life had disentangled her body from his. Respecting her decision but also desperate to feel her, Joe would sneak beneath the covers to where the air groaned with the smell of sweat and yet tingled too with the scent of vagina and cock. Joe would hold his face against Life's buttocks and smile himself back to sleep.

But on Christmas morning something was wrong with Life's arse. It's hard to say what exactly, but something was certainly different. It was almost, Joe had thought, it was almost as if her arse contained emotions and that these emotions were sour towards him. As he kissed Life's arse in the dark, kissed it cos he loves her, he had sensed red anger burning in each cheek.

Joe pulled himself out from under the duvet and Life turned to look at him, her warm face framed by her golden hair.

'What?' said Joe.

'What?' said Life.

A bad start. Life's eyes contained no temperature. Bloodless. You could see the doubts of her brain.

'Sleep well?' Joe asked.

No reply. The traditional morning lovemake in the spoon

position was already out of the question. Life just lay there until:

'I've been thinking,' she said.

It is hell to meet a person who's been thinking. Waking up next to a person who's been thinking is the worst. What they mean by 'been thinking' is simply that they've realised they're in the shit. In the shit, lifewise. Life is crap. You shouldn't have to have been thinking to figure this out. All this *been thinking* bullshit has been pissing about with people's lives for ages. I've been thinking – we should kill all the Jews, bomb all the cities, fuck with the countries. I've been thinking – we should start a band. I've been thinking – we should try for a baby, get a better car, do it up the arse. I've been thinking – we're drifting apart.

'What have you been thinking about?'

'Oh, you know,' said Life, sitting up on one elbow with a hand on her cheek. 'I've just been thinking about the Wild World and everything. What I'll do.'

Just been thinking is the worst. You're fucked if someone's *just* been thinking.

'I've just been thinking about your job,' Life said. 'Working in a theatre isn't going to get you anywhere, is it? And I've been thinking that the Wild World is really going to need well-managed events.'

Life, by the way, has almost completely lost her accent. The Scandinavians are good at this. Shit hot at English.

'What are you saying?' said Joe, knowing that since Life had *been thinking* it was his job to ask, *What are you saying?*

'I don't know what I'm saying,' replied Life.

Of course she did. Joe knew it. Life knew it. Yes you do, thought Joe, turning over in bed and staring at the ceiling. You're saying that you've realised and you're saying that

11

the sex has gone to shit. The struck match of love has become twisted, scrawny and black. You're saying that you've noticed. Take no notice. You've noticed that I've been clinging to your arse every night for a year. You're saying that at twenty-four, I work a poorly paid job and that I've lost the beauty contest. You're saying that it's over.

'I'm moving to London,' said Life. 'I've been offered work with the Wild World.'

'What?'

'Helping with the launch. I interviewed. They said I was great fun.'

'But, what about Manchester? Can't you help out with the launch here? I mean, can't you . . . What about Manchester?'

Joe watched from the bed as Life prepared to leave. She took her suitcase from the top of the wardrobe and began filling it with her clothes. Leaving on Jesus' birthday was mean. Mean on Jesus, I mean. But all statistics showed that Joe and Life weren't the only ones breaking up. Everyone was at it. Rejection got purchased early in November and sat wrapped under the tree until Christmas. Jesus was a tit for getting the whole Christmas thing going. Christmas gives people just enough space and just enough time to realise that they are completely disappointed. Capitalism keeps us busy while religion makes us see. No one wants to see. But once a year, at Christmas, we do see. Our eyes are allowed to focus. We choose to separate.

'I love you so much,' Joe had said, as Life packed at speed. 'Lie, please, I love you so much.'

They'd met two years ago at the Royal Exchange theatre in town. The play was *The Seagull*. Joe had approached Life at the bar and told her that he was Constantin. A beautiful boy of ideals. A brain. A hero. A hope. They'd got together. They'd been happy. Life stuffed a fistful of knickers into her suitcase.

'I'll call you. Don't take this too hard, Joe. I promise I'll call you soon.'

Life spent twenty minutes in the bathroom before finally coming to say goodbye. Joe had heard two flushes. What an insensitive shit to take, he had thought, frozen alone in the warm Christmas bed.

'You're special to me, Joe,' said Life, from the doorway. 'But . . . you know it's all about the Wild World. You do.'

Joe nodded. Glass shattered inside him. He covered his nose and mouth with his hands as Life left the room. His eyes were so wide. The door slammed. He cried.

He found the crumb in the toilet an hour or so after she left. The only piece of crap that Life had left behind. He considered eating it. Then decided that it had to be preserved and lowered both seats.

Joe will return to work tomorrow. Back to the theatre. The pop star Asa Gunn is starring in Corneille's *The Illusion* and full rehearsals begin in the morning. Returning to work will be tough. Normal life will lick him with its warm, rough tongue, and Joe will want to scream.

2

AS A TEENAGER, Anka Kudolski looked set to lead a brilliant life. She was named in the *Sunday Times* 'New Millennium Talent' feature at the age of just fifteen. There was a picture of her, stern-faced, wearing a beret and Doc Martens boots with a paintbrush in her hand. To the question, What would you like to be?, Anka answered, somewhat precociously, A poet, a playwright, an artist. I want to live a brilliant life.

At the age of eighteen Anka got a place at Goldsmiths College to study Fine Art and Philosophy. She cut a cool figure in south-east London. She wore shades in the studio and was a virtuoso smoker (Lucky Strike). She taped long alcohol-fuelled rants about the misery of contemporary art and left unmarked cassette copies around the bars and on the doorsteps of New Cross. Anka Kudolski was known. Known for her quick brain, bleached-blonde hair and impeccable half-German genes. She was on her way. She was pointed at in bars throwing tequila down her neck or swinging round lamp posts late at night screaming Talking Heads lyrics at parked cars. But what is youth and what can we say about it? Its drum roll is tribal. There is a solitary hit on a snare and you take your deepest breath. Then what?

Two years ago Anka Kudolski went to take a laxative-induced shit on her family toilet and fell through the wooden seat and got stuck. She was too thin. She couldn't get out. Too weak. As she sat there, completely trapped, pelvis wedged, waiting for her parents to return home from work, she decided it was time to have herself sectioned. This was a good idea. Two months of monitored eating in an Ealing clinic got her weight up dramatically and she never fell down a toilet again.

A psychiatrist told Anka that her anorexia was underpinned by manic depression and by a desire for control. Had she considered getting a job? Building a routine? She hadn't, but she could see the sense in it. Anka finds little comfort in the activity of shopping. It's too anarchic, she feels. There's too much choice which, for Anka, means indecision, self-doubt, panic, a loss of control and then weeks of living on mineral water and one Jacobs Cracker a day. Anka is twenty-two now. She moved from London to Manchester in January '05 and began applying for as many jobs as the week would allow. She works at Selfridges, selling designer bags. She works as a barmaid at the Press Club, an all-night celebrity dive on Deansgate. She's also the presenter of *QUIZ TV* on the Urbis-based TV station, Channel MANC. She's not sure what any of these jobs have got to do with the Wild World.

Anka leaves Selfridges via the staff exit on Corporation Street. She turns left.

Anka does enjoy selling. Shopping is like shitting; it feels too normal, but selling is much more fun. Anka particularly enjoys selling the designer bags at Selfridges. She likes the laughable designs and she gets to meet a gone-off bunch of leather-loving piss-drinkers.

It's a short walk across Exchange Square to the Urbis building. On arriving, Anka eats a gratin of mussels with melted Camembert and foaming hollandaise. She drinks a bottle of Indian beer. She's downing the dregs as she enters the Channel MANC studio and approaches her producer, a ginger-faced boy called Ben.

'Which one was it today?'

'Flogging bags,' says Anka, taking a sheet of instructions from him.

'You eaten?'

The studio is basic. Two cameras and a cheap set designed to mimic what might best be described as a boudoir. There is a bed draped in imitation velvet which Anka often lies on, tits puffed out, imploring people to phone in and answer questions. Behind the bed is a false wooden wall painted gold.

'Well, there's nothing new,' says Ben, pointing out to Anka the usual spots marked with red tape where she is permitted to stand. 'But please, babe, do your best. We have to triple the amount of calls. Yeah?'

Ben is a boy that shouldn't say 'babe'.

The background music for the show is already playing. It contains atmospheric synth strings and a foreboding bass line. The bass line goes dum dum din dum, dum dum din dum. Anka and the young crew find its incessant promise of disaster very annoying. It's the first thing they switch off at the end of the show.

'We're all going to Room for dinner after if you fancy it,' says Ben.

'Room?' Anka replies, raising and bending the pitch of her voice. 'Very Wild World. I can't make it.'

Ben nods and turns from where Anka has begun to perform her pre-show breathing exercises to where the two cameramen are awaiting his instruction. Anka can't be certain because she's breathing so loudly, but she thinks that Ben whispers, 'Keep the cameras off those limbs. Tits and face, right, tits and face.' Anka's about to ask Ben how he can be so rude when he spins unexpectedly and addresses her abruptly through a smile.

'Anka, unbutton, we need a tit shadow.'

'Right,' she replies, looking down at one of her arms, assuring herself that it is coated in flesh, as limbs should be, yes, we humans should have flesh. Satisfied, she releases two of her shirt's buttons so the white rim of her bra becomes visible. So simple, she thinks, the channel-hoppers will see this bra. They will. They will see the shadow cast by my pushed tits and they'll reach for the phone.

'Try not to speak too much,' says Ben, putting Anka into position. 'Just stare. Open your eyes wide. We have to get them calling!'

When Anka got this job she was required to speak a great deal. It was her pretty face and her ability to speak in sentences that made her such a strong candidate.

'OK. On in ten, everybody,' shouts Ben, retreating out of shot and placing a hand on the shoulder of the principal cameraman.

But *QUIZ TV* is changing. The public has become wise to the format. They've been fucked over too many times. People watch it for the funny guys and the fit girls but don't bother calling any more. There are too many horror stories of people going bankrupt because they couldn't stop calling.

Hundreds of times a night. Quid a pop. Pile of shit. TV's dead.

Anka corrects her straight blonde fringe with her fingers and stares down at the first question on the card of instructions. Gold lights illuminate the scarlet boudoir. 'Five,' shouts Ben. Anka stares into the camera. The cameraman zooms in on her pretty face, her blue eyes, her happy tit shadow and her red cheeks, not knowing that two years ago this face was only bone and the flesh that cared to remain was grey. The clock on the studio wall says ten. 'Action!'

'Good evening!' Anka explodes with enthusiasm. 'I am Anka. Anka as in wanker. Welcome to *QUIZ TV*!'

She'd used this line at her audition and it quickly became her catchphrase. Anka points at the thin air beneath her tit shadow, saying, 'This is the number you need. This is the number you're going to dial. Isn't it, guys?'

QUIZ TV has been getting more and more forceful as the number of callers falls. Anka stares into the camera with a look of contempt. She pictures the late-night losers slumped on their sofas, staring into her top, into her pretend eyes, hands round cans or hands round cocks. She purposefully eyes them with disdain. To make the pretty girl speak, you have to make her happy, you have to make the call.

'Tonight's question is simple,' she says, climbing onto the bed and appearing to relax amid the cushions. 'What beats beyond your ribs?'

She turns away as if bored by the camera.

'The question is easy: what beats beyond your ribs?' she yawns.

Two work-experience girls are hunched over the telephone switchboard, waiting for red lights. 'What beats?' says Anka, staring down the camera with a sudden and slightly evil enthusiasm. 'Come on. For five thousand pounds. What beats beyond your ribs?'

Time passes.

'I'm getting very bored here.'

Anka Kudolski stares sternly into the camera. Shit shows like this are one of TV's final attempts to get cash. Advertising revenue is declining rapidly. The talent/reality shows like *The X Factor*, *Celebrities on Ice*, *Best Twat*, they're good because people pay to vote for their hero or their villain. But they're more expensive to produce than shows like *QUIZ TV*. The profit margins aren't as easy to realise. Anka Kudolski stares sternly into the camera.

Around Greater Manchester, people sit on creamy leather sofas. They watch as Anka attempts to bleed and intimidate them with silence. Give in. Go on. Reach for your phone. But the people on their sofas know better than to call. They're desperate. They're not desperate. They're desperate.

Behind the camera, Ben whispers into his mouthpiece and Anka presses her finger against her earpiece to listen. 'Anka,' she hears, 'try slagging them off, yeah? Try taking the piss, babe.'

Oh, Ben, never say babe again! Anka smiles and returns her gaze to the camera. She knows what's going on. All her life has led to this moment. The talent. The art. The beret. The *Sunday Times*. The eating. The not eating. The falling down the toilet. Now, look at us, here we are!

'Go on,' whispers Ben. 'Try it.'

'You lot,' Anka mutters, picturing her audience, shaking her head a little, exhaling in pretend disbelief. 'Sometimes I don't know why you bother. I mean, you sit there on that sofa you haven't finished paying for. You tip all that shit into yourself every single day. You're mad. Take a look out of your window, if you've got one. Look at the world, sniff it, walk on it; it's changing. You're going to need the money. You're really going to need the money. What beats beyond your ribs?'

Anka gets a round of thumbs ups from the Channel MANC crew. The two work-experience girls smile at her in genuine awe. Red lights are already beginning to ignite on the switchboard. The wankers will always rise. The economy told me so. Anka suppresses a rush of pride and excitement. She grimaces into the camera.

'The fact of the matter is this: you're a loser. Deep down you've always known. All day every day you are two things. You are noisy and you are boring. Every night you are two things. You are alone and you're a wanker. You really need this money. The Wild World will watch you drown. Tell me what beats beyond your ribs?'

The more TV channels people acquired in the early twenty-first century, the more the large audiences of the past were broken into pieces. To watch TV, particularly late in the evening, particularly complete crap, is to feel inconsolably alone.

'It's a scramble. It's always a scramble,' snaps Anka, exaggerating the vindictive tone in her voice. 'And the fact is you're too fat and too thin to scramble to safety. Your bank account is a joke. You daren't check your balance. Your debts to the old world will make you unviable in the Wild. I hate to be the one to tell you this, but unless you win some money soon, you're fucked.'

'Keep going,' mouths Ben through a smile. The girls by the switchboard are leaning backwards in amazement.

This is the economy getting angry, thinks Anka. I am the old economy getting angry. This is fun, she thinks. I'll remember this when I'm safe and working and eating in the Wild World. I'll tell this story. I'll tell it to people, in the future, when I'm happy.

'Come on,' she shouts, leaping off the end of the bed and skipping close to the camera's lens. 'The one thing you don't have is time. It's New Year's Day. What beats beyond those ribs of yours? How will the debts be paid? Come on. I'll give you a clue: it rhymes with tart. It beats dirt around your tracksuit. Put your cock down. Take that cushion off your fat tits. Call in. I just know you want to keep living. Call in and tell me what beats beyond your ribs? For five grand. What beats beyond your ribs?'

Ben nods to the switchboard girls. They can afford to take a call. The pre-recorded voice of a crazy bastard shouting 'WE HAVE A CALLER!' echoes round the studio. The crew are in hysterics, they've gathered round the camera to watch Anka deal with the caller. Anka's finding it difficult to keep a straight face. She's completely forgotten Ben's remark about her limbs. Her reddening cheeks keep rising into a half-smile.

'Hello, who's there?' she says.

Silence. Then the sound of accelerated breathing. Ben flicks to the next line.

'Wanker!' shrieks Anka.

'WE HAVE A CALLER!' shouts the pre-recorded, craziest of bastards.

'Hello, who's there?' says Anka.

Same again. No answer. Just breath. A slight groan. Vague ecstasy. The line goes dead.

'Wanker!' shouts Anka.

'WE HAVE A CALLER!' shouts the wacky, recorded shithead.

'Hello, who's there?'

A Northern woman: 'You skinny southern slut, why don't you try –' Cut!

'WE HAVE A CALLER!' Zany-brained, dead cunt.

'Hello, who's there?'

The sound of breath being drawn through a very dry throat.

'Do you have an answer?' asks Anka. 'Come on, what beats beyond your ribs? Come on. Quickly. What beats beyond your –'

'Nothing,' interrupts the voice.

'Nothing?' says Anka, smiling.

'Nothing beats there,' says the voice. It is male and panting. It is almost completely breathless.

3

JANUARY 2. JANEK Freeman is sitting in silence in the dining room at Reel World. Reel World is a state-of-the-art recording studio, built by the former Genesis frontman Peter Gabriel on the site of an old watermill in the Wiltshire village of Box. Gabriel saw the point in Wiltshire. He was happy to settle here. 'Seriously,' he told his friends, 'it's actually quite nice.' He's here now, Peter Gabriel, he's staring out of the dining-room window at the lake that lies at the centre of Reel World. Behind him, Janek is pouring himself coffee. The atmosphere is tense.

Janek Freeman has been waiting his entire life for something to matter. Twenty-five years in total. He's numb. Numb from all the waiting. Janek's yet to slip and fall and get soaked from head to toe in reality. Nothing matters, he thinks. So weird that nothing matters! Janek is preoccupied with this idea. He has lived his life with his breath held, waiting to burst and breathe with enthusiasm when something, anything, finally seems important. But this hasn't happened. It's incredible. A quarter of a century on earth and you'd expect something to seem important. But nothing has.

During these twenty-five unimportant years, Janek has been circumcised, schooled and raised in Bristol by his Polish father, a keen Jew, and his mother, a West Country native with very shallow lungs. He was taunted while at secondary school in Bridgewater. The other pupils called his mum 'the breathless willy-wanger'.

What else hasn't mattered? Loads. Janek won a scholarship to study music at Berkeley in California at the age of sixteen. It didn't matter. By the time he returned at the age of twenty he'd become one of the most sought-after session bass players on earth. This didn't matter either. While in America, he'd recorded bass lines for Stevie Wonder, Gwen Stefani, Bruce Springsteen, Snoop Dogg and many others. This seemed very unimportant. He'd even released his own record: 'Twelve Decisions in the Key of Bass'. It had enjoyed critical success, made him a legend in the world of bass guitars and, incredibly, hadn't really mattered at all. Shame, Janek constantly thinks, shame that nothing matters.

Janek's image, which certainly doesn't matter, comprises a jet-black beanie hat that he never takes off. It fits snugly over his curly brown hair, framing his chestnut-coloured eyes and accentuating his strong, handsome, Polish jaw. Apart from his incredible musical talent, this hat accounts for Janek's appeal among America's leading hip-hop artists. It lends him a frisson of unimportant cool and they love him for it; the likes of Snoop and Jay-Z, they pay him for it. He's wearing the beanie now, of course, in the dining room at Reel World. He's looking up at Peter Gabriel and smiling. Janek knows full well that, for Peter, loads of things matter:

world music, entertainment, performance, African instruments, sex, family, Janek's career, music technology and probably much else besides. Janek finds this touching but strange.

Peter is still staring out at the lake. He's watching as a gigantic swan parades around on the small island, hissing at the reeds that grow there. This swan is as much a feature of Reel World as the antique sound desks and the acoustics and reverberations of the live rooms. Peter smiles, remembering how the swan had once hissed at Brian Eno and petrified him, how the swan had chased Kylie Minogue across the patio, into the games room and then pecked at her through the glass door. Peter sighs. He massages the back of his neck with his hand. He's bald nowadays, what hair remains has turned grey. But his skin is still smooth, his eyes attentive. He is trim. Still virile somehow. There is life in him. Outside, beside the lake, the vegetable patch is covered in January frost. Inside the air is cold, scented with coffee.

'Would you like a cup, Peter?' asks Janek.

'No. I don't drink that stuff any more.'

Janek watches as Peter continues to stare at the swan. Peter's lips are quivering a little, as if he's letting out dozens of small inaudible words. Janek places a cigarette into his incidental smile.

'I don't know,' says Gabriel, turning from the window and walking across to the stone carved fireplace. 'Things are changing. I do think that things are changing.'

'There're no bands here at the moment?'

'We've had to let Mary go. The kitchen's closed. Such a shame.'

Peter takes a seat beside Janek. 'It's a shame because they eat terrible food, these young musicians, nothing natural.

They need to be fed. I'm eating the vegetable patch single-handedly.'

Janek lights his fag and drags an ashtray across the table. The cigarette packet tells that 'Smoking Kills'. To Janek these words mean nothing.

'You see,' says Peter, wafting smoke, 'they make the music in their bedrooms nowadays, on their laptops. There's even software that claims to replicate the acoustics of Reel World. And it's a good thing, of course. Technology for all. The creative democracy, it's a marvellous thing. But . . .' Peter sighs; his eyes are once again drawn from the room to where the swan is clambering out of the lake. It beats its enormous wings and shakes the water from its white feathers before marching proudly across the patio. 'Good music,' says Peter, 'and good life for that matter, requires great performances. People need inspiration. They do. *You* need inspiration, Janek. And so . . .' Peter trails off.

'And so here I am?' offers Janek.

'Yes. You've returned.'

'I have.'

'But for adverts,' says Peter, lurching forward in frustration, offering Janek his crooked, gesturing hands. 'I didn't build this place to record advert jingles and I didn't help you so that you could –'

'I'm doing this for the money,' interrupts Janek. 'You know how much these people pay.'

'I do,' says Gabriel, instantly subdued, leaning back in his seat. 'I couldn't believe it when I got the call. The Wild World? I said. No thank you. But when they told me the price I had to reconsider. I had to say yes. Since the kids stay in their bedrooms, money is thin on the ground.'

The two men drift into silence. Janek grinds out his

cigarette and finishes his coffee, confirming as he does so that neither activity matters. Peter Gabriel tries to get lost in thought. He occasionally turns suddenly, prompted by some noise, and stares at the window or the door. He's seen some grand days, Peter has. The video for his 1986 hit, 'Sledgehammer', is commonly regarded as the greatest music video of all time. He did some magnificent stuff onstage with Genesis. He dressed up as a large and very entertaining flower. A sunflower. People laughed at him. Enjoyed him. He performed with his head peeping out of a gigantic yellow cone, too. He actually did that. To entertain people.

'These videos on the Internet,' Peter says suddenly.

'What about them?'

'It's good, isn't it, yes, it's a good thing, everybody getting a chance to make them and see them. And, of course, TV is terrible.'

Peter gets up and peers out of the window, away from the lake towards the car park. 'It's just . . .' he says, straining to see. 'It's just I saw one the other day that was just . . .' He turns to Janek. 'It was just a cat falling off a bookcase over and over again to an electronic beat.'

'OK.'

'That's all it was and I thought, well, I thought, you know . . . it took three days of hard work to shoot the "Sledgehammer" video and, well, you understand. That video. It's very entertaining, isn't it?'

Janek smiles. 'Yes.'

'And this clumsy cat has been watched millions of times by millions of people and I thought . . . well, I thought . . . so much time. Such a waste of time.'

'I imagine "Sledgehammer" gets its fair share of views.'

'Does it?'

'Of course.'

'But time, Janek, you don't realise. Look at me. We're short-lived. What's that?'

The grandfather clock begins to chime. Outside, a car horn sounds. Peter leaps away from the window. Janek can hear a heavy vehicle pulling onto the gravel car park.

'They're here,' says Peter. 'It's been lovely to see you again.'

'You're not staying?'

'No. No, I'm not. I'm going to pick my boy up from school.'

Peter Gabriel is at the door, but he's still looking cautiously towards the window. There are footsteps on the gravel.

'The Wild World has come to Reel World, Janek,' says Gabriel through a regretful smile. And before Janek can reply the one-time superstar has vanished. He can be heard dashing down the main corridor and making quickly for the manor's back door.

'Goodbye,' mutters Janek to himself, lighting another fag.

Moments later the door to the dining room is opening and a brunette in scruffy jeans and an Aerosmith T-shirt is walking towards Janek with a straight face.

'Janek Freeman?'

'Yes.'

'I'm bossing today.' They're shaking hands. 'I'm going to be making sure we get what we want. I'm sure we will. I'm told you can play anything we put in front of you, right?'

'Right,' says Janek, quickly deciding that no amount of cash is worth this. Nothing matters. This is going to be another pointless and day-shaped occasion. One of many in my life. My life that repeats and repeats. My life, where nothing matters, where nothing really means it. He immediately decides that the bossing woman is a delightful bitch with bored eyes, a bored nose and a bored mouth. Barely alive. A tired heart. A flirty but dry cunt. Janek stops listening.

'Oh, you smoke,' the woman is saying. 'Wow, cool, OK.'

Over her shoulder the door opens again and Janek watches as a rather grand-looking girl enters slowly, her back slightly bent, peering into the room with enquiring eyes.

'Come on in,' says the bossbitch. 'Come on in, Lie. Meet Janek.'

The rather grand girl straightens up and approaches Janek with an outstretched hand. Bossbitch watches as the two of them, Janek and this girl, shake hands and swap smiles. 'Wow, cool, OK,' she says. 'Janek, this is Life. Once we've set up we're going to plug you into her brain. Your guitar, I mean. We'll get your guitar plugged into Life's brain. OK?'

'No problem,' says Janek, pulling out a seat for Life and taking one himself.

'Wow,' says Bossbitch, her voice descending on the notes of some predictable major key. 'Wow. Cool. OK.' She leaves the room and seconds later Janek can hear her screaming demands across the car park. He and Life sit in silence for five heavy seconds. Janek pulls his beanie hat down so it's touching his eyebrows.

'You should know,' he says, 'I've been waiting twenty-five years for this.'

'This is my first week.'

'No, I mean . . .' Janek checks himself. He offers Life a cigarette and changes the subject clumsily. 'Your boss seems like a bitch.'

'She is a bitch,' Life replies, pulling a fag from the packet. 'So how long have you been involved with the Wild World?'

'Oh, I'm not,' says Janek, admiring the size of Life's facial features. Do they matter? Her big mouth. Big eyes. Her big beautiful teeth. Do her big tits matter? 'I'm here for the money,' he continues, distracted. 'They just called up, said the Wild World needed bass lines. So here I am. It's as pointless as that.'

'Well, I'd just like to say . . .' Life pauses to exhale the first lungful of smoke into the new year's light. 'I'd just like to say now, that . . .' She pauses again, briefly, before declaring firmly, her voice tinged with Scandinavia, 'I like your hat, Janek. I do. And I hope you feel the same about my brain.'

The two of them make a noise together. A breathy, chuckly, shifting-in-your-seat-type noise. It's nice to hear and nice to see.

Janek's had sex. Naturally, he has. He's done it, had it off, shagged, etc. A girl in California, a talented cellist called Judy. A girl back in Bristol, a Business Studies student. And, much more recently, a group of roadies pressured him into sex with a groupie on the Jay-Z world tour. But he's not prolific. He's not Mr Sex. Sex is submerged along with everything else in the grey, meaningless sauce that strips Janek's existence of all flavour. Nothing matters. Sex doesn't matter. Tits and arse don't matter. Love is nothing. But now, quite suddenly, after twenty-five porcelain years, something is starting to crack, to shatter. Janek stares across at Life Moberg, her huge, glorious, curving body reclined on the seat, cigarette in between her fingers and a smile, weight-less on her lips. And then her head. Her great big head. Her golden hair. Her large things. Janek feels different. He closes his eyes in time to watch as two words are dragged by ropes from his mind's deep and pointless sauce. They drip, these words, they shed the thick grey sludge and slowly reveal themselves. Janek smiles. They are rude words! Romance begins and, yes, two rude words are silently imagined. Both words begin with an 'F'.

4

A ROPE OF semen leaps from Roger's rather pale penis and clings to the television screen.

'Nothing,' he says, panting, the phone gripped between his shoulder and his ear. 'Nothing beats there.'

Roger treats his penis to a few pleasurable touches and then straightens his head, catching his mobile one-handed as it falls. 'Right. OK . . . Right,' says Anka Kudolski on the television screen, oblivious to the stream of semen that's completely obscuring her tit shadow. Roger turns the television off.

Roger Hart is thirty years old. He has an oversized head and curly black hair. He wears thick, square glasses, the type that would give normal people headaches. He lives in what was once Parker's Hotel on the corner of Miller Street and Corporation Street, central Manchester. Nowadays the hotel rooms are small flats, cheap to rent.

Singing one of the songs from the hit musical *Les Misérables*, Roger Hart goes to his kitchen and tears a few sheets of kitchen paper from a roll. Still singing, he dabs the solitary white tear from the tip of his scarlet bell-end and, returning to the living room, sets to work cleaning the semen off the television screen.

As a child, growing up in Lancaster, Roger loved the musicals. His parents often took him to London or Manchester to see a show. *Phantom of the Opera, 42nd Street, Cats*. Those were some of the best nights of his life. His favourite, of course, is *Les Misérables*, because the tunes are great and so is the storyline. Pop music and rock music were lost on the young Roger Hart. They seemed to come from a different world, one too separated from reality where the people invented their emotions in the absence of anything more pressing to do. With the musicals, the songs matter, thinks Roger, referring specifically to when Javert serenades his own suicide and to the tragic death lament of Eponine. Both in *Les Mis*.

But the musicals have gone to shit nowadays, Roger believes. There's no way he'd travel to London to see some half-arsed, shoe-horning spectacle like *Mamma Mia!* or *We Will Rock You*. Would I fuck. Pop's crap. That's it. Roger thinks pop is crap.

His television screen is now clean. The wank, over. He flushes the dirty rag down the toilet.

Besides the bathroom and the kitchen, Roger's flat comprises one square room. There is a single bed in the corner with a neutral grey cover. There is a two-seater blue sofa in front of the television. There are large posters from West End musicals on every wall. But the room is sparse. Every eye is drawn to one busy corner next to the window. The corner where his computer stands on a desk, surrounded by empty bags of crisps, tissue paper scrunched like flowers, large amounts of notepaper covered in Roger's scribble. This room, originally a fairly opulent surrounding for human beings in transit, built in 1905, is now dominated by a computer. Roger takes his seat in front of the screen. He opens a bag of pickled onion Monster Munch and stuffs a handful into his mouth. He grips the mouse with a dirty hand. Click-click. Knock-knock. Scratch.

Allow me. Allow me. I have just had the most cracking wank over this SAD bitch on Channel MANC. Got my mobile out and dialled up. I got thru!! Didn't even bother to answer the piss-easy question. Don't need the money. Hahahahaha. Do really. But I was wanking anyway right in front of my television screen. She's saying all this stuff about how I'm a sad twat and I'm thinking, don't allow that, bitch. She was trying to be massively cool, banging on about the Wild World. I was like, fuck that ho, El Rogerio doesn't give a flying donkey fuck about no wanky Wild World. So I was about to put my niggle juice all over the screen when, fuck you, my phone call connects and I'm thinking, allow that. I can hear her talking to me down the phone, asking me the stupid question. What beats beyond your ribs? I was live on TV and I was just like, fuck you, slut duster, and then I fired niggle juice all over her face on the screen. It was bare good. Allow me.
SUBMIT.

Roger leans back in his swivel chair which stands on four multidirectional wheels. He finishes the remainder of the crisps. He adjusts his glasses, pressing them back against the bridge of his nose. Next to his keyboard, a newspaper is open on the theatre adverts. Who, wonders Roger, would go and see a musical based on the songs of the Bee Gees?

He's aware that, in the past, large consensuses were built around all sorts of things, even politics and Michael Jackson. But a consensus built around a Bee Gees musical? It's strange. He's a cynic at heart, Roger, but even he can't help thinking that such audiences will have little to do with the Wild World. With this in mind, he returns to his blog.

Allow me. Allow me. I've just eaten a bag of pickled onion Monster Munch. And I was thinking about all those SAD fucking twenty-somethings that are like, ooh ooh, I love Monster Munch, remember when we were young and ate Monster Munch after school? Remember the TV programmes that we used to watch? Oooh oooh. *Grange Hill*. Little lost cunts. Don't allow them. Losers. Let me tell you one thing, for sure: When the world ends, it won't be people like me who bring it to an end. Oh no. And it won't be men in suits either. It'll be fancy haircutted cuntsealers in Soft Cell T-shirts, munching ironically on Monster Munch and talking total shit.

   SUBMIT.

Roger is about to tell his readers about a video he's found online featuring Hillary Clinton blowing the fuck out of a snake. But then a pop-up window pops up on the computer screen.

'. . . hiccup . . .'

A hiccup. One of those solitary, painful ones. He closes the pop-up window and logs on to the *Les Misérables* chat forum where his name is, as ever, El Rogerio.

Anyone see tonight's show? he writes.

I did, El Rogerio, comes the reply. *It was the best ever!*

Glad to hear it, writes Roger, closing the forum's window immediately.

A pop-up pops up.

'. . . hiccup . . .'

Allow me. Allow me. All this bullshit about the environment. Switch the lights off. Get twenty-four different dustbins. Wash in your own piss. It's a load of crap. El Rogerio says, let the world end, let the Dickhead come. Let him tell us our future. I'll be the first to ring his Cheddar bell. Fuck the ongoing world.

SUBMIT.

Roger can understand why *Les Misérables* sells out every night of the year. It makes perfect sense. Victor Hugo's novel is a great basis for a musical. Cameron Mackintosh's production is probably the best in modern times. But it still seems bizarre that every night people walk through the streets of London in their best clothes, then file into the Queen's Theatre until not one seat remains. After thinking about it for a second, Roger Hart concludes that mankind is still capable of assembling an audience, getting into groups. Yeah. He guesses they are. Just.

Roger shifts in his seat, scratching at his backside.

Allow me. Allow me. I've just had to scratch my arsehole cos I got a really bad itch. You know when you have to scratch with a finger using the gusset of your pants? Yeah, well, that's what I just did. Then I smelt the finger. Let them have it. I'd rather scratch my arse than go and see that slut Minogue. She's doing six nights at the Arena next

week. She calls it her 'Showgirl Tour'. Right. It's fifty quid a ticket. Total bollocks. She only had cancer a year ago. She should be resting up. Oh, but she's so inspiring! I feel inspired to embark on a career in killing myself. Six nights at the Arena means an audience of ninety thousand losers. El Rogerio says, get the bombs out. Allow me. Allow me.
    SUBMIT.

Roger Hart leans back in his chair. Then he leans forward.

Allow me. Allow me. I've been leaning back in my chair. Anyone going to the Cradle of Filth gig? It's gonna be well bare. The government is shit. When Blair sees a child he's just like, shit, how can I get this tit-toter into bed. He's a dick sucker. Allow it. I could do with another wank. Allow that. Stick it to them.
    SUBMIT.

Roger uses all his strength to push himself away from the computer. He goes flying backwards across the room on the wheels of his chair. He hits the wall opposite his PC with a moderate bang and then bends down towards his CD player. He puts in the *Les Misérables* soundtrack and awaits the opening song. It's called 'Look Down'. It's brilliant. It's sung by the downtrodden, Parisian poor. They sing about the squalor that has bound them together and made revolutionaries of them. When it begins, Roger leaps from his chair and spins around the room with his arms outstretched. He is dancing with real abandon.

After a lonely youth in Lancaster, Roger found himself in the late 1990s. He had thought his computer-programming skills would open up worlds of opportunity to him.

Web design, he thought, is the future. I'll master the art and then I'll master the decades ahead. I'll rake it in, designing websites for major corporations, massive rock bands, charities, pornographers, governments. Only it didn't work out like that. He did OK at first, got a few contracts. 2001. 2002. He even did some programming on the Selfridges UK website. He thought he'd cracked it. The cash was rolling in. But things change. Trust things to change. Nowadays, most thirteen-year-olds can build flashier websites than Roger Hart. He has failed to move with the times. There is a dot bullshit generation behind Roger that is better with computers than he is. He speaks a programming language that is already out of date. By 2004, he'd lost all his major contracts. The cash had stopped rolling. He started going from door to door round Manchester offering to build websites for normal individuals. This proved to be a punt up a dark arse. By this time, social networking sites were taking off. Every individual could follow simple programming instructions and build an all-singing all-dancing web page dedicated to the details of their very own life. The door to the market had been slammed in the face of Roger Hart. It bust his nose. That's when he started blogging.

Roger is still pirouetting round his room to 'Do You Hear the People Sing', track 2. He sweeps by his computer, uploading more words as he does so.

Allow me. I'm dancing to 'Death by Design' by Tit Kill. It's fucking late but time doesn't bother me. I might go out. My plan is simple: drill an eye socket. Allow me.
SUBMIT.

Blogging, like shopping, is essentially like shitting. Except it's a little bit more public. I suppose it's like shitting in a bag and showing it to people who'd rather not see. Everyone is blogging. The problem with everyone blogging is that everyone is too busy to read. Only a few lucky individuals have the pleasure of being read, of having an audience. Roger is becoming one such individual.

The truth is, Roger hasn't left his flat in months. It is his apparent ability to blog constantly that has led to a small army of young fans subscribing to his site. He has developed a reputation for *telling it like it is. Telling it like it is* is a much-loved activity in human civilisations. People love being told it like it is. No nonsense. No flowers. Just reality in all its faded glory.

Roger lives a virtually sleepless life. He will occasionally doze off at the computer. When he wakes he is quick to describe his dreams to his readers. Research has shown him that most of his fans are aged between twelve and nineteen. They are the teenagers. The same dot bollocks generation that made him redundant. It also seems, judging by their clothing, their eye make-up and the comments they leave beneath his blogs, that they are fans of a genre of music called EMO. EMO is shorthand for emotional. They are the emotional teenagers. EMO is commercial metal with soaring, melodic vocals and sentiments ranging from loss to heartbreak. Its followers hide their heads in haircuts and hoods. A fashion followed by other fragments of British society.

'Empty Chairs at Empty Tables' is the one of the saddest songs on the *Les Misérables* soundtrack. It is the lament of a young man who has lost all his friends to the revolutionary siege. The vocal is accompanied only by a piano and the melancholy call of distant violins. Roger Hart slumps down in front of his computer the moment it begins.

> Allow me. Allow me. The people in the streets are behaving like robots. When it rains, their circuitry will get wet and malfunction. I hate the way I always have black dirt under my fingernails. El Rogerio says, let the heavens open.
>   SUBMIT.

A pop-up pops up on the computer screen. AND WITH THE WILD WORLD, A BEAUTIFUL PROPHECY, A BEAUTIFUL FUTURE, A BEAUTIFUL DICKHEAD.

'. . . hiccup . . .'

At times Roger regrets that he never sleeps and never leaves his flat. He regrets that he has made a recording of himself saying, 'Whatever it is, just leave it by the door', which he plays on full blast whenever anyone knocks at his door. The postman with a parcel usually, or the Tesco delivery man with more crisps. His only interactions are with the thousand or so fans that read his continuous blog on the Internet. His audience that grows each day. They are fascinated by his comedy and lurid detailing of life. My life has taken an unlikely turn, he thinks, his fingers hovering above the keyboard. Tell it like it is, Roger. Tell it like it is.

5

JOE ASPEN MISSES the little crumb of shit when he's separated from it. He is walking down John Dalton Street in the direction of the Royal Exchange. His mind is fixed on the area of porcelain to which the evidence of love and Life still clings. He can't wait to get back home to check on it. He ignores the people who pass him on the pavement. They are subdued. They lack the personality and the romance of the crumb.

The sky is an outdated streak of piss. Joe Aspen walks under it. He turns onto Cross Street. Maybe, thinks Joe, in this Wild World we will all get our own private piece of sky to hold above our heads like an umbrella. I can't bear to share this sky with others. I can't bear to share it with Life. I can't believe she's marching about under the same sky as me. It's painful to think about. Let's hope the Wild World has sky-cutting tools. I will take my little section home and be happy with it. I will hold it above my head and get rained on. I will be quiet. I will be a happy puffin.

Joe spots the pop star Asa Gunn the moment he enters the Royal Exchange. He's over by the bar filling a plastic cup with water and then downing the contents quickly. The theatre was once the world's biggest room. Nowadays it is Manchester's most beautiful. Three enormous stained-glass domes cast a blue light into every corner. On days like this, when the sun has got its hat on, the Royal Exchange contains the perfect light for life.

Joe approaches his colleagues who are beginning to congregate around a table near the entrance of the huge room. These people are not Joe's friends. They are the new group who replaced the old group, Joe's group. Joe is the only non-student who works here as an usher. His group, his friends, have all gone off in search of real jobs. Somehow Joe has not.

'Good Christmas? Good New Year?' asks David, a tall, posh, brown-haired drama student with a fancy spoon where his brain should be.

'Not so bad,' says Joe, deciding not to share the story of the bit of shit with these people and wondering whether David realises that he is destined for an upmarket, silk-lined casket and a surprisingly low-key funeral.

As well as David, there are three girls. They're very excited to see each other again having been away for the Christmas holiday. When they talk their fingers claw at each other enthusiastically like rat hands. They touch each other's Christmas clothes. All four people, it transpires, received MP3 players from their respective parents.

'Did you get anything, Joe?' asks Merrill, a bouncy-titted girl with a pretty face imprisoned in frantic acne.

'I got a calendar. But I bought it myself,' says Joe, running his fingers through his dyed black hair. 'It's a wildlife one.

January is a leopard. February is a crocodile. April is a puffin so I'm looking forward to it. April, I mean. I'm looking forward to April.'

Joe rubs his lips, scraping off the flaked remains of his awful sentence. He spoke for too long, he realises. Merrill nods and points her tits and acne scars at someone else. Another shame. I spoke for too long, thinks Joe, getting up and leaving his colleagues to a fresh conversation about the Wild World. Students love the idea of the Wild World because they have a sense of detachment towards most things: wars, worlds, trends, survival.

Asa Gunn is still drinking water at one corner of the square bar that juts out into the theatre's foyer. He's wearing baggy green combat trousers and a tight-fitting black T-shirt. Joe approaches him, takes a plastic cup from a stack and gestures that he'd like to fill it with water.

'This week in America,' says the pop star, filling Joe's cup, 'a man came second in a water-drinking contest and then died. He died from overconsumption of water.'

'I know,' says Joe. 'And the winner survived.'

'Winners do,' says Gunn, refreshing his own beaker once again. His voice is high in pitch, his jaw is a little overwhelming and reminiscent of the word *mammal*. 'It's just a huge competition, life. There's a fine line between victory and suicide.'

Joe nods. Asa Gunn bares his teeth as he slurps from his water, his strong jaw protruding like freshly baked bread.

'Well, good luck with the play,' says Joe.

The pop star tuts noisily, wiping his lips with the back of his hand. 'Pointless,' he mutters. 'Probably pointless.'

'I guess,' says Joe, almost accidentally, walking away.

In 2002, Asa Gunn was the unlikely winner of *Pop Head*, a TV talent competition that took Britain by storm. To the surprise of many, he went on to release quite a few hit records and firmly establish himself in the industry. His songs were usually sweet, sentimental little tunes that he succeeded in singing with a persuasive emotion and in a delicate, genuine-sounding voice. By 2007, many have forgotten Asa's talent-show origins.

After years of frolicking around in the tides of pop, where the undertow is vicious and where children sometimes shit, Asa Gunn wants to dip his finger in reality and sample its flavour with a thoughtful suck. This is why he's come to Manchester. He wishes to act, to see people up close, the audience, he wants to pretend to be someone else in front of them.

He's just a jangling bag of nerves as Joe leaves him at the bar. He's tapping his thigh with a flat hand. His cheeks are drained of colour. Probably just nerves, thinks Joe, as he walks towards the disabled toilet to take a luxurious and spacious crap.

In the months leading up to Christmas, Life had become obsessed with the Wild World. Any article containing a reference to it she would cut out of the newspaper and pin to the noticeboard in the kitchen. When the Wild World was mentioned on TV she would nudge Joe and say, 'See?' in that beautiful voice of hers. She began stealing clothes from the vintage clothes shop she worked in. When she was finally sacked in mid-December she didn't give a shit. 'It doesn't matter,' she said to Joe, staring at her reflection in the wardrobe mirror. 'Because everything is changing.'

Thinking back, Joe realises that Life always hated the old world, or 'the world' as it was then called. She hated talking, for example. Life could not see the point in people talking at all. ('What is there to talk about?') Life thought talking was complete crap. She used to yawn loudly if Joe strung more than two or three sentences together.

Life did enjoy sex. But she wasn't massively bothered about the emotions of it all, the bond it created between her and Joe. She was fairly indifferent to the idea of orgasm. It's true that she demanded that Joe finger-fuck her to climax on a daily basis but that was simply pragmatic. Her love of sex had nothing to do with desire for pleasure. No. Life seemed to think that if you kept having sex then life was somehow being lived, you were succeeding, you were happy. She wanted to fuck constantly only because sex was the cheapest, most exciting and readily available event that was on offer in Manchester. It didn't matter that Joe was fairly shit in bed. Having sex meant life wasn't passing Life by. That's why her and Joe were forever fucking outside. If a conversation in a pub went on too long, she'd drag him to the toilets and bend over the cistern. Once, in an art gallery, she'd been so worried they were wasting their lives that she'd insisted they fuck in every disabled toilet in the building. There were six. It was tough. Life needed to be constantly living inside events.

When an article in the *Media Guardian* suggested that the Wild World would have less to do with talking and thought and more to do with actual events she was over-joyed. 'See?' she said to Joe. 'See?' Within a month she had left for London.

Joe wipes his arse and drops the dirty paper into the

toilet. As he stares into the bowl his thoughts naturally turn to the crumb. The darling crumb.

'Proof of Life,' he whispers, waving his hand in front of the circular sensor, causing the toilet to flush. It crosses his mind, as the dirty waters turn, that his love for the crumb might not represent his love for Life at all, but something quite different – his love for *life*, which he is sure still exists at the very centre of his torso, as far away from the outside world as it can get.

Half an hour later and the rehearsal is in full swing. Joe is standing with David guarding the entrance to the stage where Asa Gunn and the other actors are performing their play to an empty theatre. Only the director and her assistant sit making notes in the front row.

'You might as well know, David,' says Joe. 'Life left me on Christmas Day and I've taken it badly. I feel like I've been shot and I'm in shock. I can't find the entrance or the exit wounds. Without Life, I'm going to hate being alive. I love her. I now know that my life will never be genuinely good. Do you know what I mean?'

Joe turns to David who stares back at him with blank eyes too big for his posh face.

'I can't hear you, mate,' he mouths, fingers pointing to the white earphones that snuggle fizzing inside each of his ears.

'You're a cunt, David,' Joe says. 'You're a cunt and they should bury you alive.'

'What did you say, mate?' says David, removing the earphones from his large, rugby ears and letting them hang from his neck, near to his well-brought-up nipples.

'I said, David . . . I said . . . what exactly is the Wild World?'

'The Wild World?'

'Yeah, what exactly is it?'

'Well, we don't know, do we?' says David, poshly. 'That's the whole point. We just know the rumours. If you're asking me, then I'd say it'll have something to do with virtual reality.'

'Really?'

'Yeah. In the Wild World, you'll almost certainly be able to have sex with Marilyn Monroe.'

Joe shakes his head. He doesn't agree. Fucking dead film stars virtually, or living ones for that matter, is a lot like pissing shit off toilet bowls. Every man knows they could not resist doing it. But whereas cleaning toilets with piss is harmless, even helpful, virtually fucking the famous would certainly lead to every man being permanently plugged into the necessary machine for the rest of his life. It would be inconceivable to spend time doing anything but receiving heartbreaking tit-wanks from Marilyn Monroe. It would bring civilisation to an end. This is a fact. There's a tacit agreement among leading scientists and computer programmers not to make film-star fucking possible. Joe is certain he will die having never pushed his penis into an advanced piece of technology. He's right.

It's dark and it is ten to eight. Joe gets the bus from outside the Palace Theatre on Oxford Road where a large poster is advertising the Abba musical *Mamma Mia!*.

It's freezing on the bus. Shoulders hunch and point inwards. Buttocks turn to stone. Joe sits on the back seat downstairs. For the first time since she left, he's not thinking about Life or even her excremental legacy. He's thinking about what David had said about shagging

51

virtual celebrities. He definitely doesn't agree. Fucking celebrities is the old and not the Wild World. Even Joe, when he'd been living with Life, had enjoyed a few midday masturbations over celebrity magazines. We've been screwing fantasies for decades now. We're bored by it. Deep down, we're angry about it. The sexual dreams of the old world will, thinks Joe, be broken in the Wild.

He gets off the bus on the Rusholme/Fallowfield border and walks to his front door at the top of Platt Lane. As he enters the apartment complex his thoughts return to Life and to the toilet bowl. It had been her idea to move to Rusholme. She enjoyed the multicultural atmosphere and how you could still buy unpackaged food from some of the stalls. He climbs the stairs up towards his flat. Footsteps. I want to scream. Life is simple. I want to scream.

Joe finds the front door of his flat ajar. He pushes it open with an outstretched foot and peers cautiously down the hall. In secure complexes like this one, burglary is rare. Joe steps slowly into his flat. To his left is the bathroom door. He realises how little he cares about getting robbed. Bathrooms, famously, are the least robbed rooms in houses, and the only thing of value Joe possesses is a piece of shit. No black market trades literally in shit. Not even in Manchester. Joe takes a deep breath.

'Hello,' he says, in a tone of voice designed to ring out, unanswered.

'Hello,' comes the reply, a second later, followed by the uncontrolled shriek of a child.

Joe doesn't recognise the man he finds in his living room. He doesn't recognise the baby that the man is holding and feeding either. He watches for a moment as the child's chugging cheeks suck black milk from an upturned bottle, held gently in the fingers of the man. Why is the milk black?

'How did you get in?' says Joe, stepping forwards into the room.

'Life gave me the key. I couldn't risk waiting around in the cold with this one with me.' The man nods at the child in his arms. He is scruffy, the man. Ripped jeans, a faded Rolling Stones T-shirt short enough to reveal an inch of his midriff and a few straggling pubes. His head is shaved, maybe even wet shaved. He's about twenty-nine. One of those. Not quite thirty. He removes the bottle from the baby's tiny lips. A trickle of black milk descends into the baby's shawl. A series of black bubbles spreads across its lips.

'There you go,' says the man, placing the baby into a travel seat on the floor. The baby's face creases, its eyes get desperate. Seconds later it is sucking on a dummy.

'Now, Joe,' says the man, standing up and shaking his arms back to life, 'I'm sorry to barge in like this but I don't have much time. We need you to look after Sally here for a week or so. Life says you're good with secrets, that you don't go out much and that you're looking for opportunities in the Wild World. You're perfect. And your academic record is excellent, we've checked. Any questions so far?'

'Have you used my toilet?'

'I'm sorry?' The man puts a hand on top of his hairless head.

'Just tell me,' snaps Joe. 'Have you taken a piss since you got here?'

Looking perplexed, the man nods his head. Joe sighs.

53

Why is life impossible? He sits down slowly on one of the wooden arms of his sofa. He puts his head into his hands and leans forward. It's gone, he decides. Would I fit round the U-bend? he thinks. Could I just about squirm round it and then swim through the pipes and drop into the Mancunian sewers? I could spend a life-time sifting through shit, interrupting rats, throwing up, getting poisoned. I would gladly spend my lifetime just searching for crumbs.

'I was absolutely bursting,' says the man. 'It's hard to find time when you're caring for a baby.'

Joe says nothing. He knows that there is no point in going to check. The man has pissed in his toilet. A man has pissed in his toilet. The rules of the competition say that the crumb has been pissed away. He dreads to imagine this man's pride as he increased the power, got the aim spot on and then strained to fire the crumb away before he ran out of juice. He was probably panting when he'd finished. It would have held on pretty tight, that lovely bit of crap. But there is no point going to check. Because people succeed.

'Listen, Joe,' says the man, impatiently. 'Sally needs feeding six times a day. I'm leaving you enough milk to get you through two weeks. She's very well behaved. Everyone says so. You'll be paid, of course, and Life says you could do with the cash. This is a great opportunity for you. You're just the type of person we need at this stage. Low-key, unattached, no real reason to endanger –'

'How is she?' interrupts Joe. 'How is Life? Is she OK?'

'She's fine. She said to say hello.'

'Why is the milk black?'

The man smiles a frown. 'Sally needs certain things that

other children don't. In fact, I should say: don't take Sally south of Birmingham.'

'Where are her parents?'

'Dead. Sally's an orphan, see. Just keep her safe and in the north. You'll be doing us a huge favour. Life said you're the most caring guy she knows.'

'It's true,' says Joe, getting up off the sofa and crawling in the direction of the travel seat. 'I do care. I'm over-sensitive.' He leans over Sally. 'What's wrong with her eyes?'

'An infection. Nothing serious. They'll have some colour in them soon, for deffo.'

For deffo? Sally's eyes are only black and white. Joe presses her nose lightly and Sally giggles a little, a few more blackish bubbles are blown about her mouth. 'Hello there,' Joe says to Sally. 'Hello there.'

'So you agree?' asks the man, unloading large bottles of the black milk from a rucksack on the floor. 'I bet you never thought the Wild World was this easy, I mean, bloody childcare, piece of piss, eh?'

Joe quickly decides that Sally is the perfect replacement for the crumb of Life's shit. I'll take her. I need her. For so much of life, you are capable of nothing. Anything's possible, sure, only it isn't. Hardly anything's possible. But right now, thinks Joe, I could, I could do anything.

'Who are you?' he asks the man.

'I work in marketing, with Life, for the Wild World.'

'I see,' says Joe. 'And what is the Wild World?'

The man taps his nose like twats tap their crotches or killers tap the handles of their guns. 'Top secret,' says the man through a smile. He's probably shagging Life, thinks Joe. I bet he's banging her with a mask on with his white and weirdly massive dick. Who entrusts a total

55

stranger with a baby? A bell-end. The kind of man who takes shits on fans. Baby Sally lets out a deep, painful burp.

'Wait a minute,' says Joe, turning from Sally and grabbing the man by the wrist. 'I'd do anything for Life, she knows that, I guess that's why you're here. And I'm not stupid. I'll keep your secret. But Sally, she's not . . . you know?' The man shakes his head. Joe continues in a whisper: 'Sally's not the new Jesus, is she?'

The man is almost bursting with laughter. The man is saying, 'Don't be an idiot,' then he's saying, 'Is she fuck.' Moments later and Joe is chuckling too. He is asking the man what his name is and the man is saying that it doesn't matter. He's putting on a battered leather jacket and saying goodbye to Sally who is almost smiling. Joe shows the man out of his flat. After, he checks the toilet, and yes, it's vanished. Gone. No more crap. He remembers how Life had said to say 'hello'. What a terrible thing to say. 'Hello.' He calls her on her mobile but it goes straight to answerphone: *Hey, this is Life. I'm busy. Leave a message.* Next Joe is looking in the mirror, trying to work out if his roots are showing at his scalp yet. They are. So soon. It's a miracle. There is a millimetre of pure white at the bottom of each strand of hair. Jesus. My natural colour is a perfect white. Fuck me. He's thinking. Fuck me. Going white at twenty-four. What a tiny little nightmare. Now I've got Sally, he thinks, I won't be able to go and nest with the puffins in the Faroe Islands. Ha. I probably won't even grow wings now. He goes into the living room and watches Sally as she kicks and struggles in her little chair. She is beautiful. Even her poorly eyes convey a very convivial

56

character. He starts making funny noises and Sally starts laughing. She is trying to smile. More funny noises. More touching. Within minutes, the adult and the child are squeaking, giggling, squeaking, giggling.

6

ANKA KUDOLSKI LEAVES the Press Club on Deansgate at six fifteen in the morning. It is becoming day. The sun will rise. Odds on. But, for now, a half-light hangs sleepily between the new buildings and above the grey road.

The coffee shops are coming to life with first blinking and then constant yellow light. Through windows, knackered youths in aprons carry trays of muffins. Hanging mouths and barely open eyes.

The Press Club is Anka's least favourite of her many jobs. It used to cater for members of the press, theatrical types, people in television, but it doesn't any more. Anka spent last night selling warm cans of Red Stripe to aspirational gangsters from Longsight and Moss Side. Chunky chains; too gold. Revolting rings. Trails of cocaine snot from each nostril. Dead women falling off their knees in dirty old miniskirts. Nowhere near enough fun. Where are the laughing humans, Anka? Where are the laughing humans?

Not in the Press Club, thinks Anka, heading south

towards St Peter's Square. I think I might quit. I need jobs that kick reality like a goalkeeper kicks a football. Into the air. Out of reach. *QUIZ TV* works. It detaches me from the world. So does selling overpriced bags to posh pigs at Selfridges. I thought the Press Club would be the same. It's not. I think I might quit.

Anka skips between the town hall and the Library Theatre and into St Peter's Square. A minute later and she is sitting down at a square table in Luciano's, saying hello to Nic, a large, blonde, Italian-English part-time lesbian from Anka's London days. Nic works nights, too. She deals with nocturnal room service at the Midland Hotel. It's normal for the two of them to meet like this. Nic orders a sausage sandwich from the olive-skinned waiter. Anka orders a boiled egg with broccoli soufflé, red-onion tarte tatin, some frizzled shallots and a pancetta garnish. The waiter shrugs his shoulders.

'How is the eating going lately?' asks Nic in north London notes, tweaking her slightly large but necessary nose. 'Your tits are still big, but your arms, Anka, you're not eating.'

Anka smiles. 'I am. I'm working loads, eating loads, I'll be fine. Did you see me the other night?'

'I watched the first half-hour before I went to work. Whose idea was it?'

'Not mine, sadly,' says Anka. 'The producer's. We got triple the amount of calls we normally get.'

'I bet, but how many of them were just wanking down the line? I was blushing, all those horrible little groans every time you took a call.'

The food arrives. The sandwich for Nic and, for Anka, just one lonely boiled egg that rolls around the plate.

Luciano's, by the way, is an Italian cafe whose Italian menu has been eroded by the staples of the English breakfast cuisine over the three years since it opened. It is now run by Greeks.

'The sad thing is,' says Anka, ignoring her egg for the moment, 'is that a lot of the genuine callers we got last night were Romanian. They haven't figured out it's a con.'

'Foreigners are fucked. The Wild World will see to them and their fucking work ethic,' says Nic, already halfway through her sandwich. 'The Wild World is gonna save the English, the depressed. Do you know if you speak English, you're more likely to suffer from depression? It's been proven. The Wild World's gonna stop that, surely. It'll help us to deal with affluence, make it more pleasant for us to obsess over appearance, celebrity, money and status, stop us hanging from beams, shooting bullets through our brains or just moaning and moaning and moaning. I mean, Anka, look at you.'

'I don't moan.'

'Maybe not, but you're succeeding in starving yourself to death. I hope the geniuses behind the Wild World realise that there is a definite link between the English language and suicide. Or else, I should go back to Italy. Or the English should start speaking Italian. Italians don't give a fuck.'

'I'd rather speak French.'

'I'd rather you ate your egg, you anorexic English psycho.'

'Are you a lesbian today, Nicola?'

'I am, yes, your tits have given me a huge erection.'

The two girls laugh. The sky outside gets lighter, encouraged, no doubt, by the sound of female laughter.

'Speaking of the Wild World,' says Nic. 'Did you ever meet Life Moberg?'

Anka shakes her head. She has an egg in her mouth.

'I'm sure you did.'

'Only on the Internet,' says Anka, swallowing. 'I once looked at loads of her family photos, but we never met, for deffo.'

Nic leans across the table. 'I spoke to her last week. She's working for the Wild World in London. It sounds amazing.'

'What does?'

'The Wild World, dickhead. Life's helping to organise the launch party. You'd love that, Anka.'

'Would I?' Anka is sucking each of her fingertips and letting out a huge sigh. 'I'm well and truly trapped in this world. I got an email this morning asking me to strip for a mobile phone porn site. They saw the show last night and were impressed. But that's got to be the old world, right?'

'Are you going to do it?'

'Probably. As long as they buy me lunch.'

The conversation returns to Life. Nic gives Anka her email address and suggests she gets in touch. She describes how Life recently dumped her boyfriend, Joe, saying, 'Apparently, he stopped kissing her. He just used to peck her lips like a bird and flap his arms like they were wings. Also, she suspected he was trying to make a nest in her arse. He became fixated with her anus, not fucking it, just staring at it and holding himself against it at night.'

'That's pretty normal, isn't it?' says Anka, pulling on her coat and flicking her blonde hair over its khaki-green hood. 'All boys are obsessed with anal nowadays. Fannies will soon seal up – evolution!'

The two girls leave Luciano's laughing. Once in the street,

Nic does a little fart and both girls bend over in hysterics. They separate with an affectionate kiss outside the Palace Hotel. It's eight in the morning and the streets are full of people.

It's hours before Anka is due back at Selfridges. Having worked solidly for over a day, she decides to return home and sleep through the morning. She lives in Parkers Hotel, the glamorous and dilapidated Georgian building on the corner of Miller Street and Corporation Street. It's a dump, of course, but she's hardly ever there.

As she enters her corridor Anka sees a postman knocking on the door opposite hers, a large parcel at his feet. Through the wall a recorded voice is looped and screaming: 'Whatever it is, just leave it by the door!'

The postman turns away in frustration. Anka smiles as their paths cross.

'He's a lunatic,' says the postman, in an old Northern accent. 'Wants locking up. Would you mind?' The postman hands Anka a biro and gestures that she sign for the parcel.

'You should hear his music,' says Anka, smiling, signing then printing her name. 'Nothing but *Les Misérables*.'

'Nice one, love.'

Anka has never seen the occupant of Flat 126. Judging by his behaviour, she's glad.

Once inside her flat, Anka switches on her computer and then lies on the bed as it boots up. She's tired. So tired that she yawns. She takes a picture frame from her bedside table and holds it in front of her sleepy eyes. Inside the frame are the mantras her therapist gave her on the last day of her treatment. *Anka*, it reads, *love yourself. You are talented and wonderful. You are beautiful. Feed yourself. You deserve food. Love yourself.*

At first, when she got given this, Anka thought it was a load of bollocks. She didn't go in for the 'love yourself' approach to survival. Her therapist used to force her to tap each of her scrawny limbs for minutes on end, chanting 'I love you' as she did so. Anka felt like a tit. But lately, she has begun to take a shine to herself. As instructed, she has read these mantras to herself each day. At first, her voice was full of irony as she told herself that she was beautiful and talented. But nowadays, she succeeds in reading the words with some conviction.

'You are talented and wonderful.' She spies her reflection in the glass of the frame. She smiles and her eyes shine. 'You are beautiful. Feed yourself. You deserve food. Love yourself.'

Chaperoned by employment here in Manchester, it's hard for Anka to believe in her memories of Goldsmiths and London. Two years ago, she was thrashing around with other thrashing young on loud streets and in crowded bars that rattled with ambition. She wore difficult clothes, rebelliously wrapped around her body. Her outfits all uniforms for a fantastic future. She called herself an artist. She blagged invites to exhibition openings in Hoxton Square and walked with a confidence that made a Xanadu of all her destinations. The lives of others were bad TV; woozy bollocks that could be scoffed and sneered at by Anka and her friends, all of whom had fresh brains inside their new skulls and light in the palms of their hands. But youth is a journey with no destination; its road trails off to dust and early nights. Perfect certainty gives way to cautious missions through empty towns of empty bars and empty clubs where you stand, motionless, and wonder, quite reasonably, when was it lost? When did it all go wrong?

My brain tried to starve me, thinks Anka. It wanted me dead. Maybe ambition is unnecessary. I wanted to be Jackson Pollock. I am not Jackson Pollock. Maybe craving success is slightly pathetic and, in any case, it's become a bit like shitting. Whatever makes us happy makes us happy. Whatever turns you on turns you on. There is either more to life than being brilliant or there is less. Hedge your bets. Anka sighs. She squeezes out a trump.

She climbs off her bed and moves in on her PC. Her room is bare, save for the old desk and its computer and for the wardrobe that explodes with clothes. Two large windows look out over Victoria Station and the various tracks that fan from it in the direction of Rochdale, Clitheroe and Leeds.

First she checks her personal emails. She replies to the pornographers, saying she will strip for the mobile phone porn site providing she is taken to lunch afterwards. She writes a quick email to her mother detailing her eating habits and mentioning that she intends to get in touch with Life, a contact she's made in the Wild World. Next she writes to Life herself: *Hey Life, I'm a friend of Nic's. She says you're making it in the Wild World. Congratulations! I'm still taking my clothes off in the old world. Can you help me? Anka Kudolski.* Anka clicks to send then turns from the computer screen and looks out of the window. She can see Strangeways Prison in the distance. The Boddingtons Chimney. The Manchester Evening News Arena. In the foreground a tram is pulling out of Victoria, aimed at the brand-new and instantly old apartment buildings of the Green Quarter.

Life replies almost immediately: *Sure. I might be able to*

help you, Anka. Meet me in Wow-Bang any night this week around 10. Come to the Real Arms. X

Next Anka logs on to her *QUIZ TV* account. She has received a long list of emails. Some people complain about her bad language and the insulting tone she adopted on last night's show. These are the minority. Most people pay her compliments. They request stained underwear, signed photos, stool samples, her home address and clumps of her pubes. Many request that she continue to insult them via email. *Call me hopeless. Tell me I should've been born cockless. Really hurt my feelings. Stamp on my balls. Say you'll cut my penis into manageable chunks.*

El Rogerio has only sent her a web link. Anka follows it to the El Rogerio blog spot and finds a detailed description of a man wanking over her. At first, this seems weird. A bit disgusting. Anka feels a very traditional anger tickling her throat and aggressively moving her features around her face. But as she reads about the semen that leapt onto her televised body, she feels dirty and cheeky. She likes the way it's written. Arty. Fucked up. A small amount of red pride grows on each of her cheeks. 'You are beautiful,' she reasons. 'Feed yourself.' She reads on a little further but El Rogerio quickly changes his subject and Anka realises that she's extremely anxious to return to the topic of herself. She experiences a rush of guilt. She rides the rush. She reads ten more emails in which men and women have written accounts of how they wanked over her last night. Anka giggles audibly at each one then returns to El Rogerio's blog to reread it. The information age, thinks Anka, is a fucking flirt. My knickers, she realises, are a little moist.

Wow-Bang, it turns out, is the latest in a series of

Internet-based virtual worlds. Anka runs a search on it and then begins to download it onto her hard drive. Crucially, simulated environments like Wow-Bang and Second Life have got little to do with wearing electronic underpants and receiving alarming blow jobs from famous women. No, these places are convincing worlds containing continents, cities, mountains, shops and bars. They are communities. People participate in these virtual worlds in order to enjoy themselves, meet new people, play with existing friends and family and take time out from reality, that is to say, from planet earth, yes, planet earth, where people sob, where sexual organs pong and where you only die once.

Anka registers on Wow-Bang and finds Life's profile without much trouble. It says that Life has been a citizen for around a month and can usually be found in the Real Arms in the late evening. The Real Arms is described as 'one of the coolest bars, popular with media types'. It can be found on Wow-Bang's west side.

The graphics of Wow-Bang are good, but not quite up to reality's standards. Not far off though. The buildings, roads and shrubs of Wow-Bang look reasonably real to the eye.

Anka types 'El Rogerio' into the Wow-Bang search engine. He, too, is a full citizen and, like Life, is currently offline. He also seems to have a very large head, Anka notes, staring at his pixelated avatar. El Rogerio is often found in the Rib Cage, which is described as 'an EMO dive'. Users are warned that the Rib Cage is a hot spot for 'the Dead Animals', a terrorist organisation intent on ruining Wow-Bang and encouraging people to return to reality to do real things.

Anka sneers at the screen. For Anka there is something

overwhelmingly geeky about Wow-Bang. There was a time, only recently, when a virtual world would have been nothing but a nest for the nerds, a base for the bullied. But things change. Or rather rules get forgotten. And computer technology is a fucking flirt. It's embarrassing, thinks Anka. I'm full of myself. My knickers are moist.

She spends fifteen minutes designing her Wow-Bang appearance and identity: her avatar. This involves uploading photos of herself from her hard drive, choosing clothes, recording standard greeting phrases. She is pleased with the results. Her 3-D avatar rotates on the screen in front of her, its arms reaching sideways into the black background. I feel like a nerd. With a smile spread thoughtlessly across her face, Anka submits her application to become a citizen of Wow-Bang.

She returns to El Rogerio's blog and leaves a comment below the description of his wank: *See you in Wow-Bang, wanker. Anka x.* She returns to her bed and begins to undress. She lifts her legs into the air in order to peel off her jeans. She's wearing silk red knickers. And they're moist! Oh, Jesus and God, bless the moist knickers and tented kecks of civilisation.

It is clear, thinks Anka, closing her eyes slowly and relaxing into the cushions, that my knickers are moist. A finger travels down her tummy then swims under the red silk like a child seeking solitude under bedclothes. I have become a girl in moist knickers, she thinks, and I wanted to be Jackson Pollock. I wasn't entirely sure moist-knickered girls existed. But obviously they do. I am one.

I was young and ambitious, then, from nowhere, came the disease. Anorexia. And now, she thinks, and now the recovery is coming at a cost. First came self-acceptance, then came . . . not self-love, as such. How can I put this? What has occurred inside my mind? First came self-acceptance and then came many people who masturbated to my movements and my sounds. That's about it, she thinks. Old world or Wild World? No idea. Anka's finger starts to move quickly inside her knickers. Her other hand is pinching her left nipple through her T-shirt and her bra.

Minds are not empty. That's exactly the problem. Minds are crammed and detailed. The individual is a dropped vase. I'm so complex, it's disgusting, thinks Anka, eyes shut, picturing the wankers typing with fast fingertips. We are becoming very technical. The humans, she means. Skins and veins pulled into shapes. A cool identity for every square inch of organ, pipe and blood. We are things, detailed and unique, we must love ourselves. That's the trick, thinks Anka. Have time. Be complex. Fuck yourself. Tenderly.

Anka is approaching orgasm. She is remembering the descriptions. She is imagining the moments the descriptions describe. She can't fight the urge any longer. She climaxes. She is thinking. I love you. You are beautiful. I love you. Feed yourself.

7

AFTER THREE DAYS of constant shagging in the Columbia Hotel near Hyde Park, Life left Janek Freeman playing bass guitar alone in the devastated bed. He'd received a phone call from his aunt Sophie telling him that his mum was dead. He told Life about his mother's breathlessness and about her very shallow lungs. Life got a bit depressed and decided to leave.

'It's a bit too soon,' said Life before she left. 'I feel a bit guilty about Joe.'

This seemed a bit rich to Janek and even a little heartless, however breathless and doomed his mother might have been. She'd just died. And it seemed a little late in the day for Life to be feeling sorry for the ex-boyfriend with the bottom complex. And after all, things were starting to matter. My life the Fuck Festival. My brilliant life the Fuck Festival.

But nevertheless Janek was polite. He didn't kick up a fuss. Nothing matters again, he reasons in the bed. Mum is dead. Life is feeling guilty about her ex-boyfriend who, so she says, tried to build a nest in her arse. Nothing matters. Janek had told Life that he understood. They exchanged numbers and then had distracted sex before she finally walked out of the room.

Janek lies on the sheetless mattress playing chords on his bass, thinking about his poor mum. You need to have a neat technique to play chords on a bass. You need to have strong fingers and tough skin. The sound you create is strange, somehow unmusical.

'Poor Mum,' he murmurs. 'Oh dear.'

It's been four days since Janek met Life at Reel World Studio. His bass guitar was plugged into an amplifier. A signal from this amplifier was plugged into a neuro-monitoring unit. A wire ran from the neuro-monitoring unit to a contraption that Life wore like a hat. Her wavy gold hair flowed from the machinery. The bossbitch from the Wild World was searching for the A-HA moment.

The A-HA moment is discovered early in the twenty-first century. It relates to certain activities in the roof of the brain, caused when certain words and certain music are combined together perfectly. Advertisers discovered that if you could generate an A-HA moment during an advert, you were virtually guaranteed to sell a product. They researched the moment when a brand is identified, understood and desired and called it the A-HA moment. It's hard to predict. But with the right technology, we can now detail such irrational instances of desire. The scruffs from the Wild World are convinced that bass lines are the key to unlocking it.

Janek was instructed by Bossbitch to play all sorts of different genres of bass line into Life's brain. Jazz. Rock. Hip hop. R 'n' B. Meanwhile, boards with different coloured text on them were held up for Life to stare at while she listened.

They searched all day for the A-HA moment. Life stared at the word 'LOVE' as Janek drilled his bass in an array of styles. Nothing happened. Life stared at the word 'BEAUTY'. Janek plucked. Nothing happened. Word after word. 'SEX', 'COOL', 'DREAM', 'FUTURE'. Fuck all. Nothing like an A-HA. Finally, they tried the word 'LIFE'. Janek started moving through the styles. First rock, then hip hop, then R 'n' B. Nothing. Then he tried funk. He slapped his way through the funkiest of bass lines and Life's brain went crazy.

'A-HA,' cried the guys at the neuro-monitor. 'Got it!'

Bossbitch looked confused. 'All right,' she said. 'All right, Janek. Stop playing. I need to think.'

Life smiled as Janek flicked a subtle V at Bossbitch. Life hadn't been aware of her brain's radically different response to the FUNK/LIFE combination. But nevertheless she accepted the fact that her brain had gone wild.

'What do you reckon?' Bossbitch asked. 'Funky life? Is that what people want? Or is she just reacting to staring at her own name?'

Janek smirked. This seemed remarkably unscientific. Guesswork, really. Nothing matters, he remembered. It's amazing.

Bossbitch took the grey machinery from off Life's head and knelt down beside her.

'Answer me this,' Bossbitch said. 'Do you like "life"? I mean, were you thinking about the world, being alive and stuff, or were you just thinking about yourself, you know, your own name, who you are?'

Life wasn't sure. She restyled her hair with her fingers and said, 'Hard to say.'

Bossbitch got angry. 'This is important! This is my job! Which do you prefer, being Life or living life?'

73

Put like that, it was obvious to everyone present what the answer was. Life is a mighty, beautiful young girl with a zest for sex and having fun. Life, on the other hand, the breathing, living, dying life, I mean, is notoriously shit. The session ended. Bossbitch was frustrated. Janek and Life got the train from Bath Spa to London and had sex in the small toilet at the end of their carriage. Bath Spa, Chippenham, Swindon, Fuck Festival! Janek could suddenly see a way forward. A magical place beyond the cities and the fields, the shops, the streets, the web and the tedious grapple with twenty-four-hour after twenty-four-hour. The Fuck Festival: a distant land of love and sex where nothing matters in the most perfect way. Janek felt like he was on his way.

Back in the hotel room, Janek is preparing to leave. Jews bury each other quickly and his aunt Sophie wants him back in Bristol by this afternoon.

Before she left, he and Life arranged to meet in Wow-Bang during the week. The Real Arms. For Janek, the idea of meeting Life in a virtual world is a little distressing. A virtual world strikes him as even more awkward, embarrassing and difficult to be in than this one. But who truly knows the way to the Fuck Festival?

It was a psychotherapist called Melanie who had told Janek, at the age of six, to learn to play a musical instrument. Music, she told the young man, will help you bridge the gap between yourself and the world around you. Janek agreed. 'Will it make stuff fun?' he asked, in an unbroken voice. 'Yes,' his psychotherapist had replied. 'It should do.' So Janek dutifully borrowed his father's bass guitar and practised every day for hours. He performed midday concerts for his breathless mother and entertained her fully. It worked. I suppose it worked. Nothing matters, sure, but Janek has led a fairly decent life. Bass nerds all over the world worship him and attempt to emulate his playing technique. American rap stars touch fists with him when they meet and offer him gifts of diamond-encrusted crucifixes. Janek pulls his beanie down over his head and constantly survives.

Until the glut of sex he's just had with Life, Janek's had an indifferent relationship with intercourse. He attributes this, and his general sense of apathy and detachment, to the circumcision of his penis at the age of zero. Eight days into his life, the operation was performed without anaesthetic. People think the baby doesn't give a shit. This, thinks Janek, is bollocks. Janek recalls an invisible and silent trauma. He remembers shock. He remembers being comatose. Janek believes the removal of his foreskin has left a negative imprint on his brain. He feels he was painfully robbed of the small flesh interface that would have helped him connect to the world of touch. He feels like the link between his innards and the air has been severed.

A couple of years ago in California he got a blow job off his cellist girlfriend, Judy. She closed her eyes and Janek had never felt so alone. It felt like an unnecessarily sexual form of waiting. But with Life it was different. Life doesn't *have* sex. She *does* sex. As long as they were sweating and panting, moving in and out of each other, it seemed she was overjoyed and satisfied. This attitude rubbed off on Janek. Sex didn't feel like such a quest. Just fuck. Now keep fucking. The festival is coming to a city near you.

Back in the hotel room, Janek is packing his suitcase. Beside it lies a blue duffel bag that Life left behind for him. It's some sort of Wild World goodie bag and there are few things more depressing than a goodie bag. One day you will saunter into a cool hell, the walls all finally burnt; you'll be greeted by a bending devil and a bulging goodie bag. 'Great,' you'll say.

Janek shuts his suitcase with a click. He looks into the goodie bag and pulls out an MP3 player. It's tiny. The size of a coin. It's bright red. Small black lettering reads 'N-Prang'. Other than the N-Prang, the bag contains a Wild World make-up case and some stickers. One sticker reads 'I AM WILD WORLD'.

It's another bright winter's day. Light reflects off the cars and off the white-brick buildings of Lancaster Gate. Janek crosses Bayswater Road and walks into Hyde Park. He takes a copy of the *London Paper* from a small man with a hidden face and a puffy, dirty yellow coat.

On the front page of the *London Paper* there is a picture of Asa Gunn. 'Reality-TV star Asa Gunn has retired, citing certain complications involving the Wild World.' On page 5 the story continues with the popular feature 'Five Questions for . . .'

Hello, Asa. Do you think you'll be remembered?
(*Long pause*) Yes. But not for my songs or my reality-TV days. For something else.
Do you regret the decision to abandon your theatrical debut?
(*He appears to be in tears*) I'm not in a position to talk about regrets.
What's next for Asa Gunn?
(*Still weeping*) From among us, a Dickhead will rise. At the end of our time, this Dickhead will come to us, armed with our future.

76

*Fair enough and, so, what exactly is the Wild World, any
ideas?*
The Wild World is a revolution.
Who do you most admire?
Joan Rivers.

Underneath the interview a statement reads, 'A spokesman
on behalf of the Wild World today refuted the suggestion
that the Wild World is in any way connected to the tactic
of revolution.'

Janek dumps the newspaper in a bin and walks across
the squeaky wet grass to the shores of the Serpentine.

Swans call out to the sky. Janek thinks back to Peter
Gabriel and the swan at Reel World. He remembers the
sound the neuro-monitor made when he played funk bass
into Life's brain. The sound of the A-HA moment.
Having spent three days in bed with Life, Janek is
confident her brain had grown excited because it recognised itself in the word 'LIFE'. It wasn't love of existence. If I had Life's confidence, he thinks, her ability to
affect her surroundings and have fun, then my brain
would probably go apeshit over the word 'JANEK'. As
it is, Janek can imagine his brain hunching both of its
shoulders at the sight of his name, unfolding its white
pipes like arms and raising them into a questioning
gesture, as if to say, So what?

Janek walks along the water's edge, suitcase in one hand,
bass case in the other, beanie on his head. Naturally slightly
bored, he sets down his suitcase for a second and feeds the
red earphones of the N-Prang into his ears. Janek dislikes
the realism of the whispering wind and the squawks of
swans that it carries. He wonders what music the Wild

World has to offer. Probably music made by bands full of brightly dressed kids who like the idea of living.

But Janek quickly finds that the music of the N-Prang is bass-heavy. He flicks through the first few tracks and finds only huge deep bass notes, held into place by kick-drum, hi-hat and snare. His footsteps fall quickly into the rhythm of the N-Prang and he's puzzled to find himself marching round the Serpentine at a fair old speed. On the far shore he can see elderly men and women in pink wetsuits diving into a cordoned-off section of the lake. The waves begin to dance. The trees around Hyde Park hold hands, shake their heads and begin to sway.

Walking with the music, Janek feels strange. He feels like he's biting happily on a brick. The song of the N-Prang enters a breakdown: higher bass notes stretched long under a shimmering string section. Janek glides past a bench. A group of kids in matching white hoodies greet Janek with playful finger pistols. Janek smiles. One boy mounts the back of the bench and leaps off, performing three or four somersaults before hitting the ground, pulling his hood up and pirouetting quickly with one finger held against his lips. The song of the N-Prang kicks back in. The kids dance as Janek walks on, each of them, even the girls, gripping their crotches.

There's a very old man, wearing a flat cap, a tweed jacket and with a pipe puffing bubbles between his lips. This man has skin like Bible paper. The man begins to break-dance as Janek walks by. He is spinning on his flat-capped head, unsupported by his hands and with his legs thrust into the blue sky like those of a frog. Bubbles continue to blow from the man's pipe. Large bubbles float into the cold winter air and then burst.

Two women push pushchairs and really work their back-sides for the pleasure of Janek's eyes. Great booty, thinks Janek, still striding like a smooth, impossibly cool young man en route to a Fuck Festival. Did I think the word booty? I did. And I'm right. Both women bend extremely into their pushchairs, exposing large denim behinds that bubble along to the grooves of the N-Prang. As he passes by, Janek glances into the pushchairs and notices that both babies are crying with joy.

The swimming of the elderly in the freezing lake is entirely synchronised. Janek arrives and watches as a dozen pairs of pink-wetsuited legs rise up from the murky Serpentine and dance in unison in a hip-hop style. Twenty-four pink knees bend in fashionable, robotic jerks that are difficult to pull off in music videos, let alone when you're old and you're holding your breath under ice-cold water. Janek stares in disbelief. This is what he loves about London. The way little communities like this come together and battle against the anonymity of the city with well-practised and flamboyant skills. Behind him, ten swans march in single file, all their white wings spread wide like Nazi eagles. It's funny, thinks Janek, standing at the water's edge, wondering when the swimmers will resurface.

After some time, the solitary head of an elderly man rises out of the dark water, then his pink-wetsuited shoulders, then his waist, then his legs. The man, it turns out, is standing on a woman's shoulders, she's now rising out of the water, too, lifting the guy even higher. And, of course, she's standing on top of someone else. Now they're rising. So it continues, elderly swimmer after elderly swimmer rising out of the water with their feet gripping the shoulders of the person under them until the first man is very high up and Janek is clapping in astonishment. Clapping claps he can't hear because of the bass-heavy music in his ears. But clapping claps anyway. Because this is amazing.

He takes the earphones of the N-Prang from his ears. He turns to the row of swans. They are pecking at the tarmac ground now. Or hissing. Or beating their large wings for no apparent reason. In the water, the elderly swimmers have begun to lower themselves safely back down. When the first man is back in the water all the swimmers gather round him, some gasping, some smiling, congratulating each other on the success of their performance. They are treading water and exhilarated. Janek is passed by the two women with the pushchairs. Over the tears of their babies, they are talking about Asa Gunn. One declares that no matter what, they still believe that he is a superstar.

Are these signposts? I feel happy. The drugged lions, the sawdust air and the nervous clowns. Are these the well-trained elephants of the Fuck Festival?

At the end of their world tour, Snoop Dogg placed a hand on Janek's forehead and asked if he was OK. Snoop said that he'd never seen someone have so little fun, even growing up in Long Beach. Janek had agreed, saying, 'It's odd, isn't it, Snoop?'

But Life is a better fun-haver than Snoop. Oh, Life. Fucking fun. Funny fucking. Fucking funny. Death. When they had sex, when they did it, Life made both of them crane their necks to stare at the penis and the vagina. 'Watch it go in and out,' Life cried. And they did. She and Janek stared at their interacting sexes until they felt distanced from them and entertained by the performance. They stared at their bodies like they were pieces of miraculous evidence. For the first time in his life, Janek was able to forget about his circumcision during sex. Such sensory concerns were secondary. Just stare at the proof. We live. Inside and outside.

Once his mum is safely buried, Janek decides he will meet Life in the virtual city of Wow-Bang. He decides that he will try to begin a relationship with her. But for now he is in London. He makes his way to Oxford Street where the air is solid with noise until he takes out the N-Prang and switches it on.

He is striding along with humans on the enormous shopping street. Bass notes in his brain, encouraging his feet. To move. To move. Janek is walking to the groove. The other humans join him. Crotches circle and thrust. Cars begin to bounce on the jammed road. It is cool. Some leap as high as five feet in the air. People shut their mouths and allow their heads to nod to the N-Prang beat. Janek thinks of Life. So funny to imagine happiness. Such a rare and brilliant thing, when you sense it coming.

8

Allow me. Allow me. I'm fucking glad that Asa Gunn's retired. Why? Because I've never seen such a muscular mountain of Godshit in all my life. He's a twat. But he's right. El Rogerio says, every celebrity is flammable. Strike the match.

SUBMIT.

Roger Hart leaves his computer and goes to the door of his flat. He'd listened while the postman knocked. Through the screams of his recorded message he'd heard the postman slating him to the girl who lives opposite. He'd heard her take the piss out of his taste in music, too. Simple bitch. He's never met her. Never wants to. Why don't young people see the beauty of musicals? People think musicals are cheesy. People are cheesy, thinks Roger. Musicals are cool.

Roger opens his door slowly and silently. He reaches out for the parcel and pulls it inside as quick as he can. He unwraps it in a crouching position by the door. He's excited.

Quick movements cause his spectacles to slide down his nose until they cling precariously to its moistening tip.

Roger Hart is worried about his health. His left foot appears to be turning black and his anus hurts. He's worried about his inability to sleep, too. The readers of his blog are growing suspicious. A fan recently deduced that El Rogerio couldn't have slept for more than five minutes in the previous eighty hours, judging by the frequency of his posts. The fan went on to accuse El Rogerio of being more than one person. Of being, in essence, a business. Keen to refute such claims and keen to understand certain deteriorations in his health, Roger has ordered sleeping pills, an anal cream and a stethoscope from an online pharmacy. He lays out the purchases on his bed and returns to his computer.

> Allow me. Allow me. To those of you who accuse me of deceit, I pity you. El Rogerio does not sleep because El Rogerio doesn't have time. Sleeping is for you. Enjoy it. I am wide awake. If I catch any of you doubting dipshits in Wow-Bang on Thursday I'll murder you. I have the weapons. If you doubt me, I'll just shoot you. You will be searching the graveyards of Wow-Bang for your buried body while the rest of us party. Wise up. Allow El Rogerio. Allow me.
> SUBMIT.

On the computer screen, a pop-up pops up. FINALLY, FROM AMONG US, A DICKHEAD WILL RISE. ARMED WITH OUR FUTURE!

'. . . hiccup . . .'

Returning to the bed, Roger uses the stethoscope to look for his heartbeat. He pulls up his red-and-black-checked shirt and places the cold circular head in between his ribs. It's there. I'm pleased. I still have a heartbeat. Although I have to admit that it sounds seriously faint. And where is that whirring coming from?

His stomach. The whirring is coming from Roger's stomach. It becomes amplified when he guides the head of the stethoscope down onto his belly. My stomach is making the same noise as an electric fan, or the spinning wheel of a crashed bike. I'm worried. Roger's worried. He undoes his belt and holds the stethoscope over his appendix. As a child he lived in fear of a burst appendix. There was something about that part of the body that seemed charged with energy. Too much energy. Roger dreads his body's middle bursting. He listens to his appendix. He presses the stethoscope hard against the area of skin situated north-west from his ponging dick: silence, blood. He hears the distant beating of his heart and the whirring of his stomach. Running blood. The peaceful noise of his body reminds Roger of soft radio static. There is an expectancy to it. A fragility. A need to be broken. He keeps listening. Running blood. Distant whirring. Distant beats. Then, all of a sudden, from the lightless world beneath his skin, Roger hears a bleep.

For fuck's sake. (How gay!) Roger takes the stethoscope from his ears and does up his belt. A bleep! (How gay!) What a shame. Roger runs into the bathroom and stares into the mirror. This is so gay, he thinks. His pupils shrink inside his spectacled eyes. His sleepless grey expression becomes even greyer. My bathroom is well lit. My body is bleeping and whirring. This is well shit. I wish it wasn't. I don't need my body to be making silly sounds. I definitely don't. I will never sing and dance on the West End stage if my body is bursting with technology. Is life horrific? Yes, life is horrific.

Still in front of the bathroom mirror, Roger starts picking his nose. The mission gets tricky. A thumb joins his index finger inside his nostril and the two digits pull hard on a hair bringing tears of pain to Roger's eyes. He inspects the bogey. It is green and hard at one end and colourless and liquid at the other. The hair which holds the bogey isn't black. It's shiny and bronze. It is a wire.

I'm getting all technical. My poor nose. Roger flicks the wire away, and the bogey. He listens as both land in the bathtub. There is a thin ringing sound as it lands. Bollocks. This would never have happened during the French Revolution. They ate rats. Real men. Real women. Fewer wires.

Before taking his seat at the computer, Roger presses play on his CD player and skips to track 7 of the *Les Misérables* soundtrack. 'Bring Him Home'. This is an incredibly beautiful song. The ageing Jean Valjean pleads with God to allow a handsome and injured young man to survive and to take him instead. Roger sings along with the deep, troubled vocal, momentarily forgetting that he suspects himself to be full of electronic equipment.

Allow me. Allow me. Instead of hairs I've got wires up my nose. No word of bullshit, my cheerful little friends. I've got some kind of technology growing out my fucking face. I'm still gonna shag a million girls.

I can't be arsed turning into a piece of technology. The idea bores the crap out of me. I heard a bleeping coming out of my appendix and I was like, piss off, dumb bleep. Bleep-bleep. Whatever. Fuck the facts of life.

I feel like a suicide bomber. Bloody wires up my nose.
I might explode. If you hear a loud bang, El Rogerio has
detonated in public. Allow it.

SUBMIT.

Roger Hart leans back in his comfy black chair. He puts
fingers up his nose. He can feel them. The stiff, sharp and
interlocking wires that grow in each nostril. He shudders.
His whole body wriggles with disgust. He checks his emails.
Anka Kudolski, the tit shadow from Channel MANC, has
replied. She wants to meet in Wow-Bang. Dirty bitch. What
am I thinking?

I should tell someone, thinks Roger. I should call my mum
and tell her about my wires.

But Roger can't tell his mum. He wouldn't know how to.
What would he say? I can't remember when I last fell asleep.
I've not spoken to another human in a year. I've got wires
growing in my nose and when I listened to my insides,
Mum, I heard bleeping and whirring. No. Roger can't
possibly call his mum. His mum is a pleasant-seeming
Media Studies teacher. She is a resident of Lancaster. She
wouldn't like the idea of Roger, her son, bleeping, alone
and full of bronze.

Roger returns to his blog and notices that many fans
have already posted comments under his last submission.
They want to know if it's true. Does El Rogerio really have
wires in his nose? Roger shudders again. His shoulders
shaking. Spasming. He's really worried. He's breathing
nervously through his mouth.

Allow me. Allow me. El Rogerio never lies. I swear. I've
got bronze wires in my head. I'm techno. I don't care.

I'll be off out tonight. Spying on the lagery losers. Probably meet up with one of my fuck buddies and fuck her and fuck her and fuck her. It doesn't matter.

People say that just because it's windy, the Wild World's coming. Bullshit.

SUBMIT.

On the screen, a pop-up pops up: THE N-PRANG IS COMING. HOW TOTALLY INSANE WILL YOU SEEM WHEN THE REVOLUTION COMES?

'. . . hiccup . . .' A painful hiccup. Roger feels vomit in his neck. He screams. He falls from his chair screaming and clutching his backside. His glasses fall off his face and his world blurs.

Roger's rolling on the carpet. His massive head with its messy hair, closed eyes and screaming mouth is turning red. Read carefully. On the desk, above Roger, the computer crashes and the screen goes dark. Roger screams again. The focus of his hands alternates between his stomach and his arse. Life is an ache. Roger doesn't understand. He tries to lose himself in the *Les Misérables* soundtrack but he doesn't succeed. His pain is suddenly too great.

Crawling slowly in the direction of the bathroom, he wonders whether he has, of late, eaten too many crisps. Perhaps I have, he thinks. Lately, I have stuffed my face with little but corn snacks. I can't remember the last time I drank liquid. This is pretty serious, thinks Roger, through the pain. It feels like fat people with sharp feet are angry in my pelvis. If you just eat crisps, thinks Roger, and you don't drink water, then maybe your innards become as dry as technology. I'm as dry as crisps and full of electricity.

Roger gets to the bathroom and pulls himself across the

smooth black-and-white tiles towards the toilet. He arrives. He almost wants to embrace the base of his toilet. The cold porcelain. It probably isn't porcelain. He hoists himself up onto the seat, pulling down his trousers and pants as he does so. He says, 'Ouch.' The pain is constant. He bends forward extremely until his face is hanging over his kneecaps, staring into his trousers, his boxers and at his bare feet. All smell. Roger hasn't seen soapy water in a while. His left foot is blacker than ever. Is it bruising? The blackness rises as high as his calf. He feels his big toe. It is impossibly smooth.

Thinking about it, thinks Roger. I'm thinking about it. A diet of nothing but crisps is naturally going to result in a succession of fairly agonising farts and shits. I'm just dehydrated. I shall pass a few very dry turds and be blogging about them in a matter of minutes. The pain will subside. I need a beaker of water. Roger is considering reaching into the toilet to wet his hand when his arsehole opens fire with such force and ceremony that he finds himself fast-whimpering, straight-backed, gripping the toilet seat tightly with both hands.

Drip. A liquid drips from Roger after the initial revolting torrent. Where did I find all that water? he thinks, more worried and slightly upset. Where do I get my tears from? They should be bogey-like, squirming like hung-over worms from the corners of my eyes. He peers between his legs. A penis. And through the darkness, past the penis, colourless liquid. A few drops of dark blood. I'm abnormal, he thinks; my droppings aren't brown. In the living room, *Les Misérables* ends. I should have played it from the beginning. A glorious orchestral crescendo rises like a church roof in a storm, then goes quiet. Roger is seized again by pain. His bottom exhales. It gurgles. It is starting to expel an object.

This is disgusting. And it smells. It smells as horrible as the new smells heavenly. It smells like a rotten dream; a cream dream abandoned for decades in a switched-off fridge. The expression on Roger's face is a lip-curling, blinking one. He realises this isn't a matter of a few very dry turds. He's going to crap an object. Roger just knows he's going to crap an object. He can feel it. The painful contractions begin and his teeth are gritted and exposed. It feels. It feels.

Knock knock.

Scratch.

Should I say, shitting a brick? Giving birth to an adult? Pissing a guitar? With each contraction, with every centimetre that the dry object moves, poor Roger Hart performs a 'quack' of agony. This sound, and it is a quack, seems to come from deep in his body. Thin and high in pitch, the noise contains no moisture. Roger's pain is wordless. His eyes are colourful and foul like prawns on a wino's tongue. Jesus, just look at this awful Mancunian bathroom!

'Quaaaaaaak!' screams Roger.

The terrible toilet next to the stained bathtub.

'Quaaaaaak!'

The dusty mirror above the sink that Roger could rip from the wall, squat over and peer in horror at the object in his arsehole.

'Quaaaaaak!'

The bogey in the bathtub, very near the plug. The sharp bronze wire that grew in Roger's nose.

'Quaaaaaak!'

The used bog rolls. The numerous grey tubes that clamour round the toilet like insects round their queen.

'Quaaaaaak!'

The stupid toothbrush. Never used. The foul towel.

'Quaaaaaaak!'

The lying black-and-white tiles. Nothing but cheap and continuous lino.

'Quaaaaaaak!'

The pain.

'Quaaaaaaaak! Quak! Quak!'

Roger Hart dives forward off his toilet and onto the floor. He gasps. The object is no longer inside him. He hears it hit the toilet with a clang as he himself hits the floor with a thud. He clenches his butt-cheeks tight. Shut up shop. He is reminded suddenly of the supposed rapes he's watched on the Internet. He's never sympathised much with those girls, only watched and wanked in a clockless trance as they get banged, feeling as guilty as the cameraman. He understands now. I do, thinks Roger. I feel like I've been done. An odd, inside-out rape. I feel ashamed and scared. I feel like my anus has gone all wide and gaping like those girls on the web. Poor things. Poor thing. Me.

Roger climbs into a crouching position, breathing heavily. He crawls back towards the toilet. Both eyes slanted like sword swipes. Lips and cheeks raised, smiling and quivering with shame, he stares down into the bog.

Roger's crapped a motherboard. Maybe it's a hard drive? No, thinks Roger, his eyes fixed on the object, it's definitely a motherboard. I know a lot about computers. There is a black plastic cube lodged in the toilet, above the dirty water. It's covered in sockets. Some male. Some female. It's covered in the normal circuitry. There are yellow bits and red bits and green bits. Roger realises it's a good model. It's one of the best and most expensive motherboards on the market. He sighs. Weird to crap it, he thinks. Weird to crap it.

He thinks about flushing but realises it's got no chance of getting round the U-bend. He limps to the kitchen, buttocks clenched, to fetch a plastic bag. And it's as he fishes out the motherboard with the bag that he realises he could try to install it in his own computer. I could see if it works. It would be an upgrade, he reasons. It is better than my existing one. Whatever else, it would be an upgrade.

Roger Hart yanks the silver handle. He's sobbing as the dirty waters turn.

Allow me.

Allow me. Here it is. Fact. I just shat a piece of computer equipment. Fact. What do you think of that? I told you. Technology just came out of my arse. Fitting, don't you think? I'm some sort of Second or Third Coming. Which one are we waiting for? Can't remember. But it's boring. We are boring. When will we realise? Even when I was straining out the big dry box with the wires and the sockets, I was like, boring, boring, boring.

Iraq. Afghanistan. Kids in a sandpit. Such a load of.

Do you know Keats?

Words are words and words are words.

Do you fuck?

I'm joking. Everything is a smooth green bud. Inwardly folding petals of regret.

El Rogerio no longer drinks water.

SUBMIT.

Roger watches as the comments gather at the foot of his blog, like the small shallow breaths that precede death. Someone simply writes 'Genius!' Someone else asks, 'What's with the gay poetry?' Others ask what the truth is. Others enquire as to whether El Rogerio is planning to describe his suicide over the web. If he is, then could he be clearer? Internet suicides work really well, the teenagers say, but only when the process is documented simply, not poetically. Yeah?

(Fuck off.)

Roger leaves his computer. He takes the anal cream from his bed and applies it in the bathroom. When he'd ordered it, he thought he might have piles. Because of all the time he spends sitting down and typing. But no, his bottom hurts because it was preparing to crap a motherboard.

The cream helps a bit. Though his fingertips are black when they come back from applying it. Roger returns to the main room and is surprised to find that he's reluctant to blog. Normally he does so without thinking. But he doesn't have the will at this moment. He can't summon words from where words get summoned from. He considers watching his DVD of *South Pacific*. A guilty pleasure but a great musical. The pain is too great. His feelings too bad.

Eventually he forces three sleeping pills down his dry throat and takes a seat on the blue sofa in front of the television. He watches a celebrity singing contest on BBC1. One by one the unheard-ofs come out to sing. They try to entertain with funny faces and unserious dance moves. They sing songs from the past six decades. Roger watches each performance carefully. People love people. In a way. Roger sighs. Towards the end of the programme, he picks up his telephone and registers a vote for a former football player. A black centre forward from the 1990s who'd made a decent fist of 'Are You Lonesome Tonight?'. When a recorded voice tells him that his vote has been counted Roger hangs up and begins to wait patiently for the results.

9

JOE ASPEN WAKES to the sound of screaming. His duvet is pulled over his head. He moves it down a little and stares across the bedroom. The turquoise curtain is shaking frantically, causing the hoops that connect it to the curtain rail to rattle. He tries to go back to sleep. Joe always tries to go back to sleep. But before he can succeed, baby Sally has pulled the curtain clean off the wall and her screams have become muffled.

Joe gets up. He always gets up. He pulls the thick curtain from off Sally's thrashing little body and takes the child in his arms. She stops crying the moment he points her head over his right shoulder and, with his forearm under her warm bottom, begins to rock her gently.

'There there,' says Joe, staring from the window down onto a dusky Wilmslow Road. Five men in brown boots and luminous jackets walk south to Fallowfield. They're pursued by long, tilting shadows. 'There there.'

The digital clock tells 16:45 in lines of red light.

Joe walks across the room. He stands with his back to

the full-length mirror so that Sally can stare at her reflection over his shoulder. He's been doing this since the day Sally was given to him. He figured that as a human, or as a would-be human, Sally should get to know herself.

Joe waits while the baby stares at itself. He stares at his bedroom, marvelling at the dismal stillness. We pretend time passes, thinks Joe. We meet up with people and stir time into life, like milk into coffee. Really, let's be honest, nothing is happening here.

The incident with the bold Wild World guy in the Rolling Stones T-shirt seems like a dream to Joe. But he's rationalised it: I need love. I loved Life Moberg but she left me. I loved her shit till it was pissed from the porcelain. Nowadays I love Sally. One day I'll drop dead. Loveless.

In a twist of something, maybe fate or irony, Sally never shits. Joe changes her nappy each morning like adults change their underwear – for the sheer humane hell of it. Sally never pisses either. Joe's been filling her with black milk for a few days and has witnessed no evidence of waste disposal. In a twist of something else, probably normality, he has now stopped pissing in the sink and begun using his toilet as before. He pees and poos in it then gives it a flush, like he did before Life abandoned him.

Since Sally was given to him, Joe's been trying Life on her mobile every day. He figures an event like being entrusted with a baby warrants a phone call. She never answers but yesterday the answering machine message changed to, *Hey, this is Life's phone. You can find me in Wow-Bang. Weekdays. 10pm. The Real Arms. Ciao.*

Most non-Italians shouldn't say 'Ciao'. But Life gets away with it because she's perfect. Every word is hers.

Joe returns to the bed and puts Sally into her feeding

position, cradled horizontally on his lap. He takes a bottle from his bedside table and presses the teat into Sally's little mouth. There is still no colour in her eyes. She glugs the black milk. Black eyes wide and fixed on Joe.

'There you go,' says Joe. 'My little puffin.'

This week Joe has eaten nothing but rainbow trout. He buys them whole and fresh from Rusholme Fish Market and eats them off the floor with his fingers till just the face and the skeleton remain. He has not been needed at work since Asa Gunn retired. He spends his days crawling around the flat with Sally, hunting spiders and hiding in small places.

When Sally's drunk enough she begins to overflow. Black milk begins to stream down her cute little chin and onto her podgy body. Joe removes the bottle's teat from her mouth and raises his arms, allowing Sally to scurry from his lap, leap off the bed and begin crawling in fast circles around the bedroom floor.

Earlier today, Joe made the decision to track Life down. He and Sally had found a pair of her knickers while they were busy building a nest inside the airing cupboard. They were bright blue, the knickers. Sally tried to incorporate them into the nest but Joe snatched them back, barking, turning from Sally and entwining the blue silk around his fingers with his shoulders hunched. He sniffed the knickers, sobbing a little. We're really alive, he thought. I want to plant these knickers at the back of my throat. I want to grip my heart with them. Push them inside my body as far as they will go. But he didn't. He put them into his pocket and curled up beside Sally in their nest of yellow, insulating foam.

'We'll find her, eh, Sally?' he whispered. 'You don't really mind travelling south, do you?'

Sally didn't seem to. She followed Joe out of the airing cupboard and watched him eat uncooked rainbow trout from off the kitchen floor. It tasted salty. He bent down at it and pulled at the oily flesh with his teeth. When he'd finished he cleaned his mouth with the knickers and said to Sally, 'I'm in love, Sally. Do you know? I'm madly in love.'

The two of them leave for London after Sally's feed. Around six. Outside the night has crushed the day to nothing but quarter-light and cold wind. With his rucksack on his back, Joe walks through the neon of Rusholme, Sally's travel seat hanging from his right arm. The air smells of Indian food and exhaust fumes.

At the bus stop a fat, drunk, white woman bends over Sally with buckets of enthusiasm tipping and emptying from her eyes. Joe watches as her face drains quickly of colour like strawberry milkshake up a straw. The woman turns to him. Transparent.

'My child has an illness,' Joe says, looking over the woman's shoulder at the flashing orange indicator of the bus. 'It's nothing for you to worry about.'

Joe entertains Sally on the journey into town. He plays peekaboo. He pretends to nibble at her chubby arms and presses her pretty nose like it's a button. 'Bleep,' he says.

As they walk from Piccadilly Gardens to Chorlton Street bus station, Joe's attention is drawn by a miaowing coming from a dustbin. Placing Sally down on the pavement, he reaches inside the bin and grips a delicate ribcage covered in soft fur.

'We'll call him Beak,' Joe says to Sally, removing a kitten from the dustbin, taking a small crown of chewing gum from its head and then stroking it under its chin with one finger. Joe brings the kitten's small grey face near to Sally's. Sally looks at it with those totally black eyes of hers, eventually giggling when Beak performs a cute miaow.

'The three of us,' says Joe. 'No more pretending. Let's get Life back.'

The Megabus heaves itself round the bends of central Manchester. Posters glimmer in the dark tunnels like ghosts pleading for DJs and fun. Joe, Sally and Beak share the back seat of the upper deck. By the time the bus joins the M6 just south of Tatton Park, they have the upper deck to themselves. A black couple, the woman pregnant, have retreated downstairs, frowning towards the back seat as they descended the steps. Three veiled Muslim girls followed soon after, lips muttering complaints behind their black face cloths. Through the windows, the orange lights scroll like brushstrokes of fire. And beyond the light, northern England, moonlight and moon shadow.

None of our three notice the brightly lit blue sign. 'Birmingham, 59 miles. The South.' No. None of our three notice because of the fun. The thrill of the quest. Sally shrieks and crawls under seats. Beak scratches at the dusty upholstery, sharpening his young claws. Joe is crouched at the very back of the bus, staring down the filthy aisle. He pictures Life. Such fun to imagine happiness.

'We're coming,' he whispers, beating his arms a little, then smiling and tweeting for joy.

10

IN A TERRIBLE bar with Anka Kudolski, people are speaking, loudly.

'People will still sing, I just know they will,' says a cameraman with pinhole eyes. '*Get your tits out,*' he sings. '*Get your tits out, get your tits out for the lads!* People will still sing that,' the cameraman confirms, suddenly talking quite seriously. 'Even in the Wild World. Don't look so gloomy.'

When Anka had asked to be taken out to lunch she had hoped for somewhere nicer than this. Wetherspoons. An enormous Wetherspoons on Deansgate. A dump. A crap dump. A quite crap life.

Anka stares at the vegetarian lasagne that has fallen asleep on her plate. It hasn't been cooked so much as stared at moodily by a thin yellow chef with warm cheese eyes. I wouldn't eat it if I were dying, she decides, throwing her cutlery onto the table as the director, a forty-something with an aimless nose and white skin like the inside of an orange peel, begins to sing.

'*Oh Manchester is wonderful.*' The cameraman joins in, putting an arm round the director, his smelly mouth surrounded by rusted lips. '*Oh Manchester is wonderful. It's full of tits, fanny and United. Oh Manchester is wonderful.*'

Earlier on, the shoot had begun with Anka stripping to her underwear in a cramped room above a vegetarian cafe on Thomas Street. 'Cracking bones,' said the director, before he pressed Play on a CD player, crossed his arms and said, 'I fucking love Kylie. Now let's see some dancing.'

Anka did her best to sway and look sexy. She licked her finger and gyrated a little. But, in truth, she felt like shit. She had hoped that stripping like this might feel a little like performance art, and initially, as she removed her bra in four sexy stages, she had told herself that this was so: I'm an artist. This is arty. I'm Warhol, Kruger, Manet, Magritte. When did I last see myself eat? Anka started to panic. She grew frantic and started dancing wildly and at a faster tempo than the music. I'm Warhol, Kruger, Manet, Magritte. When did I last see myself eat? In the end she must have fainted.

She must have fainted because she remembers opening her eyes and seeing the cameraman and the director peering down at her as she lay on the floor. 'Don't worry,' the director was saying. 'Don't worry, we got what we needed, don't worry, they'll spunk early because it was very sexy. Up you get now. Let's go get that pub lunch, shall we?'

Anka leaves the cameraman, the director and the lasagne in Wetherspoons. She walks across Exchange Square, near to Selfridges.

Where is it that we go to think? In this wide and meticulously gardened roundabout of history, I mean, which turn-off leads to the quiet wasteland? Where is thought possible? The coffee shop? Too much choosy bollocks and rules. The urban parks? Too much posing and sandwich sex. The library? Too tense. Home? Too depressing. Cinema? Shite. Pub? Distracting. Anywhere else? Too much one-on-one, chill-out, kick-back and kill-yourself conversations, confessions of a constructed mind; talk so dull it could bore the tits off womankind, leaving bras empty and leaving future-man groping and sucking at boobless air. I can't think, thinks Anka. Was I really just filmed in the nude? Yes. In which case I'm in trouble. The facts of life are aliens but cannot be ignored. I touched my tits with a licked finger. A camera captured my nipples. I fainted.

Anka walks past Sinclair's Oyster Bar with its brown sea of outside seating. Men and women grip beers in plastic glasses, grip too hard causing the foam head to spill onto their wrists. Anka passes a line of voguishly lonely designer boutiques, pressed like shiny self-help manuals into what was once the world's Corn Exchange. The sky is blue. She arrives at Manchester Cathedral, which winces when Americans compare it to Canterbury.

In the cathedral porch a man holds a trowel and talks to himself. He says, 'So anyway,' then lifts his trowel in a sort of benevolent threat as Anka pulls on the door handle.

During the Blitz the cathedral's north end was bombed. Every pane of glass got shattered. Trust the Germans. The south end of the cathedral is authentic.

Ancient. Anka enters and stares at the blackened columns, stretched like dead tendons from the stone floor to the stone ceiling. The cathedral is full of people, bent down, faces closed in prayer.

'And, at this time, we ask Our Lord for support,' says the reverend, in his pulpit. 'We ask him to protect the armed forces in Basra and in Afghanistan. Above all, we reject false prophets, we reject the idle tongues that talk of the coming of . . . sexual freaks or dickheads, and yet we ask Our Lord solemnly and openly for His love and His compassion, and for His fashion wisdom when the Wild World comes.'

The man with the trowel has followed Anka inside and begun tugging on her shirt. 'Leave,' he's saying. 'Everyone is praying.'

Anka walks the aisles of Tesco Metro, Market Street. She takes a ploughman's sandwich from the shelf and examines its calorie content. She puts it back.

Was it arty? she asks herself, staring with a delicate throat at fifty different types of cheese. Was it arty to strip and to dance? Am I an artist again? Maybe I am. Maybe I should tell the *Sunday Times*.

Anka buys a ham sandwich and some monkey nuts. She gives the sandwich to a tramp, slumped on the pavement outside a sports shop. The tramp seems unimpressed.

Anka nibbles on a monkey nut, walking home down Corporation Street. She becomes certain she is being followed. Anka is running. She is hurrying the key into the door of her building and running up the stairs. She is cursing herself. She is thinking, I made a big mistake. I agreed to strip for money and I tried to make it arty. I stood in front of a camera and lost myself in my performance. My art. My arse. No flesh. Just bone.

Who the fuck is following me?

She shuts the door of her flat, leans back on it and sighs. She goes into her kitchen and looks into the yellow of her fridge. It's empty. Virtually. There's a carton of soya milk, a punnet of brown cress and a black carrot.

She checks her emails, nibbling on another nut.

Anka, I need to meet you in Wow-Bang because I fear my time on earth is coming to an end. Normal shit!
Yours sincerely, El Rogerio

Great news about your eating, darling. Dad sends his love. We're both very proud.
Love Mum xxx

Looks like I can help you, Anka. See you in Wow-Bang.
Life x

Anka drifts away from her computer, to the bathroom and its mirror.

'I'm Anka,' she says, staring at her eyes. 'Anka as in wanker.'

I have felt this feeling before, she thinks. I have stood in front of mirrors, brain spinning like a copper coin on a steel surface. Eyes glazing. Face greying. She splashes cold water onto her cheeks. It runs off her face and she is quickly dry and just staring. It's back, she thinks. She's back. My brain is calling me on an unknown number and breathing deeply down the phone. 'Anka,' it's whispering, putting on a spooky voice. 'Anka, where are you?' Oh shit. My brain is arranging to meet me for lunch in a nice little cafe where they only serve organic food. But my brain is standing me up. My brain is suggesting we go paintballing with my womb and my liver. We could be on the same team and really fuck them up. My brain is laying me down.

Anka thinks about the self-help mantras trapped in the picture frame in the other room. *Love yourself. Feed yourself.* I'm beyond those, she thinks. For a while, they worked, I did love myself. But Anka is suddenly aware that her life, of late, may well have been confused.

Tomorrow, Anka will be surprised to receive a text from the director, informing her that her video has been uploaded and is already receiving a great deal of attention. She will be surprised when she uses her mobile phone to access the video, surprised to discover that her striptease has been listed in the 'Bony Screw' genre. A genre she has never heard of.

She will be so surprised. She will lie on her bed to watch and listen to her performance. She will not recognise herself. Are those my limbs? Are those my tits?

Anka will recline onto her bed in underwear she does not remember choosing. She will lie with one hand round her mobile and one hand in her knickers. Another set of knickers moistened. How ridiculous, she will think. Real-Anka will watch and wank as screen-Anka removes her bra in four sexy stages.

She's rubbing her bits with her fingertips, lying on the bed, surrounded by sucked monkey nuts, thinking about how we are all of us out of control, about how there is no control. And deep down we all know what we should be doing. Sure, Anka will think. Humans: WE ALL KNOW

WHAT WE SHOULD BE DOING. We all know we should be leading clothed lives of washed bollocks, shaved legs and opinions, served on big white plates on tables with tablecloths. We all know we should be unmurderous, light-hearted and familiar with certain trends. We should be out there, making friends. We all know that others lead wank lives so that we can lead absolute crackers. We all know that we've got to mostly pretend. We're fine with it. We all know that cash is one thing, and that we need to work or get lucky to have it. We all know that love is the other thing, and that we need to get pretty or get lucky to get it. We're fairly obsessed with fucking. On balance, this is fine.

The rhythm of Anka's finger will be suddenly shot to shit. Her emotions will be suddenly muddled up. She'll be close to orgasm, tense and concentrated, but then she'll watch in horror as, on the screen of her mobile, she starts doing things she doesn't remember doing. This must be when I fainted, she will reason. But her orgasm will be suddenly out of reach, like a chased train in a Western that has gathered speed. Anka's finger will slow and come to a stop as, on the screen, her naked self steps out of shot, then returns a moment later with a mobile phone in her hand. Real-Anka will watch with separating features and bending knees as screen-Anka appears to dial a number into the mobile. Seconds later the video will cease to stream and the screen of Anka's phone will flash with the words *Anka Kudolski ... calling ...* Anka will sigh at the sight of her own name. How can I be calling myself? Yes, she will sigh and wonder why. Why is reality so trendy, so changeable, just another fashion victim?

The air will be full of ringtone. Anka's finger will hover above the 'Answer' button. Should I? She will think. How can this be? Should I? Course I should. Life is a hop, a skip and a jump. Anka will answer the phone to herself.

'Hello,' says Anka, from the bedroom.

'Hello,' says Anka, from inside the phone.

'Why are you calling me?'

'We need to talk.'

'I don't think we do.'

Anka will go to the window, where the trains will be accelerating and decelerating in and out of Victoria Station. 'I've got nothing to say to you,' Anka will say, hand flat against the glass. 'Where are you, anyway?'

'I'm nearby,' says the voice inside the phone, in precisely the same tone. 'We need to talk about your eating.'

'We certainly don't. I've been eating,' says Anka, defensively.

'You haven't. I'm coming round.'

'Don't come round.'

'I'm coming round.'

Anka will take the phone from her ear and look at the screen. According to the timer, she's been talking to herself for nearly a minute. She will return the phone to her face.

'Why now? Why now, after all this time?'

'Because I love you.'

'And you think I feel the same?'

'I know you do,' snaps the voice, doubled now, coming from inside the phone and, more loudly, from beyond the front door of the flat. Anka will drop the phone onto the bed. She will walk to the door and place her ear next to the letter box.

'Open the door, Anka,' will come the whisper. 'Admit it. We're obsessed with ourselves. Open the door.'

11

THE GHOST OF Janek's mum is yet to swoop into his ear and start flying round the off-white tunnels of his skull. She died only yesterday, of useless lungs, and she's clearly yet to negotiate the customs and bureaucracy that dying entails. God is yet to tap the A4 evidence of her life into a neat stack and grant her ghost status with a grin. He will though, thinks Janek, walking up Bannerman Road in Bristol towards the crematorium. Mother will be haunting me soon. She'll be whispering opinions that tickle the backs of my eyes. That's all I need. A haunting.

It'll make pulling Life a lot harder, thinks Janek. To Life, I will seem even more distant and distracted with a dead mum grumbling inside me, disapprovingly. I've dreaded this moment, thinks Janek, nearing the entrance of the grey, domed crematorium.

For the first time in a long time, Janek has removed his beanie. What would Snoop say if he saw me like this? he wonders. Stupid brown curls and a black yarmulke embroidered with white cotton.

Janek sees his relatives loitering by the entrance to the crematorium, cloaking their faces from the nose down with handkerchiefs, hands drooping from smart sleeves, getting held and kissed.

'Oh, Janek,' cries Aunt Sophie. A tall ex-model with heavily hairsprayed hair. 'Give me a hug. Janek! Give me a hug.'

Janek gives his auntie a hug. In darker days, he used to fantasise about making love to this woman. But it failed. The fantasy proved weak and feeble. And a penis gripped is a problem halved. Now Aunt Sophie's hands scuttle round his back like blind animals. Trapped in her arms, Janek breathes her crisp, chemical hair. Strands scrape his cheeks and he winces inside the family embrace. Somewhere there are Fuck Festivals. Little matters. Only nothing. That will do.

'Your mother lived to see you succeed! Thank God she lived to see you become such a huge success!' Aunt Sophie holds Janek in front of her with straight arms, tears shining in her eyes, a sombre smile turning around her face.

'Little Janek,' she cries. 'We all had such low hopes for you. So quiet and so shy. You were always just staring, sat silently on the floor like a little grey stone . . . now you're a musician for the stars.' Sophie sniffs snot up towards her two eyes, adding, in a guttural voice, 'You're even more successful than me!'

Janek smiles and nods. He watches his other relatives congregate behind Sophie. His uncle Danny with the voice like a synthesiser and creepy cartoon eyes. His mute grandfather, a white quiff of hair curling round his forehead like a funeral salute. The clump of young cousins, gathered round a mobile phone, heads pressed together, watching music videos. Nothing matters, thinks Janek. But nothing is better than nothing. I'll tell Mum when she's finally paddling in the puddles of my skull, rolling up her cream trousers to the knees and dipping those shocking white calves in my brain slush. I'll tell her all about Life.

The congregation is moving into the hall. Janek nods at the rabbi at the entrance, an overweight old man with panda eyes and a beard like a scribbled storm cloud. Janek sighs at the building's interior. Bright light. Very still air. The smell of yellow polished floors. He puts the N-Prang into his ears, presses Play and waits for the rumble of bass.

The rumble of bass doesn't come. What does come is the sound of stamping feet and clapping hands. The crematorium is a third full. About forty people occupy the front three or four rows. They are making noises in unison. Two loud stamps on the floor followed by one clap, over and over again. Janek walks the central aisle, red wires leading from his ears to his pocket where his fist grips the N-Prang. In front of him Aunt Sophie single-handedly pushes his mother's coffin, which is raised on a trolley with multidirectional wheels. Sophie is slumped over it, cheek against the lid, moving dramatically to the beat of the crowd. Jesus, thinks Janek. People love themselves at funerals. The ex-model is back on the runway, dressed in nothing but her sister's death. I wish Life was here. Funerals make the grieving seem exceptionally sexy. The more the corpse loved you, the sexier you are.

The beat of the crowd does not stop. Janek's never heard a congregation be so loud and percussive before. When his aunt has pushed the coffin to the front of the crematorium, she turns to the audience and starts performing wide overhead claps. Nodding her head. Her face all serious and cool.

'Come on,' shouts Sophie, over the claps and the stamps. Janek watches as, beside Sophie, the rabbi cups an ear with one hand and sends out a bouncing Nazi salute with the other, his eyes edited to cool, enjoyable squints. 'Bring it,' shouts Aunt Sophie, prompting the rabbi to start yelling along to the beat of the crowd: 'Word. Word. Word. C'mon on. Bounce. Bounce. C'mon. Bounce.'

Janek watches, as his aunt Sophie climbs onto his mother's coffin and tears off her long black chiffon skirt, revealing red silk hot pants and violet fishnet stockings. He's reminded of why, as a kid, he'd wanted to shag her. She continues to direct the crowd from the light brown coffin lid, encouraging them to keep the beat. She turns away from them and bends over, polishing her silk red booty in a successfully sexy fashion. Meanwhile the congregation begins to strip. Men remove their black mourning blazers and then their shirts and ties to reveal very muscular bodies. Ripped six-packs. Meaty, nippled pectorals. Oiled up and shining. They tug their trousers down till they're hanging really low. Janek notes that each wears fancy underwear, waistbands embroidered with gold lettering. *Calvin Klein. Armani. Wild World. Fuck Death.* The N-Prang has become red hot in Janek's fist. Women shed their mourning costumes and find that their tits and crotches are covered in outlandish knickers and bras. Purples. Reds. Yellows. They fondle their bodies with shock and joy, as if they've never really stripped before. They bend over and begin jiggling their backsides really quickly till each buttock is just a quivering blur. No one's stamping or clapping any more, but the beat goes on. Backs get arched and boobs protrude. Nipples dance inside expensive bras. The near-naked men and the near-naked women begin to dance in twos, elbows raised, hands in loose fists; they bring their crotches together, staring down at them, smiling. Janek watches as, from on top of the coffin, Aunt Sophie begins to sing.

> 'No Wild World for my sister,
> I wish I could say I'm gonna miss her
> But I won't.
> She's dead and she can't bend over,
> Our lesbian cabaret's finally over.'

Aunt Sophie's melody is simple. She rhymed 'over' with 'over'. Bit shit. But it's pop music. Catchy. Rammed with basic resolution. Janek has no time to ponder the lyrics. He's holding his yarmulke in his hand. He contemplates blocking his mouth with it. I feel a bit horny, he thinks. In fact, I'm going to get an erection. These elderly Jewish ladies all have fantastic bodies. And so this is me: getting an erection at Mum's funeral. This is fate. Sophie begins to rap.

> 'We grew up in the Bronx where we always rocked an Afro,
> My sister and me, we never had no cash flow
> We worked all day doing shows, playing incest,
> Mock-fucked all day, became Ghetto Princess.
> Our sexy black asses hard screwed every pervert
> Leaning over glass, sipping drinks, sniffing sherbet.'

To Janek's knowledge neither Sophie nor his mother ever rocked an Afro. They were born and raised in Somerset. They were never ghetto princesses. Neither ever had a black ass. Mum went to an all-girl school near Salisbury. It's unlikely she ever performed incestuous lesbian shows for New Yorkers. Janek's standing beneath Sophie now, he could reach out and touch his mother's coffin. He watches his aunt's feet tapping around on the lid. Out of the corners of his eyes he can see the congregation, grinding away at each other because they're all so fucking sexy. He watches the rabbi with his bobbing beard and his hand, fingers splayed, covering his crotch. Janek is getting more and more turned on. He is chanting to himself. Nothing matters. Welcome to the festival. This is nothing. I might have to tuck my erection into my belt. Aunt Sophie, meanwhile, has sung another chorus and is ready for verse two.

'This one's for all the bitch ass niggers in the house. We know whassup.
Yeah. What?
We were 69ing back in 1986
Our shows was in decline, yo, we were in a fix.
We started singing as we licked and suck-suck-sucked
We were back on top. We were laced in bucks.
Although eating out my sister made it difficult to sing
We had diamonds round our necks and we were sister-fucking bling.'

To complete her performance, Aunt Sophie leaps from the coffin and over Janek's head, performing somersault after somersault in mid-air. She lands behind Janek and before he can turn round to ask her what is going on and ask her whether she and his mum really did perform lesbian cabaret, she is grinding her crotch against his backside, both hands up his T-shirt, teasing his nipples.

The rabbi is next onto the coffin. He's jumping from side to side, getting into the rhythm, waving at the dancing crowd, getting ready to rap.

'Yo yo yo. Time to feast, motherfuckers, time to feast. Come on.'

The rapping style of the rabbi is more aggressive. A bit Busta Rhymes, Janek thinks, as his auntie notices his erection and pulls a very wide smile. The congregation has moved closer towards the coffin on the rabbi's instruction. He is bending down to them and all except Janek are smiling up at him. The rabbi begins.

'Check out my sermons, they're fresh as a daisy,
Check out my balls, they're aching, baby.
Just get freaky, licking on my Jap's eye,
Y'ain't got taste till you're sucking on a rabbi.
I'll fill your mouth with swollen gland
I'll take you to the Holy Land.'

The crowd are loving the rap. They are shutting their eyes and smiling. For the chorus, a group of ancient Jewish hags with unbelievably smooth, sexy bodies and matching yellow underwear get in a line next to the coffin and sing in a style that reminds Janek of the Supremes. They sing:

'Feast. Yeah.
Feast on the priest. Yeah.
Feast on the rabbi.
Shake. Yeah.
Shake off the sheikh. Yeah.
Shake off the rabbi.'

Janek is fighting off Aunt Sophie. She's not saying anything, just writhing and grinding. Janek feels like he's got sticks in his ears and sticks in his eyes. He can feel his erection flinching like a fish out of water. He could reach out and touch his mother's coffin. He could push the rabbi off the lid and spend a moment quietly remembering her life. The rabbi is performing a headstand on the coffin now, he's shaking his legs in a cool and entertaining way. His face is squashed and red, but still he keeps the beat.

'I ain't frightened, I'm a rabbi with a dark soul
Get down to pray, I'll enlighten your arsehole.
Verse two, motherfuckers.'

Aunt Sophie has a lollipop, she sucks it like a cock. The elderly women cup their tits and Janek can't help but watch. Men flex their rabbit muscles. Women crane their necks to stare over their shoulders and watch their own arses shake and sway. Sexy, smoky eyes and three-quarter smiles. Dance. Bat your eyelashes at your anus. The rabbi's back on his feet. What a cool bastard. He's stamping on the coffin as he raps.

'I've sin a lot o' synagogues I've sin a lot o' sin,
Bin in a lot of lucky dogs and licked a lot of quim.

Here I come, avert your eyes,
I know you like it circumcised.
Jesus wept, I'm coming like an ocean,
Easy, baby, slow down the motion.
Suck my God I know you like it
Lick me like you just can't fight it.
Better clean up, bitch, don't want liable,
Better clean up, bitch, toss me the Bible.'

The rabbi's just riding the beat now. This is the climax to all the fun. He's pointing both hands towards the roof, intimating to the congregation that they should raise the motherfucker. The eighty-year-old women with the shiny cleavage are singing again.

'Feast. Yeah.
Feast on the priest. Yeah.
Feast on the rabbi.'

Janek's wondering whether he should just let go. 'Just let go!' shouts Aunt Sophie. 'Enjoy yourself!' Janek has never heard his relatives speak in this way before and he just isn't sure. The crowd are locked into the groove. Is this the playout? wonders Janek. Are we waiting for the DJ's voice? For God's voice? *That was 'Feast on the Priest' by the Rabbi of Bristol, performing today in honour of Janek's dead, shallow-lunged mum. Come on!*

Janek can't let go and he is no longer horny. This is not the festival. In fact, this is misery. 'Nothing matters,' he shouts, but no one listens. He takes off his yarmulke and frisbees it up into the rafters of the crematorium. 'If nothing matters,' he shouts, drowned out by the beat, 'then why are we doing nothing? If nothing matters we should be doing something. Rabbi! Listen to me.'

The rabbi stares down from on top of the coffin.

'God matters, Janek,' he booms. 'Don't start playa hating on ma motherfucka the Lord. Don't go pimping His omniscience.'

Janek doesn't believe in God. I believe in bass lines, Janek thinks, watching as the expression on the rabbi's face alters suddenly and completely. It changes from squinting, pouting, multi-platinum-selling hip-hop superstar to the face of a petrified soul whose footing has become unsure.

'Janek!' cries the rabbi, his voice alarmed, returning to the sharp fuzz of his Orthodox accent. 'Janek! What's happening?'

The coffin beneath the rabbi's feet is beginning to shake violently. His whole body is shifting around, arms outstretched, trying to regain balance, surfing a wave of angry death.

'Help me, Janek! Help your rabbi!'

The crowd around the coffin have become still but the hip-hop beat is louder than ever. It's deafening. The congregation watch, panting from the dance, as the lid of the coffin begins to splinter and crack under the pressure being applied from within. Janek wonders what his mother thinks she's doing. Not a lot probably. But really, bursting out of your coffin during your funeral isn't funny. It's insensitive. But Mum's doing it anyway, thinks Janek. She always was eager. He watches as the rabbi topples backwards off the coffin, making it easier for his mum to smash the lid and rise like a puppet from the red silk-lined casket. She has begun to decompose. She's lost weight. Her face has lost its rosy cheeks.

'*Word up, blood.*' His mother's voice is as breathless as it ever was. One tit looks precarious, as if it's only held on by the bikini. This is me. My dead, shallow-lunged mother has come back to life wearing a bikini. Why burn a woman looking so easy?

Janek sees the rabbi's head peep out from behind the coffin, looking up in horror at his mother's dead, gold G-stringed backside. The rabbi disappears, hiding his face with his beard. Beside Janek, Aunt Sophie is staring up at her sister through moist eyes. 'I always said she was talented, Janek,' Sophie whimpers, not taking her eyes from her sister. 'I mean, I was the *really* talented one. But given that your mum gasped a great deal, she was still pretty good at entertaining people. Just look at her.'

On second thoughts, thinks Janek, it's probably best that Life didn't come today. This would have freaked her out.

'I'm tired of cocksuckers tryin' to tell me I'm past it
Ain't no way I'm gettin' nailed inside no whack-ass
    casket.'

'Whack-ass casket', rhymed with 'past it', is, Janek thinks, the most impressive piece of hip hop we've heard all funeral.

'Don't cry. Don't cry.
Cos I
Won't die. Won't die.'

This is really brilliant, thinks Janek. Mum's really being playful with the beat, not just cramming in words like the rabbi and Aunt Sophie, who really just copied US rap circa 1988. Oh, Mum. Mum's relaxing on the beat, real chilled, maybe because she's dead, you know, because she's less anxious. She's establishing melodic, half-spoken 'hooks'. She reminds me of Snoop Dogg. His really commercial later period.

'You can call me hardcore. Cos I'm hardcore.
I'm gonna live the life I worked hard for.
I may be breathless. I'm still sleazy.
I make cheatin' death look so easy.'

Oh, you do, Mum, thinks Janek. You really do. If I had known you could lock into a groove with such confidence then I'd have come to see you more often. I wouldn't have gone to Berkeley or on tour with Jay-Z. I could have come round and jammed with you. Me on bass and you just letting your lyrics flow. I love you. I should have told you. Even when you used to cough up blood at the dinner table, I loved you so much. I never said it. But I always felt like we had loads in common.

Janek approaches the coffin and holds out his hands. His mother bends down to take them immediately. Together they sway. The sexy congregation can only watch as Janek and his mum just hold hands and sway. This is real dancing, thinks Janek. Not like all that groin-bating bollocks we saw before. It's a shame Mum's wearing this bikini. But nevertheless, he thinks, this is lovely dancing.

They sing.

'Don't cry. Don't cry.
Cos we
Won't die. Won't die.'

Janek's in seventh heaven and he's disappointed when he's seized by a sudden pain. When the huge balloon of his consciousness is popped with a lit match. When he's dragged from the melody by hands holding tightly onto each of his ears. He yelps. His eyes shut tight in pain. He loses his grip on his mother's hands and feels himself falling backwards, getting dragged down till he can tell he's on the ground. He can feel the polished wood of the crematorium floor on his back. He can hear the sound of his own screams. Human voices.

'Janek! Wake up! Janek!'

'Just keep holding him down.'

When Janek opens his eyes, he sees two concerned faces. The Rabbi of Bristol and his aunt Sophie. He glances at the floor either side of his head. The earphones of the N-Prang have been removed from his ears. He exhales. The silence is ringing.

'Death comes for us all,' says the rabbi. 'Accepting that is the first step to happiness.'

Aunt Sophie nods enthusiastically. Beyond the rabbi's shoulder is his mother's coffin. It has been damaged. A small hole has been punched in the lid, just large enough for someone to have reached in and dragged out one of his mother's arms. The arm is dressed in violet velvet. Every dead finger wears a ring.

Behind him, the congregation sit on the pews in silence. Two or three elderly people on the front row have clearly had their clothes torn. They are trying to repair them, holding collars and dress straps in place, then letting go and sighing as the ripped sections fall.

'Bullshit,' Janek whispers.

'No, no,' snaps Aunt Sophie, 'the truth.'

Still on the floor, Janek touches his tongue with the tips of his fingers. He finds words there. Three of them.

Please don't die.

A second later and Janek has shrugged off the rabbi and has pushed Aunt Sophie away. He is striding down the central aisle of the crematorium. He is stuffing the N-Prang into his pocket, walking in awkward paces of varying lengths, beatless, no rhythm at all.

Please don't die.

Janek picks up his suitcase and his bass guitar from a luggage locker at Bristol Temple Meads. He phones Life. Voicemail. *Meet me in Wow-Bang!*

Janek sits in the long tunnel of the train station. He watches as the people strain to look at the screens before being siphoned off to one platform or another. He thinks about getting out his bass and doing some busking. But everyone's wearing an MP3 player. You can hear it in the air. The thin ringing of personal music. He'd be better off begging.

I've got to find Life. If anyone knows the way to the Fuck Festival, it's her. I've got to make her fall in love with me. I've got to stop using the N-Prang. Life can be more than just a goodie bag, a music video, a funky existence, a wandering bass line. Everything matters. Nothing. Everything. They were only ever words. Fat, wet words that you got bogged down in. You dickhead. Relax. Fall in love, it's fucking agony. Sex is fine. Enjoy it. Life is fine. Be optimistic. We all know what we should be doing. Be optimistic!

Half an hour later, Janek Freeman is on the train to London. He watches the countryside scroll by. He listens to his dead mum drone on and on inside his head.

'Don't!' he shouts, causing fellow passengers to turn at him and glare.

Staring at the fast fields, he realises that little can be sustained. Ideas and desires have the lifespan of a mint, and while being optimistic is fine in theory, it can't be sustained. The N-Prang is burning a hole in his pocket. He thinks about pushing a hosepipe into his ear and filling his skull with cold water. He's not even halfway to London when he decides to lock himself in the toilet, stuff the earphones into his ears, cover his eyes and close his mouth.

'*Life,*' he sings, alone. '*Life, I'm coming to get you, baby. You're in my brain, you sexy lady.*'

12

ROGER HART HAS discovered he is difficult to move. His lower legs are now covered in black plastic. Both feet. Both legs. Up to his knees. He doesn't like it. It's heavy, for one thing; he has to lift his legs with both arms if he wants to go anywhere. But also, his lower body now reminds him of the dashboards of cars he was driven in as a child.

He sits beneath his computer in his empty flat. He's found an old photograph of his family on holiday in Brittany. Roger, his parents and his sister sit round a table in a pretty little courtyard with uneven, stony ground. There is a red-and-white tablecloth. A plate of pasta and tomato sauce sits in front of all four of them. They have turned to smile widely at the camera. Roger's sister, elder by two years, looks very pretty in a dark blue dress with small red flowers on it. His parents look like younger versions of their real selves. Their hair still lively and with colour. Their faces not yet pulled towards the obscurity of old age. Roger's head is not as large as it was to become. The lenses of his square spectacles are still fairly thin. On the photograph's reverse, it says '1990'. Roger ignores the machinations of his body and stares at the image in silence.

To go back! To snuggle inside that split second again like it was a warm sleeping bag. To force my huge adult head inside my small childhood one. To make happy high-pitched sounds. To spill red pasta sauce down my lovely white shirt. To be with my family. To be with humans. To go back!

Just when Roger's convinced he's going to bawl his eyes out, his eyes slam shut and refuse to open. He feels his eyeballs turning round and round; turning, slopping and dropping, like wet clothes in a washing machine. When his eyes do spring open, he blinks blue sparks. Roger sees that the photo has fallen from his hand. It is out of reach. He lacks the strength to retrieve it. Roger has discovered that he is difficult to move.

Turning into a piece of clumsy technology, thinks Roger, has to be the worst thing that's ever happened to me. No, no, that's an exaggeration. Most of my adolescence was worse than this. But this is still pretty awful. Roger knows he has sat at his computer for too long. He suddenly pictures the vast array of words he has produced in the last year or so. The lengthy descriptions of certain shits he's taken, certain wanks, nose-picks, pisses, etc. The words he's wasted describing his sitting position. His blog was popular, sure. But it was bollocks. Roger realises that he has screwed up too many words into hard balls and hurled them at innocent people. He realises that, deep down, he wants to continue to do this. He is addicted to blogging. He wants to write every last bit of space out of the world. He feels guilty about this, of course, but he can't deny his instincts. And anyway, he feels guilty about loads of stuff. He realises that it is time to confess, before it's too late and before all his true feelings get threaded like bronze wires inside safe and colourful plastic. He heaves his heavy body up onto his office chair and sighs and sparks.

Allow me. Allow me. My loyal readers. My gentle teenagers.

How I have enjoyed writing to you. Blogging for you. How I have enjoyed learning about your little approaches to life. You have amused me. You have. You have amused me with your funny stories about feeding your burgery backsides into your skinny jeans. Amused me with your love of American musicians who tell lies about their age and claim to love death. Your touching loathing for those around you. I have loved it all. The black hoods you tug over your impressive hairstyles. How I have enjoyed watching you grow and grow.

But I have something to confess. The blogs I wrote were full of lies. The person I created, the person you liked, El Rogerio, was nothing but an invention. I am not like him. Nothing like him. My real name is Roger Hart and I do not care for rock music. I'm a really big fan of the musicals. My ambition is to dance and sing on the West End stage.

I'm thirty. The things I have claimed to love or hate, I barely know. They are just things I discovered through researching around your interests. I became lost in the exercise, began to believe myself. I have been isolated for a while now. I'm writing to you this one last time, to warn you.

I should say that not everything I wrote was bollocks.

I am, for example, a prolific wanker. I did indeed fire semen at my TV, at the bony, busty Anka Kudolski. But let me tell you, my faithful teenagers, we are all of us wankers. So don't elevate me or feel bad about yourself. We are all of us hungry. We are all of us greedy. We are all of us starved.

For me the game is up. I have taken things too far. I see that now. I have lived without humans for too long. I couldn't return. Soon I won't even be able to talk to you, my teenagers. This makes me sad. But I'm pretty sure that very soon I will be little more than a flurry of programming, technology, devised by something that is, in essence, dull.

You see, I really did crap a motherboard. I really do have wires in my head. My legs are truly black and shiny and my belly does bleep in the same way that yours rumbles. I can't sleep. Physically. I can't sleep. Water hasn't passed my lips in weeks. These are the facts. You didn't believe me, did you? Well, come to Manchester and administer my cream. See what a mess that motherboard made of my arsehole. Then you'll believe.

The one truth I told you was the one thing you refused to believe. This pissed me off. So much so that I thought about abandoning the lot of you. Leaving you alone. But then . . . But then. But then I couldn't breathe without my keyboard. Couldn't wank without my mouse. My body's black and full of wires. I lack the guts to leave my house. I think I'm dying.

I realise, as the technology inside me gets more and more advanced, I have no one left to turn to but you. Only you lot, whom I have lied to from the start. What a sad state of affairs. You feel death winding up inside you, your foot turns black, then your legs, you give birth to technology, and the only people you can confide in is a bunch of children you've always lied to and who you've never even properly met.

I can't even be sure that my fingertips are hitting the keys. Tell me. Are they? Are you reading this, my teenagers? Is this real? I can no longer tell the difference between really breathing and describing breath, the difference between the filling of my lungs and the tapping of my fingers. The difference between my brain and the screen, my penis and the porn, myself and my text, my heartbeat and my hard drive, my arse and my elbow, my eyes and your eyes. I'm confused. I'm disgusting. Am I alive or am I describing being alive? Both. Tell me, are you reading this? If you are, then comment on it. The text, I mean. Comment on me. Send me messages.

SUBMIT.

Roger watches with anxious, humming eyes as his teenage readership do indeed begin to comment on his blog. There are a few unforgiving dicks who go down the 'How could you lie to us, El Rogerio?' route. But, on the whole, the teenagers take the news of Roger's deceits well. They claim to be quite interested and ask Roger to continue. A girl called RapidDeath says she was once taken to see *Joseph and the Amazing Technicolor Dreamcoat* and thought it was quite good. Roger smiles. Bleeps. Carries on.

Thank you. Allow me. Allow me. Still alive. Let me tell you the whole story.

I crapped out the motherboard and then I rested. I tried to sleep but I just couldn't. In the middle of the night, I removed the existing motherboard from my computer and replaced it with the one I'd given birth to earlier. I couldn't resist doing it. It was an upgrade. It is not in my nature to turn down a technological upgrade.

After screwing the new hardware into place, I switched on the computer. I watched it boot up. I listened to it bleep and whirr. I listened to myself bleep and whirr. The fact that I was turning into technology, as I have said previously, bores me to death. When I noticed that my pubic hair had been replaced by a snakepit of red and black wires, I yawned. I was so lost in my blog that I didn't care. I wasn't interested in the changes to my body.

With the new motherboard successfully installed, I felt an increased unity with my computer. We were more bonded than ever. A motherboard had passed from me to it. We were conjoined somehow. We shared each other. The attachment I felt towards this machine far exceeded that which I had felt for other humans. Just to look at the computer made me happy. It became a symbol of self-fulfilment, play, creativity, socialising, sexual experimentation, information and enjoyment. When I stared at the screen, I felt a profound lack of responsibility. I felt exhilarated. And although I try to fight this feeling, I love it.

I have taken things too far. I promise you that, effectively, I have turned into a computer. It's very gay. I'm hardly surprised now, when I go to clean the wax from my ears and I discover USB ports. Or when I think about Anka Kudolski and go to touch my penis, only to find a numerical keypad and above it, as I say, a thatch of plastic pubes. What a laugh. I'm hardly surprised any more.

It's some elaborate pisstake. Can you imagine me on the West End stage? Hobbling on with these stiff plastic legs of mine. Metal springing out from me. If the leading lady kissed me she'd receive an electric shock. My vocal range is diminishing rapidly. Soon, I suspect, I will be left with just one note. I will speak in an old-fashioned, unrealistic monotone. But speak to who? To you? To Anka Kudolski? I'm frustrated. I didn't ask to become a computer. I can barely move. Getting over to the stereo to play *Les Misérables* would be a struggle.

I can feel an impulse inside me that I cannot fight. It is an impulse to describe. Not to live but to describe. It is an impulse to fill the world with words until you just can't move for them. I will just describe and describe. Words will zip from my software brain out of my window and out into Manchester, then London, across the seas. Soon you won't be able to run in the outside world for fear of smacking into a sentence of mine and hurting yourself. People will sneak off to the countryside to try and escape the endless amount of words that will gridlock the cities and black out the sky. But words will get everywhere. Young couples will run up mountains for a bit of secretive sex, but sentences will straddle these mountains like giant slugs. Small words will flit about in the air near the summit, putting the couple off their lovemaking. They will feel awkward and watched. This is the impulse that is inside me. To describe until it hurts to breathe the air.

I'm trying to fight this impulse. Oh, really I am. But I can't fight it for much longer. I am a man. Or I am a computer. Whichever I am, I am afraid to die. You should be too, my teenagers. If you don't get up and do something soon, you'll be screwed. You'll be sitting at your computer, chatting or watching a video or whatever, when words will enter your bedroom. Big boring words will surround you and you'll get scared. Rightly scared, staring with petrified eyes at these menacing letters. Lengthy descriptions of human beings doing fuck all will square up to you and suck the air from your lungs. Idle chatty words will fuck with you. Basic flirtatious words. Sharp needless words. Jokey words. Heavy gossip. Words that advertise. Long bullshit lists of words. Films people like. Books people have read. Huge meaningless words will surround you. They will come together like the clashing rocks of ancient times and they will crush your head to dumb, dumb shit.

I can feel all this inside me. I can feel no desire to live. I can feel a desire to just gossip, chat and declare that I'm laughing. To bang on and on and on about nothing until there is nothing left to say. If you don't act now, my poor teenagers, then the human dead will bequeath little else but lists of likes and dislikes, one-word declarations of sexualities, a favourite quote and a funny joke, some abbreviated remarks, a stupid question and not a breath of displaced air.

This is depressing. Isn't it just, my little friends? You didn't think I was capable of caring so much, did you? Well, this was my last and only warning. From me to you. Our boring thoughts and our boring remarks are going to hunt us down and bore us all to death.

Hey U. U ok? U ok? Gr8. Hey U. U ok? U ok? Gr8. Hey U. U ok? U ok? Gr8.

:-) :-) :-) :-) :-) :-) :-) :-) :-) :-) :-) :-) :-) :-) :-) :-) :-) :-) :-)
:-) :-) :-) :-) :-) :-) :-) :-) :-) :-) :-) :-) :-) :-) :-) :-) :-) :-) :-)
:-) :-) :-) :-) :-) :-) :-) :-) :-) :-) :-) :-) :-) :-) :-) :-) :-) :-) :-)

:-) :-) :-) :-) :-) :-) :-) :-) :-) :-) :-) :-) :-) :-) :-) :-) :-) :-) :-) :-)
:-) :-) :-) :-) :-) :-) :-) :-) :-) :-) :-) :-) :-) :-) :-) :-) :-) :-) :-) :-)
:-) :-) :-) :-) :-) :-) :-) :-) :-) :-) :-) :-) :-) :-) :-) :-) :-) :-) :-) :-)
:-) :-) :-) :-) :-) :-) :-) :-) :-) :-) :-) :-) :-) :-) :-) :-) :-) :-) :-) :-)
:-) :-)
:-)
;-)
;-(

I invite you all to attend my wake in Wow-Bang. I'd like to say goodbye to you all before I finally become a complete computer and just start jabbering total crap. Anka, if you're reading, I'd especially like to meet you.

Forgive me, my teenagers, for lying to you. I hope you understand that I was in an odd state of mind, that I was turning into a computer and therefore honesty was a difficult policy for me. If you're angry with me for not being myself, then, well, that's a bit silly. But feel free to meet me in Wow-Bang. Feel free to exact your pound of digital flesh.

SUBMIT.

Roger is at his desk and trying desperately to sing. He tries to sing the song the people sing when they know they're going to die. When they know the revolution is over. It has been crushed. Look down. You're standing in your grave.

Roger's notes do not soar like they used to. His voice is modulated and getting crushed to a singular and irritating drone.

'I will fight. Obviously I will. But first to Wow-Bang!' he cries. 'First to Wow-Bang!'

Roger's fingers squirm onto the keyboard like fast worms

onto a warm corpse. There is a furious tapping. Tap. Tap. Tapping. Sap. Sap. Human crackling.

'Help me!' cries Roger, watching his blurred hands in disgust. 'I am hitting the keys too hard.'

Knock Knock.
  Scratch.

II

One Night in Wow-Bang

Knock knock

13

IT'S AMAZING WHAT we can do with computers nowadays. The traipsing queue of civilisation that snakes behind us in brown clothes and rubbish shoes should be jealous. (Insert smiley: the angry one.)

That lot. The dead. The past. What do they have? Mud. Silly hats. Inkwells. Glossless lips that mumble the old questions that we no longer mumble. 'Are we free?' they whisper. 'Is it good?' they groan. 'Life, we mean. Is it good?'

Don't answer.

The sky above Wow-Bang is a perfect yellow and a perfect blue. It streaks in the way that all skies would streak, if humans were able to reach up and streak them personally with large, artistic hands. The birds are excellent birds. They are birds of paradise and of prey. They fly in great numbers, silhouetted against an imaginative sun, large wings beating slowly and in unison.

The harbour of Wow-Bang is programmed well. There are white houses bathed in sunlight. There are wooden walkways. Virtual humans sit on virtual chairs. They chill and chill in the bars and in the cafes. They are looking out at whales in the harbour, just under the surface of the shallow digital sea. The large and docile whales designed and programmed, no doubt, by the whale enthusiasts of the real world. Those who have grown tired of the scarcity of whales and wish to see them more often and so bring them, wrapped in code, and tip them into the sea off the coast of Wow-Bang, shouting, 'Look, citizens of Wow-Bang! We now have whales! Soon we will have everything we need!'

Life Moberg often comes to the Wow-Bang harbour in the early evening. The harbour is the city's most peaceful district. The only part that is yet to be taken over by fetish clubs, fuck palaces and discotheques. Life likes to walk along the seashore, staring at the whales, of course, and at the perfect sky which appears most beautiful when viewed from the coast. It doesn't attract too many people, this place, so the graphics of Wow-Bang are able to scroll smoothly. One's virtual body doesn't jerk like it does in more crowded places. Here, it is easy to enjoy the impressive, well-programmed, unnatural beauty of Wow-Bang. Here, it sometimes seems possible to breathe.

But of course, in some dimly lit room in the real world, Life Moberg is sitting on a real chair, staring at a screen with her index finger pressed firmly on the cursor keys of a computer. But she sees through that reality and so should we. She ignores the air she breathes. Its taste, temperature and smell. So should we. Life is enjoying Wow-Bang.

She locates an empty jetty and walks to the end. Below her, little red boats bob in the repeating motions of the blue sea. In the distance, the sun is setting, changing to beautiful colours, completing its graphic cycle. It's strange, thinks Life, even though this sun is fake, it still makes me sombre and keen to reflect. Somehow I still feel its warmth. Life's mind turns to Joe. The boy she left behind.

He wasn't trying to nest in my arse, she thinks. I shouldn't say that to people. It was affection. It was only affection and I just crushed it. But we got too close. We were so close we were touching and the air around us was a cocktail of Joe's real smell and my real smell, and I watched him breathe that odour with closed eyes and pure pleasure. It put me off him. I sniffed it and I winced. I wanted more. I always thought there was a world and a way of life that was . . . I don't know – light without light bulbs, smiles without brains, love without odour and sex without stains. But really, if that's what you want, you can only ever live virtually. Like this.

A shadow floats on the water. Life points her graphic eyes at the sky and sees a large bird flying above her in the blue and the yellow. The bird is too big to be a native program of Wow-Bang. It is a human. A human who has chosen to appear here as a bird. Life realises that it is, in fact, a puffin. The national bird of her homeland, the Faroe Islands. She knows that it is Joe. I know it's you, she thinks, following the flight of the puffin. He does not fly too close to her. He keeps a respectful distance, just flitting back and forth with his black wings outstretched. She considers hovering up next to him. Every citizen of Wow-Bang can fly, not just those who choose to look like birds. But she doesn't join Joe in the sky. She points her head at the ground and teleports away.

Life teleports to the pier on the other side of Wow-Bang harbour and hopes that Joe does not follow her. The sun is disappearing quickly. The digital night is falling. Life begins turning round aimlessly in a circle. She feels anxious. She considers instructing her hands to cover her face in sorrow, but what would be the point? She considers making her eyes cry. Same problem though. What's the point?

Instead she keeps turning in a mechanical circle. She thinks about Janek Freeman. He'll be in Wow-Bang tonight. Is he everything that Joe isn't? He's solvent, sure, a successful musician, involved in the Wild World. But he's cold. He makes love a bit like a zombie. And he never stopped playing his bass. Nice at first, but it's not the most melodic instrument. He is handsome. But is love really just a medium-paced queue of boys in un-ideal trousers and a variety of shirts and T-shirts, bad shoes, good shoes, strange dicks, standard dicks, underwear, trips away, sayings and hairstyles? Is Janek really the kind of boy that I should kiss while I'm alive? I don't know. Pointless thinking about it, thinks Life. She does not like to reflect. I should not come to the harbour, she decides. I should not watch the setting of this impeccably programmed sun.

Life leans out over the wooden walkway and stares down at the unimpressive tide beneath her. The tide comes in and out rather crudely. Too quickly and completely. Waves should leave wet-looking, dark sand when they retreat, not bright yellow sand. Bad programming, thinks Life, noticing that, below her on the beach, a man is shooting a woman repeatedly in the head with a grey pistol. They're both knee-deep in the water. Circles of red blood keep spurting from the woman's head. They land in the sea and then disappear. You still see bollocks like this, even at the harbour.

As for the Wild World, thinks Life, turning away from

the murder and continuing along the raised wooden promenade, through the fading golden light, I'm not sure the Wild World is quite what I'm looking for. At first, I was impressed by the organisation. Everyone spoke with so much excitement and confidence. People bought me drinks and gave me advice. We snorted cocaine till early in the morning in their Bethnal Green homes. They told me I had a good attitude and that a beautiful girl would go far in the Wild World. But they're using me. I know for a fact that they're using me.

Life notices that the man with the pistol has finished killing the woman. He has climbed up onto the promenade and started killing other people who have just come to stare out at the sea. Although the man looks old, it's likely he's being controlled by a group of teenage dickheads in America, Russia or China, who knows? Life can picture them, gathered round the computer screen in a dark room, laughing, mouths full of saliva, spitting accidentally, shouting, 'Kill them, kill them all.'

Life stays to watch the man kill four or five innocent, unarmed people but then decides to teleport away. She hasn't got time to die tonight. Not with Janek and Anka Kudolski in town to see her. She hasn't got time to start searching the cemeteries of Wow-Bang for her dead body and then waiting for it to reanimate. Here, death is inconvenient.

Just as Life is teleporting away and the graphics of the Wow-Bang harbour are dismantling, she catches sight of the puffin again. It's flying through the sky above her head, flying at speed towards the murderer, its red beak open with rage.

* * *

145

Roger Hart rises to applaud the cast of virtual actors who are virtually breathless and bowing on the stage above him. There's something about the virtual performance of *Cats* that Roger really enjoys. In the real world, the cat costumes worn by the actors suggest to the audience that it might be absolutely fine to fuck a cat. It positively promotes cat-fucking. Roger finds this odd. But in the Wow-Bang production the cats are pretty much the same as cartoon or video game characters. The spectacle is less erotic, allowing one to enjoy the incredible Rice/Lloyd Webber score.

Behind Roger, also applauding, are about seven hundred teenage avatars. They are Roger's fans, or, more accurately, they are fans of the El Rogerio blog. They agreed that since Roger is turning into a computer, it might be nice for them all to go to a virtual musical together in his honour.

Most of the seven hundred have programmed themselves in quite similar ways. They are all incredibly skinny, limbs literally as thin as cocktail sticks. They are all dressed in tight black clothing with the occasional splash of yellow or pink neon. On top of their big heads, they have outrageous haircuts full of bright colours and large, daring shapes. On their faces they have programmed enormous sad eyes which contrast with their small mouths and barely noticeable noses.

They are all applauding *Cats* along with Roger, mainly out of politeness having actually found the production to be deeply boring. But they feel strangely drawn to Roger, to the man they used to call El Rogerio. In fact, he is close to being a prophet in their massive teenage eyes.

Roger turns to wave at his fans. His Wow-Bang avatar bears a striking resemblance to his real-life appearance before he started getting all technical. He has a large bespectacled head. Stocky body. Nondescript clothing. He is genuinely moved by the amount of people who have turned out to meet him. He instructs his face to smile as they all cheer and chant his name. I'd have told the truth earlier if I'd known they'd love me more, he thinks. After minutes of cheering, Roger is overwhelmed. He turns to the stage where the cast of *Cats* is a little confused by the rapturous applause. Overcome with emotion, Roger executes them all.

Janek Freeman is frantically searching for a decent dick. He's scouring the boutiques of Wow-Bang's 'Lower East Side' in a desperate attempt to find a cock that will satisfy Life.

This is Janek's first time in Wow-Bang. He's unfamiliar with the format. He's got less than an hour before he has to meet Life in the Real Arms and his avatar looks alarmingly basic. He's managed to design a head that looks like his own insofar as it's wearing a beanie. He met a man with the head of a rhino who helped him to acquire some clothes. A red T-shirt and a pair of jeans. But as they parted company, the rhino guy said, 'If you're meeting a girl, be sure to find yourself a good-looking cock.'

'Where do I find that?' Janek asked.

'Penis Street, Lower East Side.'

Janek's on Penis Street now, staring into the shop windows wondering what constitutes a good-looking cock. He can see all shapes and sizes. Pierced, tattooed, horses'. He can't decide. He's never had to pick a dick before. He's wondering whether he should try and find a circumcised one to match with real life. Or maybe I should branch out, go crazy, get a dog's dick. This is ridiculous. Life's seen my real dick, maybe she'll think it's tragic if my virtual dick deviates noticeably.

At the far end of Penis Street, a man wearing a pink tuxedo starts randomly killing people with a machete, so Janek hurries inside Cock Heaven to be safe.

'Hey there, what are you after?' says a naked man with several penises growing around his waist from front to back.

'I need a penis.'

'Sure,' says the man, performing a camp pirouette, causing his belt of penises to fly horizontally like a grass skirt would in reality. 'Well, our most popular penises are Afro-Caribbean and donkey. Can I ask, do you have a girlfriend here in Wow-Bang?'

'Yes,' Janek lies, the image of Life flashing through his real brain.

'And are you together in real life?'

'Of course.'

'In which case I suggest you splash out on a realistic and beautifully rendered phallus. One that won't disrupt your sex life in the real world.'

Janek's confused. Through the window of the shop, the guy with the machete is still killing people. Slitting their throats, causing them to disappear.

'You see,' the penis seller is saying, 'if I sell you a whale's dick your girlfriend might get used to it. We've found that frequent exposure to a novelty Wow-Bang phallus can breed apathy towards real human dicks.'

'I don't understand any of this,' says Janek.

'There's nothing to understand,' says the man. 'It's just fun.' As he says the word 'fun', every dick on the man's waist goes hard. It looks like his torso is sitting in a flesh salad bowl. A minute later and Janek has left the shop. He exchanged thirty Wow-Bang dollars for a six-inch, white, uncircumcised erection.

Anka Kudolski is eating a virtual cheeseburger in Eddie's, a popular fast-food restaurant in central Wow-Bang. She's watching people. Watching as they move awkwardly around each other, their movements stiff and quite random. She watches as people form rough circles and try to start conversations. On the table next to her, a guy and a girl sit down and speak.

'Where are you from?' asks the girl, she's wearing a latex catsuit and she has whiskers sprouting from below her nose.

'Detroit. You?' says the man. He's wearing a Chelsea FC kit with the name 'Lampard' on the back. He's even got the socks.

'I'm from Nanjing,' says the girl. 'Do you like football?'

The man in the football kit leans towards the girl, blows her a kiss and says, 'No. Do you like throat sex?'

Anka watches as the man gets up without warning and charges towards the exit. In his effort to leave quickly he ends up walking against a transparent wall for a few seconds before finally finding the door. The whiskered girl from Nanjing gets up and starts walking round the restaurant bumping into people. This is a stranger's paradise, thinks Anka. She's reminded of those people who decide to knock on the door of their childhood homes and get shown around by the present occupant. It's just not quite right. It feels wrong. Strangers are lurking in the background of your family photos. Former friends are watching from the shadows as you kiss your current lover. Your enemies are licking their lips over lists of your latest friends. The living are haunting the living.

Anka looks down at the half-eaten burger on her plate. She looks at her excruciatingly thin wrists and instructs her face to grimace. She redesigned her avatar on arriving in Wow-Bang this evening. She went to a shop on Torso Road and demanded the thinnest body available. That turned out to be an under-the-counter job. Not strictly legal, even in Wow-Bang. She positioned her new body in front of a mirror for no reason. The shopkeeper smiled, saying, 'You're nothing but a skeleton with huge tits, aren't you?' Anka nodded.

She's due to meet El Rogerio in the Rib Cage at around nine. She's arranged to meet Life in the Real Arms at ten. She wonders whether either will sense that there are two of her, that she has a double. Will they realise that in her bedroom, back in Manchester, two identical pairs of hands are tapping at the keys.

She has only made half of her cheeseburger disappear. Nevertheless, Anka leaves the restaurant. As she does so, people stare. They are horrified by the skeletal avatar. Her body is terrifyingly thin. People instruct their faces to show pain.

14

THE SKY ABOVE central Wow-Bang darkens realistically. The streets begin to get busier as, in the real world, wives, husbands, siblings and parents turn in for the night, leaving the citizens of Wow-Bang alone at their computers. Shit gets said: 'I promise I won't be too long, I just want to see who's around.'

Life walks into the Real Arms and is greeted by several people. It's a small place, just one room. There's a dance floor in the middle where people congregate and show off the latest moves they purchased on Dance Street. Around the dance floor are tables and chairs programmed to appear wooden. Against the back wall is a bar where you can buy the Cocaine Code and the Heroin Code, each as popular as they are pointless.

Life instructs her hand to wave at the people who grin at her.

'All right, Life?' says a guy with two pink erections sprouting like wings from each of his shoulder blades.

'All right, Jimmy,' says Life, instructing her mouth to open wide with excitement.

Life has met Jimmy in the real world. He's gay. In reality, Jimmy's sitting at his laptop in his parents' living room in Crawley, occasionally quitting Wow-Bang to scan Gaydar for potential lovers in the Sussex area.

'How's work going on the launch party?' asks Jimmy.

'Oh, pretty good, still a bit vague. I'm meeting that guy Janek tonight.'

'Oooh,' says Jimmy, making the helmets of his erections flash like disco lights. 'The lucky fucker himself. There isn't a digital dick in Wow-Bang that doesn't want to program its way into your pants.' Jimmy's two dick-wings spurt large drops of semen which disappear the moment they hit the floor. Life and Jimmy laugh and instruct their bodies to embrace.

Life takes a seat alone in the corner of the bar. Most of the people in here have some connection to the Wild World. Jimmy, for example, has got something to do with marketing. In fact, everyone involved with the Wild World seems to have something to do with marketing. Life has never heard anyone describe their involvement in any kind of detail. Even Bossbitch, even the bald-headed guy who asked if she knew a Northerner who could be trusted with a child. They all talk in shallow code and it makes Life uneasy.

She sits and stares nervously at the door. She's got a bad feeling that Janek is going to have a very unattractive avatar. She hopes he's had the sense to buy a hairstyle and some decent clothes. The Wild World lot all have crazy avatars and frown on those who don't.

Having thought about it, Life's decided she's attracted to Janek's quietness. In a world of too many words Life is glad to have met a man of few. But sometimes few words means more thoughts and more thoughts often means complication and then failure, lack of joy, unhappiness. But what can you do? You can't do anything. You can carry on.

Two things strike Life as odd about Wow-Bang. Firstly, the speedy growth of commerce. Originally intended as a utopian society where people could meet each other without having to be constantly buying crap, capitalism developed in Wow-Bang faster than in any other human society in history. It took about a week for most major corporations to buy land in Wow-Bang and to build huge towers displaying their logo on their roofs. Also, people quickly found that they struggled to sit at tables and get to know each other without having first bought something. Within a day or two people started opening shops and bars that sold the Cocaine and Heroin Codes, the Cappuccino Code and the Champagne Code, all of which are, in essence, total bollocks.

The second thing that Life has noticed about Wow-Bang is the quantity of penises. They are everywhere. It is impossible to walk down a street without seeing a whole bunch of people with erections jumping hugely from their trouser flies. The penis has been craving mainstream attention since the twenty-first century began and tits and fannies became as breathable as air. The erect penis is pretty invisible in culture. It is a veined source of shame. So when men entered Wow-Bang and found they could program penises onto any part of their body, they got really excited and set about doing just that. The employees of the Wild World are no exception. It's rare to meet a guy in the Real Arms who has resisted the temptation to adorn his avatar with a cock. Some avatars are only cocks: pale shafts as tall as humans with ballsacks that waddle along like fat feet. There's a few of those here tonight. On the dance floor. Life thinks it's quite sweet. The quantity of erections in Wow-Bang doesn't add up to an atmosphere of sexual aggression. On the contrary, it's almost like men want women to meet their chubby little penises in a normal environment. As if for some time men have been meaning to clear their throats and say, deep, deep down, we are only dicks.

The door of the Real Arms swings open and Janek shuffles in. He has no cocks on his body. Life sees he's wearing a beanie and finds this cute. He's replicated his real-world image. Bless him. She watches as he takes in the atmosphere of the Real Arms. The tall penises disco-dancing on the floor. The numerous people snorting cocaine off the tables or injecting heroin into their arms. She watches as people angle their bodies away from Janek when they register his normal appearance. She warms to him. When he finally scans the room and spots her, she instructs herself to smile and to blow him a kiss.

Janek steers his body through the crowd towards Life. She's not as beautiful in Wow-Bang as she was in that hotel in London. But unlike most girls here Life has resisted the temptation to program a ridiculous cleavage for herself. Janek's glad about this. The other girls here have tits like home-made babies' heads. Full of migraine, Janek takes a seat and manages to work out how to smile.

'So what do you think of Wow-Bang?' asks Life.

'Are you sure you wouldn't rather we actually met?'

'This is cheaper.'

'Doesn't the Wild World pay?'

'The Wild World doesn't even know what it's meant to be. How was the funeral?'

'I'm not sure.'

'You didn't go?'

'No. I went. I'm just not sure how it was.'

Life becomes quickly annoyed. Janek's not getting into the spirit of Wow-Bang. She goes to the bar to buy the Heroin Code. She wouldn't normally do this, but she wants Janek to see that this virtual world is more exciting than he realises. Janek watches her and wishes that this was reality. He'd like to touch her cheek and tell her how he feels. Tell her he's ready to live, to run away and join the Fuck Festival, ready to be less bogged down in the horrors of existence. Ready to have fun and fuck with an open mind. But instead he watches as a man with a scrotum instead of a head tries to force his digital dick into Life from behind. He watches as Life turns and slits the man's wrinkled throat with a knife and then returns to the table and begins injecting heroin pointlessly into her arm.

'Life, listen, I've been thinking a lot about stuff. And I'm pretty sure it's possible to enjoy being alive.'

'You are?'

'Definitely I am,' says Janek, standing up with excitement and bumping into Life over and over again. 'Nothing matters, obviously, but that doesn't mean we can't lead great lives . . . even a fuck festival. You and me, even.'

'What do you mean, a fuck festival?'

'I feel stupid saying this here, Life. But meeting you has made me realise how much I've been missing out on. The simple stuff, you know, sex and laughing?'

'Really,' says Life, wondering whether Janek is familiar with the concept of playing it cool. 'What's brought all this on?'

'The N-Prang.'

'Seriously?'

'Yeah. Because life is meant to be fun. It makes you realise. We're born, and then everything should be insane and fun . . . and you know, a fuck festival?'

Life sighs. She instructs her lips to purse and exhale. She wonders how a promotional MP3 player could have changed Janek's outlook on life in just a few days.

'I know what you mean, Janek,' she says. 'But I think I'm heading in a different direction. I've had enough of all that living-for-the-day stuff. I don't get much out of it any more, you know, drinking, going mental, shagging, breathing. I'm really getting into this.'

The two of them turn and look around the Real Arms. It's getting busier. Giant knobs nod at the bar, bullshitting each other about the Wild World. Naked girls with eyes instead of nipples snort coke from the tables causing the lids of those eyes to rapidly blink. People's clothing and appearance are constantly changing in radical ways; faces and outfits alter as regularly as second hands as avatars trot across the dance floor to talk to someone new.

'But, Life,' says Janek, 'do you not find this a little sad?'

'No. It's not sad,' replies Life. 'It's just really easy.'

The door of the Real Arms bursts open again and a loud squawking can be heard. People turn to watch as an enormous puffin enters the bar with its black wings outstretched. A few of the dancers instruct their faces to show anger. A lot of the dicks in the place become erect with rage and one guy alters his appearance so he's just a middle finger raised in insult. The Wild World lot don't like people who pretend to be animals. They hate them, in fact. They're not welcome in the Real Arms. Most animal avatars are members of the Dead Animals gang, a group of hippy terrorists who think

Wow-Bang is destroying natural human instincts. They blow themselves up in busy places, infecting those around them with viruses.

Life recognises the puffin straight away and stands up. A man with a vagina where his Adam's apple should be is firing up a flame-thrower and preparing to attack the puffin.

'Don't,' says Life, rushing over. 'It's my ex-boyfriend.'

'Are you sure?' says the guy, flame-thrower poised.

'Yeah, I'm sure. It's you, isn't it, Joe?'

The puffin nods. 'I've come to find out about Sally.'

'The baby?' says Life, smiling at the guy with a fanny on his throat and guiding Joe to the table where Janek is walking quickly against a wall. 'What's the matter with her?'

'I don't know. But I took her south of Birmingham. I thought it was bullshit and I wanted to see you.'

Joe watches as Life instructs both her hands to cover her face. 'You didn't,' she says. 'Tell me you didn't.'

'I did,' says Joe, tucking his wings into his body and attempting to touch Life with his beak.

'Don't,' says Life, looking at Janek and then turning to face the huge puffin, her former lover, saying, 'Where are you now? Where is the baby?'

'I'm in a Travelodge at Watford Gap services. We got thrown off the Megabus. Sally's back in the room. She's ill. I need to see you, Lie.'

Life doesn't say anything. She pulls Janek away from the wall and gestures that he and Joe take a seat. They do. Janek looks at Joe, wondering what Life ever saw in this enormous puffin and wondering what the fuck he's doing here, obstructing happiness with his black wings. Joe shows no interest in Janek at all. He just watches Life as she instructs her face to look like it's thinking. Eyes shut and forehead creased. Life looks at both boys and thinks about being alone. And, of course, she is alone, in reality. In reality, they all are.

15

YOU CAN'T SPOT a cock for love nor money in the Rib Cage. Among the young, the EMO kids, the fairly thoughtful teenagers, dicks are seen as sad or fucking crude. Unlike the rest of Wow-Bang, naked flesh is rare in the Rib Cage.

Occasionally you'll see two teenage avatars, dressed in black with blue hair heading upstairs or outside together. Chances are, they'll be en route to get their digital sex organs out and put one inside the other. But only in private, not like the huge Wild World knobs and the literal dickheads at the Real Arms. These teenagers still uphold a sexual morality. Mainly out of immaturity.

The Rib Cage is four or five times bigger than the Real Arms. It's a club. Pop metal is blasted out across the dance floor, which is covered in the young. They dance with chins held against their collarbones staring at the floor. If a heavy tune comes on then they mosh, stamping their feet and shaking their ridiculous hair with their eyes shut. But they're a lovely lot, these kids, despite their dark clothes, their pale faces and the slogans on their digital clothes that seem to beg for death. They're actually nice, good fun, well behaved in a cool way. There's hardly any murdering in the Rib Cage and, as I say, you can consider yourself lucky if you see a pink penis or an attempted rape. What you do get here is a hell of a lot of light-hearted suicides. The long bar at the back sells the Hanging Code, the Overdose Code and the Slit Wrist Code. None of which kill you, only seem to. They're what make the teenagers such pleasant company. They're far too busy killing themselves to kill anyone else and so it's easy to relax.

Anka Kudolski and Roger Hart are both perched in silence on two skull-shaped stools at the back of the Rib Cage. They are surrounded by gawping teenage avatars, some of which have been instructed to kneel in the direction of Roger and pray. On his way here from the *Cats* show, Roger was followed by hundreds of his adoring fans. They shouted questions about his condition in the real world. 'In reality, El Rogerio,' they asked, 'how close to death are you? When will you be only technology?' Roger didn't answer. He was a little bit annoyed by their company. His plan had been to expose them to a musical and, by so doing, lessen their adoration and fuck them off for the night, if not forever. He certainly had no desire for an audience when he met Anka for the first time. But that's what he's ended up with. Now neither he nor Anka has the nerve to speak.

It's Roger who eventually breaks the silence.

'I actually came to apologise,' he says, the crowd shifting forwards as he speaks.

'To me?' says Anka, unfolding her barely visible limbs. 'Why?'

'Because,' Roger continues. 'Because just because you're on TV doesn't mean I've got the right to wank over you, and I certainly shouldn't have blogged about it. But all that El Rogerio stuff was a lie. I mean, I did do it, I did wank over you, but only because you're pretty. Thin, but pretty. But since I started turning into technology I've realised I don't want to be horrible any more. The annoying thing is, this lot don't seem to mind.'

Roger gestures to the crowd, more and more of whom are knelt in prayer.

'Who do they think you are?' asks Anka.

'I don't know. Some sort of prophet. Since I told them I'm infested with technology they seem to think I'm the Second Coming –'

'We don't,' interrupts a boy at the very front of the crowd, his graphic eyes lined with graphic make-up. 'We don't think you're a prophet, El Rogerio. We think you're cool.'

Roger tuts and turns to Anka. 'Right. They think I'm cool. But the important thing, Anka, is that you forgive me for the things I wrote about you.'

'I do.'

'Really?'

'I definitely do.'

Neither Anka nor Roger realise that as they sit, watched by hundreds in Wow-Bang, they are, in reality, separated by just a couple of doors and about fifteen metres of space. They do not realise that they are neighbours in the real world. That the computers on which they nervously type are essentially sharing a power source in a crumbling Edwardian building in Manchester. But they do feel a warmth as each of them looks into the screen at the other in Wow-Bang. They feel a warmth, isolated and vulnerable as they are.

'So I'm guessing you live in Manchester, if you saw the show, yeah?' Anka asks.

Roger nods. 'But I haven't left the flat in months.'

'We could meet up, maybe.'

'We couldn't, sadly. I can barely move and I'm dying.'

'Yeah, so am I if I'm honest. I'm probably starving to death.'

Roger leans in to Anka, trying to hide from the teenagers.

'It's crap, isn't it?' he says. 'You're growing up and it all seems OK. You're getting taller and taller and saying all sorts of things. In your late teens you get some cheap thrills wanking, buying booze or ordering food in restaurants without your parents. And then . . . and then you just plunge. Reality's like a siren, it drives you mad, and then you're full of technology and barely any feeling –'

'Exactly,' interrupts Anka, 'or you're dancing in front of a camera, pleased that men are rubbing their cocks hard, and you're not eating –'

'I don't eat either. Apart from crisps.'

'How come you never leave your flat?'

Roger and Anka are standing up now. They have formed a triangle with the wall so that the teenagers can't see their faces, which are now held closely together so that they can both make out the pixelated colours in each other's eyes.

'I started blushing,' says Roger. 'When I was outside I'd feel my face heating up to unbearable temperatures. It felt awful. I'd remove my glasses and stare at my reflection and see that it was all red. The worst thing was, it was a vicious circle. I'd be so shocked and ashamed of the blood inside my head that I would blush more. My career was in tatters. You only had to look at me to know that I was unsuccessful and had only the slimmest chance of ever being happy.

Then one day I logged onto the Internet as El Rogerio. I started writing. Now I can't stop.'

'What do you mean?'

'If I'm not writing, I'm only dying. It's hard enough being here.'

'You know what I think?' says Anka, raising her skeletal fingers and touching the inexpensive skin tone of Roger's cheeks. 'I think we're lonely.'

Roger locates the Bashful Grin Code from among his facial expressions and executes it, saying, 'I think we're lonely, too.'

The two of them turn to face the large crowd of teenagers. They watch as heads rise from their praying positions and faces open. Lidless graphic eyes that seem to stare through everything at nothing. Lips that can't taste. Shitless bodies that will never feel a thing.

Roger is trying to work out how he can disperse this crowd of admirers. He's wondering what he could say. He notices, suddenly, that Anka is holding his hand in hers. She must have programmed them into this position without him noticing. He smiles. Suddenly ecstatic. It only takes a second. Life is shit unless people are holding you or stroking you. Roger feels like the small featherless bird that lives inside his heart might be coming back to life, trying to open its sealed-up eyes.

'Leave me alone,' he shouts, wishing this wasn't Wow-Bang but the real world instead. Wishing he could strengthen his grip on Anka's hand as he shouts at the crowd of teenagers, all their bodies dug like dirt into angles of fashion. 'Please,' he shouts, hands in the air. 'I'm running out of time. Leave us alone!'

Just as the crowd of teenagers begins to smile in protest

and to grumble with too black lips, 'But you're so cool,' there is a commotion at the entrance of the Rib Cage. A man with a naked, neutered, dickless body and the head of an Alsatian dog storms across the dance floor. He's enormous. He's muscular. He's barking loudly over the American pop metal causing the little graphic people to turn in aimless circles, panicking, attempting to teleport away. 'Dead Animal!' they scream. 'Dead Animal!'

In the commotion, Roger turns to Anka, placing his hands around her straw-thin waist. 'I've still got a bit of warmth inside me. Do you like musicals?'

'No,' she replies, half an eye on the blood that drips then disappears from the Alsatian's jaw. 'I hate musicals, Roger. But I have a little bit of warmth left, too. I've been such a dickhead lately.'

'I've been a dickhead, too. We've got things in common. Haven't we?'

'We have,' says Anka, remembering the black carrot that haunts her fridge and how she had answered her phone to herself. 'You and me do have things in common!'

Roger laughs. His lips parting quickly in what is a commendable imitation of happiness. He is leaning in to kiss her. He is craving that senseless moment when his red, programmed lips will meet with hers.

Too late. The Alsatian detonates his virus and Roger finds himself ripped back painfully into the real world. Suddenly Manchester. In his flat, his lukewarm flat, Roger watches as his and Anka's avatars freeze and dismantle on the computer screen, lips just inches from each other. He cries out. With his real voice Roger cries out. 'But I was making a connection!' he screams, at the ceiling. Screams at the god who crouches on the ceiling making hoax calls on a shit-hot mobile. 'I was making a connection, you wanker! Anka!'

Roger tries to get up from his office chair but his huge, heavy legs won't budge. His stomach bleeps and he punches it in anger, causing it to whirr. 'Fucking bullshit,' he mutters, tears in his voice. 'Anka!' he screams again in abject frustration, before settling painfully in his chair to reboot his computer.

'Roger?' comes a voice from the distance, somewhere beyond the door. 'Roger, is that you?'

Both Ankas had heard a voice calling out their name. They had heard the cry and turned to each other, staring at themselves like the normal stare at their reflection. One Anka is terrifyingly thin and the other Anka is a healthy, responsible weight. The problem is that neither of them can agree who is the skinny one and who is the healthy one. They argued about it all last night. Similarly, neither can agree as to which of them is the *real* Anka. Since they spoke on the phone and moved in together they have both staked a claim to being the genuine, authentic Anka Kudolski. Neither ever agrees with the other. But as they turned away from the crashed computer screen, they both agreed that someone was calling out their name. Neither had any idea who it could be. Certainly they know none of their neighbours and they're only on second-name terms with the caretaker. 'It's Roger,' said one Anka. 'It could be, I suppose,' said the other. 'Think about it. He said he liked musicals.' There was a silence as both Ankas put two and two together, made four and then crept towards the door.

'Answer me, Roger,' says an Anka, out in the corridor now, staring uncertainly at the flat opposite hers. 'Is that you?'

'Please,' adds the other Anka in an identical voice. Both Ankas are suddenly nervous about meeting a person. Since they were reunited, they have stayed indoors.

In his flat, Roger is staring at the door and then staring back at his computer screen. He's wondering whether it's finally happened. It must have done, he thinks. My brain can't distinguish reality from reality. Am I still in Wow-Bang? Fuck knows. Who cares? I care, thinks Roger. I haven't used my voice to communicate in a year.

'It's me, Roger. It's me, Anka,' says the voice beyond his front door. When he hears that name, Roger's belly makes an embarrassing noise, like a loud electronic fart. How can it be? wonders Roger, like we all wonder when the empty carousel of coincidence is spinning around us.

'Anka?' Roger shouts, neck twisted, anxious in his office chair. 'Anka, is it really you?'

'Yes!' shout both Ankas in unison. 'Come to me, Roger. Let me in.'

Bugger me, thinks Roger Hart. One day you're crap-ping a motherboard and the next you're falling onto the floor, dragging yourself wilfully in the direction of happiness.

'Open the door, Roger.'

I'm trying, thinks Roger, gripping the hard carpet with his fingernails and pulling himself frantically towards the front door. But his legs are so heavy. It feels like they're full of cement and not computer technology, it's like trying to lift a fridge.

'Just hold on . . . I'm coming.'

On the other side of the door the two Ankas are staring at each other. Both look nervous. They offer each other stark, open eyes. Identical thoughts pop like washing-up liquid bubbles inside their heads. What are we going to say? How will we begin to explain?

'You should go and hide,' whispers one Anka.

'Me?' says the other, pointing at her protruded collar-bone. 'Why should I go? You're the anorexic.'

'You are, you mean. You're just a skeleton.'

'Bollocks. I'm a good weight. Look at yourself. It's painful to see.'

The two Ankas hiss at each other. How did this happen? they both think. I was fine. I was eating. I'd recovered. Sure, I was working hard, burning calories, but I was eating. Suddenly, a memory hits them both like a snowball to the ear. The memory of going into Subway for lunch. The memory of asking for a fistful of watercress and being told abruptly that Subway is a sandwich shop. The memory of saying, 'Then I'll get something later on, and in any case I only eat organic food nowadays, I only eat seafood, only eat nuts, rye bread, popcorn, water, black coffee, zero dairy, I'm a vegan at the moment, you know the shit they put in food, I'm going to grow my own leeks, become a farmer, a self-sufficient superstar, I'm thinking about trying to get a recipe book published and, the thing is, I ate before I came out. I did, honestly. I ate a shitload just before I came here. It's ridiculous really and that's the truth. It is. That's the truth.'

'Bollocks,' says one Anka, shutting her eyes then covering them with a hand.

'I know,' says the other.

'We haven't been eating at all lately, have we?'

'We ate an egg. We sucked on monkey nuts. But other than that, nothing.'

Knelt down in the corridor next to Roger's door,

both Ankas hold hands and share their worried eyes. On the other side of the door Roger is making slow progress. He's looking at the different coloured lights that blink beneath the skin of his hands. Blue ones. Red ones. Yellow. Will she mind? he's thinking. Will Anka find it foul that my bronze wires have grown so long from my nose that my lips can hardly be seen? She might think it looks weird. Or worse, ugly. She might not be attracted to the thick black cables growing from my ears, or the mouse that's growing out the back of my head. She might not find me sexy. Nothing new there. But she knows, Roger recalls. I told her all about it. She understands. We both felt a warmth. We made a connection. We are both alone and desperate, desperate!

'I'm almost there, Anka. Hold on.'

Roger is almost there. He is lying like a dead seal beneath the door. He's panting with exhaustion. Every piece of equipment is muttering inside him, desperately processing. He's staring up at the lock. It's like staring at the clouds. I won't be able to reach it. He rolls onto his back, breathing at the ceiling, wondering what the best plan is. How will I get beyond the door? To Anka. To sex. To a human moment.

'Roger?'

'Yeah, I'm here.'

'Before you open the door, there's something I need to tell you.'

That's handy, thinks Roger, trying to breathe a sigh of relief.

'Have you ever had a threesome?' say both Ankas, hands held tenderly against the wooden door. 'You know? Have you ever tried it with two girls at once?'

Roger, pinned to the carpet, is finding it hard not to laugh.

A threesome? There's more chance of me bumming the Queen. He stares at the space around his eyes, examining it with darting glances. He puts a hand on his crotch and starts tapping at the numerical keypad where his penis should be.

'Sure,' he says. 'A threesome. Absolutely. I've done that. Why?'

'Because, well . . . Roger, I'm quite ill.'

'You've got an eating disorder.'

'Yeah.'

'I figured.'

'And you see . . .' Both Ankas are pulling frantic faces at each other, shaking their hands, fingers crooked like they're gripping invisible hearts. 'It's hard for you to understand, Roger, but, basically, when you open this door, you'll see that there's two of me.'

Jesus Christ. This is all a bit much for Roger to take. He's tapping frantically at the keypad that replaced his cock.

'What's that noise?'

'It's my teeth,' says Roger, 'they're chattering. I'm cold.'

'Do you mind it being a threesome?'

'No,' squeaks Roger. He's thinking. If you can call it thinking. He's thinking: a threesome with two Anka Kudolskis. What a concept. The mere idea of it undermines all the hardware in Roger's skull and he briefly feels sixteen again. Brain like a trumpet with boobies in the bell. He remembers how Anka had looked on *QUIZ TV*. He duplicates that image and begins bleeping and whirring for joy.

'I think I can deal with it,' he says, trying desperately to get to his feet and open the door. 'It will be odd, but I think I can understand.'

The Ankas can barely hear Roger's voice over the sound

169

of clinking electrics and clattering plastics. 'At least we're human,' whispers one of them. 'Listen to that. He's just a sack of technology.'

'Shhh,' hisses the other. 'He's a nice guy. I know he is. And you and me need to be touched. We've forgotten. We've lived in our brains too long. Our brains are fucked.' She raises her voice. 'Roger, are you gonna open this door?'

'Yeah,' says Roger, through a high-pitched wince. 'Just as soon as I can . . . get . . . up . . .' Roger is yet to leave the floor.

'I think we can help each other, Roger,' say the Ankas, suspecting Roger might need encouragement. 'We're all in a right state. We need to behave simply. We need to just feel each other.'

Definitely, thinks Roger. We need to have a frantic three-some that'll convince me beyond doubt that life is a big wooden barrel of laughs. Roger's face is purple with strain. His teeth are gritted. His hands try desperately to lift his legs.

'Come on, Roger. Hurry.'

'I'm trying.'

Roger's on his feet. Almost. He's trying to straighten his legs. Straining for the door handle with a shaking hand.

'Don't be embarrassed,' say the Ankas. 'We're ready for you.'

'I know,' hisses Roger, through a closed mouth, reaching up, fingertips straining, brushing the grey metal catch, desperate to get a grip.

'We're here, Roger. We're really here. We're ready and waiting for you.'

'Aaaaaaagggghhhhh!'

Roger throws his failing body upwards at the lock. His

170

hand grips it for a second. He feels the latch and tries to drag it down. Drag it down and unlock the door, throw it open and fall on them, the two beautiful girls, his first humans in months, their soft flesh, damaged by disease but still silky and warm and actually alive. I'll see them, he thinks. Sex and hope. Smiling faces. I'll open my eyes and feast on the light of beauty.

'Roger?'

Silence. Roger nibbles on the shadows of his lonely apartment. The lock above his head is still locked. I failed. I can't do it. I'm too far gone.

'I haven't got the strength, Anka,' he says. 'I can't reach you.'

More silence. On the other side of the door the two identical girls shake their heads in frustration. They each push their blonde hair off their faces and make temporary ponytails with their fists.

'Can you get back to your computer, Roger?'

Roger sighs. 'Always.'

'Then let's go back to Wow-Bang. Meet us at the Real Arms.'

Roger places a hand against the door. The two girls do the same. The lovers are separated by just an inch or two of wood. 'It'll be OK,' say the Ankas, in that soft London voice of theirs. 'It'll be OK, Roger. But be sure to bring a penis. In fact, bring as many codes as you can afford.'

16

BACK IN WOW-BANG, Joe Aspen is deliberately trying to piss Janek Freeman off. They're both in a small, red-walled room above the Real Arms. They're waiting for Life. After Joe dropped the bombshell that he's taken baby Sally south of Birmingham, Life insisted they hide up here while she probed her colleagues from the Wild World for the likely consequences of this. For a while the boys, their avatars at least, shared an awkward virtual silence. They were both relieved when two men in suits walked in and started snogging each other. They watched with relief as one man's appearance altered completely and he became, in fact, a woman, with black suspenders, crotchless panties, big tits, brown nipples and blonde hair. Joe and Janek watched as the other man bent the woman over a table and began screwing her with a stripy zebra dick. They watched as the woman struggled, her arms flailing and her legs kicking. They heard the man say, 'You love it, mate. You fucking love the Rape Code.' But watching the rape only kept Janek and Joe distracted for a little while. Not long enough.

Soon they turned to stare at each other again. They both tried to work out exactly what Life saw in the other. This is when Joe started to wind Janek up. He spread his large puffin wings and began flying around the room, over the rape, then round and round above Janek's head, occasionally pecking at his digital beanie.

When Life arrives she's quick to put a stop to the rape. She produces a small pistol and points it at the man with the zebra dick. He withdraws from the woman, smiling, dick nodding, putting his hands in the air. Life shoots him anyway. She shoots the woman, too, as she's clambering back to her feet. Joe and Janek feel a little ashamed.

'No one knows,' says Life. 'No one knows what'll happen to Sally in the south.'

'She'll be fine,' says Joe, flying towards Life, landing just in front of her. 'I'm a good dad. I love her. I'm gonna raise her.'

Janek watches Life with her former boyfriend. He's getting annoyed. Since his revelation that being alive could conceivably be quite good, he's yet to get off the mark, notch up a few happiness points. He needs Life. She's the key. He stares at her graphic breasts and recalls how the breasts they imitate had shaken in that hotel bed. How the two of them had craned their necks. How Life had shouted, 'Watch it go in and out.' That was living. Fast, shaking flesh. Stuck in Wow-Bang, Janek can't figure out what to do.

Joe can. He's wrapped a wing round Life's shoulders. Life can't help but be amused. This is typical of Joe, coming to her disguised as a puffin, the emblem of her home country. It reminds her of when the two of them visited the Faroe Islands to spend Christmas with her family, over a year ago now. Joe had enjoyed the food: the rotten mutton, the herring, the fresh salmon, the puffins themselves. He volunteered to help catch the puffins and he and Life's dad had gone off to the coast with large nets. It's likely that that trip to the Faroe Islands kick-started Joe's preoccupation with the natural world. He was fascinated by the rotten sheep's ribcage that they collectively devoured during the two-week stay. He'd insisted that he and Life walk daily in the green-black mountains, tracking long-haired sheep for miles, drinking ice-cold water from the countless falls, kissing Life's full, frozen lips, their feet sinking into the spongy waterlogged grass. When they returned to Manchester, things just weren't the same. Joe stood nightly at the black winter window, eyes shut, flapping his arms. By day he filled his pockets with handfuls of what soil the city produced. The relationship had to end. It's amazing it took a whole year. Life hadn't left the Faroes to shack up with a boy with a puffin complex. She came to Manchester for the pavements and the English language. The coffee shops and the clothes. As she stares now at Joe the puffin and, beside him, Janek, Life realises she's affected both boys in almost opposite ways. She has turned Joe into an animal and Janek into a classically modern, carefree, thrill-seeker. She wonders which of them, if either, she wants.

'If I wasn't a puffin, Life,' Joe says suddenly, spreading his wings so as to obscure Life's view of Janek, 'and if I wasn't standing in this bullshit virtual world, whatever it's called, then you'd be able to see I've changed. I've matured. I'm the only moral person in England. I'm the only one who wants to live simply and be happy. I've got no hang-ups. I'm a good guy. We were in love. I know we were. You said we'd call our first child Magnus, if it was a boy. You said that, Life –'

'I don't want to do this, Joe. We only broke up two weeks ago. I care for you, I love you, but –'

'But what?' pleads Joe. 'You're not sure? You're going to fuck off with this guy in the hat and forget all about me, forget about the time we spent together? Is there no chance we can just go and be happy somewhere, anyfuckingwhere? We could make a Magnus that could play with little Sally. Fuck fun, it's bollocks. Fuck all this tap, tap, dip, shit, wappy, fucky, clothed crap. There are only two things worth doing in this world, Life: being in love, and hiding!'

Janek's had enough of this. He pushes Joe to one side and stands in front of Life.

'Don't listen to him, Life, he's a complete dick. Five minutes with an N-Prang and he'd be fucking fine. A couple of weeks ago I was talking this kind of shit.' Janek turns on Joe, saying, 'I bet you're weeping in the real world, aren't you, Joe? Crying at your computer. I bet you wouldn't even buy a ticket for a fuck festival.'

Joe smirks. 'Shut up, you dick.'

'Piss off, puffin boy.'

Janek turns to Life again. She's standing completely still.

'Think about it, Life, I'm the one. You've made me realise that life is only about moving from one hilarious moment to the next. And don't forget, I know Jay-Z, and Snoop Dogg, I'm mates with Peter Gabriel. Think of all the fun we could have.'

'No one cares,' says Joe, red beak snapping. 'She doesn't even like hip hop, do you, Lie?'

Life says nothing. She doesn't even move.

'She'll like Snoop,' blurts Janek, before silence can get its teeth into this moment. 'He's really funny. He's really, really funny.'

'Big deal,' says Joe. 'I'm offering her a real life; children, love, soil, shelter from all that bullshit.'

'Yeah?' says Janek, intonation rising like scraped guitar strings. 'Yeah, puffin boy? Well, get a load of this.'

Janek has altered his appearance: his recently purchased penis is bursting, fully erect from his trouser fly. He's twizzling round, showing it off to Life and Joe. This'll show her, he's thinking. This'll show Life that I'm serious about being a fun-haver, a leggy giggler, a flippant and funky human. Get a load of my big digital dick.

'Well?' says Janek, crazed circular eyes. 'Well?'

Life is motionless and Joe is rummaging in his feathers. Seconds later and Janek's isn't the only well-programmed penis in the room. A proud human erection is poking out from Joe's puffin groin. The atmosphere seems suddenly doomed. The two boys stare at each other's graphic sexes, inspecting them nervously and in detail.

Mine's longer, Janek notices. Is that a good thing or a bad thing? Does that mean I'm insecure? Is it wish fulfilment?

Pubicly, thinks Joe, mine is more impressive. Janek's pubes look like a black stain, whereas mine, well, the pubic detailing I acquired was worth every penny. Each strand perfectly rendered by the geeks who design these things. I mean, obviously I don't care, thinks Joe. What I care about is catching rainbow trout and cooking it in lemon juice on an open fire while Life feeds baby Magnus milk from her breast. But it's still nice to be winning this contest. It could matter. Though his dick is bigger than mine. I'm fairly sure that's a bad thing.

'Mine's nicer,' says Joe.

'Bollocks.'

'Of course it is.'

'No,' howls Janek, 'I mean, you don't have any balls.'

'I don't?'

He doesn't. And Janek does, not great ones, but he does definitely have balls.

'We'll let Life decide,' says Janek, falling into line beside Joe so their erections are side by side, grinning at each other.

'Whatever,' murmurs Joe, realising that he has sunk once more into the wet black tar of the social and that he's desperate to be out of Wow-Bang and back on all fours in the real world with baby Sally and his kitten, Beak.

'Well, Life?' says Janek, hands on his hips, arching his back. 'Tell us, which is better?'

Life hasn't moved an inch in minutes.

'Life?' says Joe.

Nothing. The two boys edge closer towards her, both their erections nudging pointlessly at her stomach. Her graphic eyes contain no soul, no meaning, no movement.

'She's gone,' says Joe. 'She's left her computer. What did you expect, hassling her, getting your dick out?'

'Piss off,' Janek groans. 'She arranged to meet me. We're together.'

'You're not together. You're too boring to be with Life,' snaps Joe. His comment hits a nerve because Janek knows it's true. 'We are together,' he shouts in retaliation. 'We shagged in a hotel. I watched it going in and out!' This hits a nerve, too, because Joe knows it's true. He knows Life couldn't go long without sex. It's part of her sublime nature. He brings his beak up close to her face. He stares into her eyes, imagining her computer screen and the real room she must be living in. Where is she? In the real world, Joe feels each of his rag organs twist and twist until they're very thin and dry: why can't she just decide to be with me?

As he backs away from Life, Joe sees that Janek has a pistol pointed at him. He shrugs. 'What are you doing?'

'I'm just killing you,' Janek sighs. 'I'm just killing you because I want to fit in. For the fun of it, you know?'

'Fine,' says Joe. 'I've had enough of this place anyway. It's shit. I need to get back to Sally, and to my kitten.'

Janek cocks his pistol, saying, 'The thing is, Joe, this girl is a happiness machine.' He waves the gun in Life's direction. She looks like a statue of herself. 'You must know what she's like. She makes happiness; spits it, shits it, sweats it, makes its noises. I need a happiness machine, Joe . . . I need a happiness machine!'

Joe closes his large puffin eyes and awaits the sensation that comes when a bullet travels through your head in Wow-Bang. But what he hears is the clatter of a door. His eyes open with a blink: a big-headed boy in spectacles and a blonde with limbs as thin as cigarettes come falling into the room, hands moving all over each other. Janek's distracted and Joe takes his chance. He puts his beak through the small window at the end of the room, hops out onto the ledge, spreads his wings and flies off; bullets from Janek's pistol chase him through the purple sky. If I get hit, I get hit, thinks Joe, staring at the night. Every bullet misses.

Back in the simple red room, Anka Kudolski is standing in front of Life, saying, 'Life, is that you?' But Life is not responding and Anka notices that Roger is almost naked in the corner of the room. 'Life?' she says one more time, before concluding that Life is not at her computer and therefore can wait. 'Would you mind leaving?' she says to the young man in the beanie who's shooting maniacally through the smashed window. 'We'd like some privacy, please.'

Janek turns to her, gun in hand.

'Don't even think about killing us,' warns Anka, hopelessly trying to shield the naked Roger with her scrawny body.

'I won't,' mutters Janek, dropping the pistol noiselessly onto the floor. 'I need the N-Prang. I need to go back.'

Anka and Roger watch as Janek thrusts his erection several times against Life's vacated body, before rushing out of the room muttering the word 'festival' over and over again. Weirdo, they both think. What's an N-Prang?

Anka turns to Roger and places kisses on his cheek. 'Are you ready?' she whispers, into his large and undetailed ear.

'Not quite,' says Roger. 'Look. My dick's bigger than your body. How's this gonna work? Would you be prepared to –'

Anka closes Roger's mouth with a delicate finger. A second passes. Anka switches to the larger avatar she'd first designed before she realised that the anorexia had returned. Roger smiles, saying, 'You see? You can do it.' Anka shuts her eyes and nods. Then she grins at her tits and at her curvy limbs. 'What codes have you got?' she asks.

'Let me surprise you,' says Roger, embracing Anka and executing the Arse Grope Code; taking a handful of her buttock and twisting it with force. 'All right,' she whispers, and before she knows it, she's completely naked and Roger's steering both their bodies towards the painless black floor.

It had taken Roger a while to drag himself back to his office chair in the real world, but once he was back in Wow-Bang he knew exactly where to go to get good prices on numerous sex codes. Anka couldn't have chosen a better-equipped virtual lover. But buying sex codes is easy. Using them can be tricky. Down on the floor, Roger is struggling to make decisions. He's wondering whether it's presumptuous to begin with a blow job. He has, generously, brought along the 69 Code and the Pussy Licking Code as well as the Blow Job Code. He's thinking he should start with one of the former, the 69 maybe, make a case for equality in the hectic world of oral sex. But he really wants a blow job. Really, really wants to watch his cock being sucked.

Roger pushes Anka's legs apart and executes the Pussy Licking Code. He buries his bespectacled face in her digital loins and licks her first tenderly, then vigorously. A minute or two of this and maybe she'll mutter what most girls mutter while being badly licked out: 'Stop – let me suck your cock.' Lick in hope.

Both Ankas are enjoying themselves. It's ages since they've had any kind of sex. Anka's adult sex life never got off the ground because of her eating disorder. Most of her sexual memories date back to her Goldsmiths days, falling into bed with fine artists, far too fucked, high on coke, waking the next day not knowing whether they'd done it or not. Then before you know it, you're wasting away, your sex drive stops and no one wants to kiss you. Being with Roger makes sense, even given the origins of their relationship, even though they've never met in the flesh. They are both in trouble and in need of support and love. Anka looks down her body at Roger's bobbing head. She touches his cheek. 'Stop,' she whispers. 'Let me suck your cock.'

Roger is excited. He executes the Blow Job Code and watches as Anka crawls down his body and drapes her lips over his oversized penis. He's not had a blow job since the 1990s, when an overweight IT student with invisible tits had licked half-heartedly having met him at a Gilbert and Sullivan Society meeting. But that hadn't lasted long, she'd barely licked the tip before she stopped, saying, 'It doesn't taste right.' Roger is pleased that this virtual blow job is progressing nicely, with meaning and good rhythm. If his real-world penis hadn't been replaced by a numerical keypad he's pretty sure it would be standing tall and that he'd be stroking it joyfully, having curtained off the nerdy, less erotic sections of his brain. Yes, this is great. And with Anka Kudolski, too. The girl on TV who's as fucked up as me. We're mates. Virtually lovers. Roger is happy and confident. He executes the Deep Throat Code and watches as his huge erection disappears down a non-existent throat.

The motionless body of Life Moberg stands above the blow job, but Roger and Anka have forgotten about her. They are both wrapped up warm in the programming language of human sex. In the real world, both Ankas watch, hands held, as their avatar performs oral sex on the screen. They picture Roger in the flat next door and realise that this is as close to romance as they have been in a long time. They are pleased when Roger executes the Deep Throat Code. After living so precariously under their own influence, the Ankas are elated to be moved and influenced by someone else.

In the absence of any real physical pleasure, virtual sex demands regular aesthetic change, just to keep the excitement levels up. The same is true of real sex, I guess. Roger knows the blow job has lasted long enough. Where do I go from here? He thinks about the Tit Wank Code but that just can't be right. He needs to keep it intimate. This is meant to be romantic. He's finding it hard not to imitate the sexual choreography of the Internet porn he's spent years of his life glued to. He fights off the urge to double-click the Fisting Code. This isn't porn. We are real people. In a sweet homage to average intercourse, he gives Anka ten seconds of the Fingering Code, rubbing at her detail-less loins with his simple fingers, then he launches emphatically and unexpectedly into the Missionary Code. The Missionary Code! The cheapest of all the sex codes. Roger pushes and pulls between Anka's legs, his head bent upwards above hers like the head of a swimming dog. This is wonderful. If romance is anything, it is imitating ordinary old missionary in a world where anything is possible. Anka and Roger both realise this. They watch themselves having such simple sex and feel an incredible empathy for each other. Sometimes you need to step outside yourself to realise just how cute and phenomenally unserious you actually are. Anka smiles. She does a little moan like she used to while having nervous teenage sex. Roger grits his teeth, just like the real boys do. It is at this moment, as they obediently replicate normality, that Roger and the Ankas feel that this may indeed be a kind of love, come to rescue them both.

And, of course, love is little more than a green light to perversity. Having dug love up, scraped it clean and having agreed between the two of you that it is, beyond doubt, true love, anything is possible. The dirty becomes clean. Crap becomes romantic. Fists become affectionate. Arseholes become beautiful and spanks become kind.

'Can I turn round?' says Anka.

'Sure,' says Roger, double-clicking on the Doggy Code, almost adding, 'I love you,' but checking himself.

So Roger's behind Anka now, she's on all fours. But because it's love, this isn't dirty. Oh no. Because it's love this is metaphoric. Both lovers looking in the same direction, staring into the distance at their shared future. Though in actual fact, Anka and Roger find their attention drawn to Life, who is still motionless in the middle of the red room. This is a little weird. But because of the genuine sense of affection, they bang on unashamed.

A minute or two of doggy and Roger knows what to do. What else can you do after missionary and doggy? Roger double-clicks on the On Top Code with such a sense of pride. Anka, suddenly riding Roger triumphantly, once again gets a rush of empathy for herself and for Roger. How sexy and lovely the normal is, she thinks. To follow such a standard progression of sexual positioning in a world where he could be fucking me with a seal's dick and badger's balls and Gwyneth Paltrow's face. It's so sensitive. Just what I need. He even resisted anal. So he should have done. But it would have been so easy to have clicked it in. Anka smiles as Roger feigns serious excitement, just like lovers in the real world do.

By this time, Roger is planning the finale. He can make Anka come whenever he wants, simply by feeding her the Orgasm Code. He can even dictate the volume of her orgasm. But should they come simultaneously? This would surely be the most romantic thing. But then again, Roger remembers, we're experiencing romance when we replicate the real. Is it realistic to orgasm together? It's certainly ideal. But I'm out of touch with this sort of thing, he thinks. I've been watching too much porn, where sex ends in other ways. In the real world, on the computer screen, Roger's cursor hovers over the Facial Code, then the Pearl Necklace Code. It would have been different if I'd got that door open, it would have been a threesome. This might be my last chance, he's thinking. My last chance to be daring and disgusting. By tomorrow I could be technical and dead. Love is one thing to experience, but dying without having been very perverted might be difficult to bear. He looks down at Anka. I could just use her. I could just come on her face and leave her on the floor.

Above the sex, Life's avatar comes back to life with a jolt. She turns and looks down to where a girl is riding a boy. Her first instinct is to kill them both. Life dislikes the constant shagging in Wow-Bang. In the real world, she loves it, but she becomes bizarrely moral in virtual places. She takes out her pistol and points it at the lovers. They're about to come, Life realises. And then she notices how banal their sexual position is, how normal and unadventurous. She's never seen such standard sex take place in Wow-Bang. The sex here is usually barely recognisable as sex, or else it's rape. Life puts her pistol down by her side. It's so romantic that this isn't rape, she thinks, and that he only has one penis, and that no part of her is animal or bleeding. Life watches with squinted, smiling eyes as the blonde girl and the bespectacled boy climax simultaneously, as both bodies spasm with pleasure. She watches as their eyes open with quick, joyful blinks. Roger executes the Affectionate Kissing Code and Life is overcome with emotion. The two lie naked, Roger and Anka, side by side, legs entwined, leaning towards each other; they give small kisses to each other with digital lips.

'That's so beautiful,' says Life, walking backwards towards the door.

'Life?' says Anka, placing a hand on Roger's shoulder while turning to the door. 'Life, it's me, Anka.'

By the time Life has walked across the room both Roger

and Anka are fully clothed. She and Anka embrace and Life executes a Cheeky Smile in Roger's direction.

'Yeah,' says Anka. 'This is Roger. Roger, this is Life. She works for the Wild World.'

Roger shakes Life's hand without taking his eyes from Anka. He realises that double-clicking on the Simultaneous Orgasm Code is the best thing he's ever done in his whole life. It wasn't strictly an honest thing, he would like to have ejaculated on her face. But honesty is not the thing. The thing is to be creative, kind and dishonest.

Roger's deep in real thoughts. Can there really be two identical creatures sitting in the flat opposite mine? How am I ever going to get to them? He becomes ambitious: Before I die, he thinks, or before the technology takes me over, I am going to actually feel them. I am going to kiss them both and then fall into all their arms.

'Nic told me about your eating problems, Anka. Is that going to be an issue?'

Anka puts an arm round Roger. 'I don't know.'

'To be honest,' says Life, 'I don't know whether anyone should be getting involved with the Wild World.'

'What do you mean?'

'I'm worried about a child and, if I'm honest, I'm not even sure what the Wild World is.'

17

IT'S LATE NOW in the Real Arms. Most people have left for the sex dives, the brain brothels and the skeleton clubs. At the bar, only a single helping of humans remain. Avatars slump, tired, pointlessly using the Cocaine Code, asking the barman if he sells the Slit Wrist or the Overdose Code, then sighing when he shakes his head apologetically. It is the end of the night.

Only Joe Aspen has left Wow-Bang and returned to the real world. Having flown from Janek's bullets he abandoned his puffin avatar. Now he's stroking Beak in a Travelodge on the M1, watching Sally nervously. But the rest of them are still here. At a table in the corner of the Real Arms, Anka and Roger sit with Janek and Life waiting to talk to a group of men that Life is calling the 'key players in the Wild World'.

Roger has lost count of how many times he's used the Passionate Snog Code with Anka. He can't stop himself. She keeps asking for it, too. They feel a sublime frustration.

Life has never witnessed such sincere passion in Wow-Bang.

When Roger and Anka inevitably start snogging she turns to look at Janek. Janek is behaving strangely. He is not the boy who smoked cigarettes and sipped coffee with Peter Gabriel. He is not the boy who played his bass dispassionately into her brain in every imaginable style. Janek has discovered talking. When people discover talking, it is terrible.

'So when I next see yer, I'm deffo gonna shag yer, it feels like years since I last had yer.'

'Stop doing that.'

'Doing what, princess?'

'Talking in rhyme,' snaps Life. 'And don't call me princess.'

'But we made a connection, I got an erection, and I'm so tired of introspection,' says Janek, shooting the air with a finger pistol and then blowing away the imaginary smoke.

'What's happened to you?' says Life. 'I liked your introspection. And just to make it clear, we're not together.'

Janek sighs, half smiling to himself, nodding understanding. 'Maybe not today, bitch, maybe not tomorrow, but one day soon I'll be forcing you to swallow.'

'What?' says Life, in disbelief. 'You'll be forcing me to swallow?'

'Suffice to say,' mumbles Janek, his real brain feeling like it's doused in vinegar. 'Suffice to say, I'm a sex buffet and you sure look ready to feast.'

Life pulls out her pistol and presses it into Janek's side. 'Shut up. I don't know what this is, but shut up.'

Janek doesn't tell Life that in the real world, as they speak, he is using the N-Prang. That since he arrived in Wow-Bang he's found it difficult to fulfil his desire for a brilliant, easy-going fuck festival of an existence. After the incident with Joe Aspen and the digital dicks, he didn't know what else to do but put the N-Prang into his real ears. The N-Prang changes the world. Janek wants the world to change.

'Remember what happened with that machine, Life,' says Janek, trying desperately not to make his words rhyme. 'Remember what we learnt. Funky life, that's what we all need. We're here to have fun. This is fun. So ride my cock . . . until . . . you . . . come . . .'

Life ignores him and turns to watch Roger and Anka Passionately Kissing. When they've finished, Roger puts a hand on each of Anka's cheeks with the intention of executing the Thoughtful Kissing Code. But he doesn't. She's changed her body again, he notices, staring at the same pencil-thin limbs that Anka had been wearing earlier.

'Why?' he says. 'Why would you go back? You looked beautiful.'

'Because,' squirms Anka. 'Because this is me, Roger. Seriously. This is me and I've got to be myself when the Wild World people arrive. Haven't I? I want a job. If I can't be Jackson Pollock then I'm going to work for the Wild World. OK?'

Roger shakes his head, suddenly anxious, slightly disturbed. 'I've got to go,' he says. 'I've never gone this long without blogging. It's like an itch. I've got to go.'

'Are you angry with me?' asks Anka.

In the real world, neither Anka can believe they've just said this. Are you angry with me? Jesus. They both deny saying it, but one of them must have. It's the kind of question idiots ask other idiots. Back in Wow-Bang, Anka looks at Roger, thinking, this man wanked over me. He wrote a description of it. I wanked over his description.

If that was madness, how have things become so suddenly normal?

'We've both got our problems, Anka. Wait for me in your flat. I'm going to figure out a way of opening my front door.'

Roger's getting up, pursued by Anka's hands. 'Are we OK?' she says. Again, neither Anka can believe they've just said this. In life, they decide, you're either fucked up or you're a fucking idiot. It's that simple. 'Go. It's fine,' they say, emotionally backtracking. 'We've never even met each other.'

'No,' says Roger, glaring at Anka's limbs. 'We've never even met each other.' And with that he disappears.

When the 'key players in the Wild World' arrive, it comes as no surprise to anyone that three out of four are literally dickheads. Longish, brown, digital penises grow from their foreheads and fall between their eyes. Testicles hang tight above their eyebrows. The fourth man, the one who's not a dickhead, is literally a wanker. That is to say, one hand is rubbing up and down on the digital dick that's poking out of his flies. When he sits down with his dickhead mates, he doesn't stop wanking. Life can see his hand moving swiftly under the table.

It's Life who introduces everybody. She's met the three dickheads and the wanker before. She's even met them in the real world. At a house party in Clapham shortly after she'd started working for the Wild World. All of them have made at least one attempt to have sex with her, either in reality or in Wow-Bang. None of them has succeeded. Not even the wanker, who in the real world is quite sweet and called George. Life lied to them, said she was going out with the bass guitar protégé, Janek Freeman. In view of

Janek's current behaviour, she's regretting having done this. She watches as Janek tries shaking hands with the dickheads in an American, hip-hop style. But he doesn't have the right code. It's a fiasco. He's rapping. '*I see you're a dickhead, how have you found it? I like my cock with lips wrapped round it.*'

The dickheads and the wanker look confused. They look at Life and shake their heads, the end of their penises bouncing around their noses.

'So you're Janek, you're Life's boyfriend?' says Dickhead 1.

Boyfriend? thinks Janek. The N-Prang rhythms in his real brain accelerate and then syncopate with joy. She told them I was her boyfriend!

'No doubt,' says Janek. 'I'm her lover, I'm the one who sucks her titties when we're underneath the covers . . . check it out . . .'

Janek's about to launch into a romantic rap about the sex session he and Life had enjoyed at the Columbia Hotel, when his computer screen suddenly goes blank. In the real world, he starts slapping his monitor with one hand, turning up the volume on the N-Prang with the other, shouting, 'What the fuck? What the fuck?'

In the Real Arms, Life puts away the pistol she used to shoot Janek and takes a seat next to Anka. To be honest, she's got half a mind to kill Anka, too, given the state of her body. But then one of the dickheads shakes Anka's hand and says, 'Anorexic chassis,' in the same way that boys sometimes say 'Ferrari chassis.' So Anka survives. She and Life sit opposite the three dickheads and the wanker, who incidentally, is still at it underneath the table.

'In fact,' Dickhead 2 is saying, 'we really want to rebrand eating disorders in the Wild World. Anorexia, we reckon, is a good way for women to enjoy short but successful lives. High death rate, sure, but other women envy you before you die, which is quite pleasant, you know, pretty cool.'

On hearing this, in the real world, one Anka frowns, the other smiles. In Wow-Bang, her avatar doesn't move. She doesn't want to say the wrong thing in front of the Wild World guys. Life, on the other hand, is full of energy. She puts two fists on the table and leans forward.

'Listen,' she says. 'It's time I was told what the Wild World is. It's getting ridiculous. It's embarrassing.'

Dickhead 1 smiles. He pushes his penis back over his head like a greasy strand of hair. 'You should relax. I can't believe you just shot your boyfriend.'

'Answer the question. What's gonna happen to Joe's child? She's practically in London. Do you guys have any idea what you're doing?'

'Of course we do,' says Dickhead 2, twisting his penis round with his finger and thumb then releasing it, letting it unravel and spin. 'It all begins in a matter of days. I think it's going to be great.'

'You hired me to throw a party,' says Life, 'and I'd really like to know what the fuck I'm throwing it for. I've got three days and I'm on my own. I think it's time I heard the truth, you know?'

There is a silence. All four men turn to each other, confident that one of them is going to speak up and offer a simple and accurate description of the Wild World. None of them does. The Wanker stares down nervously into his lap at his blurring hand.

'Well,' says Dickhead 1, tentatively breaking the silence like an egg tapped against the edge of a bowl, 'I'm only really involved in the marketing sides of things, you know, distribution and whatever. So . . . well . . . the Wild World is about empowerment, isn't it, guys? It's about giving individuals complete responsibility for the creation of their identities. Giving people total control over who they want to be. The way we do this is simple. We dismantle all hierarchies. Celebrity, government, the economy, beauty. Any system that differentiates between individuals is going to be abolished. After that, it's dead simple. We just have to stop people from getting into groups. This'll be a piece of piss because we're going to give them loads of great ways of designing really strong images and personalities for themselves. Consequently, they won't want to get together with others that much because, well . . . they'll be too afraid of others finding out that their identities are basically bollocks, you know, that they're technological, in essence, just a complete invention. It'll be great. The Wild World will be full of wacky, fascinating people, all of them separated and cheerful, all of them silently sustaining society's central lie –'

'Which is what?' interrupts Life.

'Which is that human beings are in some way interesting,' says Dickhead 1.

Dickheads 2 and 3 and the wanker all started giggling the moment Dickhead 1 started talking. When Life and Anka began nodding with comprehension, the three of them started rolling around in hysterics.

'What's so funny?' asks Dickhead 1, angrily. 'That's basically it, isn't it?'

'No,' cries Dickhead 2, the penis flying round his forehead like a lasso. 'You must have missed a meeting. That whole idea was only a joke. We were on drugs. I can't believe you took that seriously.'

Dickhead 1 has instructed his cheeks to glow red. His penis

shrivels upwards towards his hairline. Life is still leant forward, staring with annoyance across the table.

'The Wild World,' chuckles Dickhead 2. 'The Wild World's got nothing to do with any of that. If anything, the Wild World's just old-fashioned moneymaking. After all, we're heading for a recession. You see, and I will try to be brief, research recently revealed that hatred no longer exists. We couldn't believe it. To us, everyone seemed to hate immigrants, terrorists, natural disasters, death, economic meltdown, being alone etc. But we dug a little deeper, and found that, basically, no one really gives a running fuck about any of those things. We found that most people consider life to be slightly overrated, so-so, a bit dull, you know, fairly pointless but, essentially, not that bad. And this is a bad thing, this kind of indifference towards being alive. The cornerstone of the economy has always been a firm and widespread hatred of being alive, particularly among women. Hatreds of various kinds are often fundamental reasons to spend money. But things are changing. People are increasingly less willing to buy away their hatred of life. They're no longer willing to try and be happy. They just bob along, pointlessly, thinking it's OK, not that good, not that bad, average, which doesn't inspire the necessary consumption. And so the Wild World is just a threat, a way of scaring people, an attempt to frustrate them and cause them to worry and to revive their hateful approach to the issue of living, get them into the shops, get them talking to each other, get them speculating about the world again, hating it. It'll be great, right?'

'Wrong,' says Dickhead 3, neatly tucking his penis behind his ear and shaking a pitying frown at Dickhead 2. 'The Wild World has got nothing to do with the economy.

And, in any case, the living will always buy.'

Across the table, Life shrugs. Anka plays with her minuscule wrists while the wanker wanks.

'The Wild World,' continues Dickhead 3, 'and this is an absolute fact, is nothing more than an excuse for a party.'

Life instructs her hands to cover her face in frustration. With each attempt to describe the Wild World she has become increasingly annoyed. After all, she sacrificed a lot to work for it. She left Manchester. She left Joe. She's spent every night schmoozing in Wow-Bang trying to make connections.

'Think about it, Life,' says Dickhead 3. 'Just lately, all the big parties have become a bit boring. People just aren't enjoying them as much as they used to. For example, everyone's pretty much figured out that Christmas is crap, that it's very depressing. Even little kids are pretty cynical about it. Easter, obviously, is rubbish, completely meaningless. But the problem goes much wider. Stuff like the football World Cup, the Oscars, St Patrick's Day, the MTV Awards, the Proms, the Queen's Jubilee, right down to things like birthday parties, weddings, office summer parties. People just aren't getting much out of these things any more. They try and everything, but, you know, they tend to feel pretty let down, like they've seen it all before. The idea behind the Wild World is simply to tell the people that the world is new and wild and to encourage them to party in celebration of this fact. The Wild World is little more than something for people to do. And that,' says Dickhead 3, 'is the truth.'

The word 'truth' hangs in the air like stubbornly stained underwear on a backyard washing line. Anka doesn't know what to make of any of this. Each dickhead's explanation contained the rickety, creaking sounds of lies. She and Life watch, confused, as the dickheads nod to each other and whisper sagely, that, in effect, they're all right. 'Yes, of course, in a way, all of us are right.' Then over the course of a silent minute the atmosphere around the table sinks like an object accidentally swallowed and everyone is briefly pleased that the wanker has decided to speak.

'What about the human engineering?' he says, wrist still working overtime beneath the table. 'What about the N-Prangs?'

Life bursts into life. 'Well? What about those things? What about Joe's child?'

The wanker stands and, quite reasonably, everyone wishes he'd remained seated. It's a bit disgusting and off-putting, the constant masturbating. But still they listen.

'The idea of Wild World,' the wanker begins, 'came about because of certain scientific developments. Mainly, the ability to build human beings to any specification. They thought about putting this ability to all sorts of uses. Honestly, for the past few years they have thought long and hard about the different types of humans they could build. For example, they thought about growing organ donors to cure the ill, but they couldn't muster enough enthusiasm. They thought about designing intelligent, diplomatic creatures, strong ones, servile ones, loving ones. They even thought about creating beautiful, sexually flawless creatures, perfect boyfriends and perfect girl-friends for everyone. But none of these things seemed quite right. And no one involved had any strength of vision. In fact, the rumour is that everyone thought it was a bit old-fashioned to be scientifically engineering perfect humans and radically affecting the future. They couldn't agree on anything. It was ridiculous. In the end, having failed to build a consensus for any of the more ambitious plans, it was decided that the creatures should just be engineered in the interests of a very humorous future. You know, they all agreed that they could just design funny creatures, half-human, half-scientific joke. They figured it would be pretty cool if the creatures could provide those that met them with a bit of amusement, not in terms of what they say, as such, but in terms of what they are, what they do. Everyone involved agreed that this was the best idea. In fact, they saw it as the only option left open to them really. And so they got on with it. The job of dictating the behaviour of the creatures was given to mates of the scientists, guys who they considered to be a right laugh, really funny, or eccentric, or fucking nuts. You must know the types of people. Those half-young men from pubs, well known for their amusing stories.'

The wanker is wanking more vigorously than ever. Life leans in and whispers to Anka: 'You don't want to work for the Wild World. Trust me, it's not worth it.' Anka has already jumped the short distance to this conclusion. She has returned to other concerns, like which one of her real-world selves is the anorexic. Which of them must she try to destroy? And what of Roger? Could he be one of these Wild World jokes of human engineering? She hopes not. She hopes that he is becoming electronic naturally and that he's real and that when she sees him, she likes him, and maybe they can help each other. The wanker is wanking more vigorously than ever.

Life is thinking about Joe. She's looking at the fuck-ups and the literal dickheads she dumped him for and wondering whether it was worth it. She's wondering whether there is less to life than meets the eye. Less to herself and less to life itself. Maybe the Faroese have it right. Maybe they're right to dry out mutton in small outhouses and eat it through the seasons. Maybe the world of events management and three-dimensional social-networking environments is the biggest pile of shit of all. Maybe we should embrace the simple disaster of being alive by curing meat and planning meals.

'Why don't I believe you?' says Life, sickened by the fact that the three dickheads have become erect and are clapping and nodding to the accelerating rhythms of the wanker. 'In England, everything sounds like a fucking lie. And what about the baby?'

'If it's true,' hisses the wanker, through gritted teeth, 'and she has been taken south of Birmingham, then there's nothing your friend can do. Chances are the baby is already pregnant.'

In the virtual city of Wow-Bang, in the Real Arms, the wanker ejaculates and the dickheads cheer. Life and Anka stare at each other. There is a virus contained in the large, unrealistic drops of semen that settle on the table and then disappear. Yes, there must be a virus in the liquid because within seconds Wow-Bang crashes. The walls and decor of the Real Arms freeze on the computer screens of these people. Its graphics dislocate and die leaving each of them, the two girls, the three dickheads and the wanker, breathing quickly in England, in actual rooms, on chairs, each of them truly alone, and suddenly real.

THREE DAYS PASSED. These days behaved like recipients of intensive care. They were rushed in on stretchers to the distant sound of sirens. They screamed. They were sedated, surrounded by a chaos of keen and skilful humans who did everything they possibly could to revive these days and make them last, if only for a little while longer. But they died. The days died one after another and the humans regretted this. Tired and desperate to make amends, they scrubbed their hands with soap and stared at their reflections. But the fact was, what no one seemed to notice, was that the days were happy to die. They were more than willing. They were, in truth, desperate to die. Because although their lives were short, each had seen as much of human life as they could take.

To think that all this happened in January. It makes me laugh. Just another nervous January. We can collapse as fast as buildings. We can be demolished fairly safely. I was still calm, as I remember. I was knock knock and I was scratch.

I was, as we often are, thinking of other things. It's like I said at the start, the Wild World meant nothing to me.

Life invited Anka, Roger, Janek and Joe to the Wild World launch party in London. She emailed the invites with a click and then leant back in her chair and closed her eyes.

It was January. What else was going on? What else was going on?

Knock knock.

I remember the Premiership title race was exciting, as it tends to be after Christmas. It was Man Utd against Chelsea. Manchester against London. United were playing the best football. Scholes was on fire, Ronaldo and Rooney, too. And then you had Chelsea, dull but resolute. Shevchenko had been misfiring all year but Drogba was unreal and Lampard was getting more than his fair share of goals. I do not know who won in the end. If beauty matters in this corporate world, then it would have been United. And, yes, everyone was invited to the launch party, to the Event in London.

It was January. The Wild World competed for the newspaper headlines with kidnapped children, car bombs in Iraq, hostage disasters, university massacres and the news that former pop star Asa Gunn was selling six-inch sections of his veins over the Internet and encouraging their use as friendship bracelets. The weather was sunny and it was winter, prompting people to worry about global warming and offset their carbon consumption by writing songs about natural beauty and posting them on the Internet. It was January. Selfridges started to sell small scraps of paper with the words 'You're a thick twat' written on them in a stylish font. They cost a tenner. They were popular. Channel 4 commissioned a programme to help a group of young people to reinvent the West End stage musical for the modern world. The programme's commissioners had brains that looked like sheep shit, which, if you've seen it, looks like hand grenades. They called the programme *Musicool*. It was January. Someone filmed a really fat bloke in a crop top dancing to Peter Gabriel's 'Sledgehammer' and posted it on the Internet. A million people around the world watched this video. It was January and, Jesus, I could talk like this all day. I know my bollocks off by heart and the past is in my head, the birthday cake is in my fucking head. But what matters is . . . well, I'm tempted to say nothing, but.

Knock knock.

Scratch.

What matters is the living.

III

The Event

Scratch

18

JANEK IS BACK at the Columbia Hotel. It's three in the
morning. The manager's head belongs in a taxidermist's
dustbin. His clothes, a dying pair of blue pyjamas, belong
in a ghost's wardrobe. Janek stares into the man's seventy-
year-old nostrils, at his cheeks, sucked colourless by night,
and at the countless, miserable folds of his forehead. Janek
can't understand why the manager's eyes are disappearing
with rage.

They're standing at the reception, in the light of an orange
standard lamp. Janek's shoulders are gripped by a huge
night porter. At the foot of the stairs, Janek can see the
maid in her pink dress with her apron wrapped around her
hands, her head bowed.

'If her status in this country wasn't as delicate as it is,
you'd already be in a cell.'

Janek does hear the words of the manager, his voice a
violent whisper, but everything that enters his mind lately
gets set upon by a gang of minstrels with cloaks and musical
instruments; they seize each word from behind as soon as

one enters Janek's head, they retreat to a brothel in the cellar of his brain and play new meanings into their prisoners. Lately Janek listens to the N-Prang even while he sleeps.

Tonight, a dreamworld mixed effortlessly with a real one, like the harmless combining of two vaguely different airs.

Janek had been smiling in an outdoor jacuzzi with several women of every different race. It was somewhere in California. The sky was cloudless and deep blue. Behind the jacuzzi, a new, white mansion echoed with music. Women and men danced on every balcony. Women lay on the bonnets of fast cars in the driveway where men also congregated, guns tucked into their underpants. A large film camera hovered, unheld and unsupported in the air above the jacuzzi. Janek looked into the lens. He brought his fist out of the hot, bubbling water and made it dance for the floating camera. On such occasions when one of the women would clamber over Janek's lap and display her damp backside for him much like the court painters of the seventeenth century might hold up a still wet canvas for the king to behold, Janek would stroke it as one might a much-loved pet. He dirty-grinned at the camera.

Janek left the jacuzzi dripping and pulled on some jeans. He led the camera inside the mansion where he showed it the contents of his fridge, pointing out for specific attention the champagne, the foie gras and some old-style bottles of Coca-Cola. He led the floating camera to the indoor swimming pool where men and women played volleyball half-heartedly, making their wet muscles ripple and their wet breasts yell. He showed the camera his gymnasium where he climbed onto an exercise bike and pedalled furiously for a while, pulling a serious grimace at the camera. Janek showed the camera every room in the mansion. The dining room, the games room, the home cinema, the home studio, the basketball court, the library. All was going nicely until he took the floating camera to his bedroom and nodded with odd eyebrows at the large and psychotically made bed, intimating that this is where the magic happens, you know, this is where I stick it in. He made a quick call on the phone beside the bed and, having hung up, he leapt horizontally onto the bed itself and plunged his backside down into the mattress, making it depress and bounce, as if to say, this is pretty much how my mattress moves when I'm having sex on it, absolutely, it's almost exactly the same. He used a remote to make a TV screen descend from the ceiling. He winked at the camera, smiling, suggesting undoubtedly that it wasn't unknown for Janek to watch television on this massive television, maybe even while naked and with a girl, maybe even porn. Meanwhile, a girl's arrived holding a tray of bread and miniature chunks of vacuum-packed cheese. The girl is plain, her complexion full of Eastern European shadows and soft yellows. To impress the floating camera, Janek begins grinding on the girl's behind, holding her hips, guiding her clothed bottom around his denim dick area. And he's smiling, oh, he's really beaming with pride, even though the girl is slapping his cheeks with desperate knuckles and trying to get away. In fact, it's only when the girl is really beating the shit out of him that Janek becomes a little embarrassed by the presence of the floating camera and, amid the throws of the girl's punches, intimates that it doesn't need to see this and should probably float elsewhere. Next thing he knows he's being marched down the grand mansion staircase by a man with fingers as thick as wrists. Only it's not the mansion now, it's a hotel, and outside the windows is night.

'Get your stuff and fuck off,' says the hotel manager, his grey face slashed by red pillow lines.

'Easy,' mutters Janek, his voice weak, dragged through sleep. 'I ain't a player hating motherfucka,' he whispers, with no conviction.

'Pardon?' shouts the manager.

'Nothing,' says Janek.

Half an hour later and he's walking through a deserted Hyde Park. He tries Life on her mobile, knowing it's far too late for her to answer. He listens to the ringing, desperate for that moment when the tone is interrupted by a human voice, Life's voice, a sleepy inhalation and a croaky hello. It doesn't come: *Hi, this is Life's phone. Leave a message.* Janek chooses not to, but he does register yet another change to Life's recorded message. No more bright and breezy invitations to the Real Arms, Wow-Bang. He's pleased about this. But still, since she killed him, Life has ignored all his calls.

Janek makes immediately for the shelter of a large poplar tree. He lays out his coat on the rough ground and sits on it, pulling off his beanie and covering his face with it. Where have I been? he thinks. What have I been doing? He recalls the past week, his attempt to get giddy and find the festival. His attempt to live for the moment. The moment, thinks Janek. Better to live curled up in a car boot than kicking and screaming inside a moment. In fact, there are no fucking moments, only sickly sweet cocktails of solitude. There's boring truth in the complex crap that we contain. It gets pumped round our body, makes our dicks and nipples hard, makes us blush, makes us faint. Janek's beanie is wet with his tears. No real life, he concludes, should ever be lived in moments.

Janek looks up through the branches above him at the purple sky. The leaves randomly sway and the sky randomly arcs and alters its colours in small ways. Not even the hopeful humans can connect all this shifting debris together any more. We can't be arsed.

Janek inserts the N-Prang into his ears, confident it will never be removed.

19

AFTER A GIGGLY reconciliation and three days of nervous negotiation, the two Anka Kudolskis have acquired a sledgehammer.

'Do you really want this?'

'You know I do.'

'OK then. Here we come.'

Roger waits. He has propped himself up against his computer desk. He's standing up for the first time in ages. He's loving it. He's thinking, this is living. If living is anything it is standing the fuck up, nervously preparing a friendly facial expression and waiting for a girl you've never even met to smash down your front door.

'Aaaaaarrrrrgggghhhh.' Out in the corridor, the two Ankas bring the sledgehammer crashing down against the door to Roger's flat. The effect is charming. The boring brown door gives in after just one stroke because it hasn't got the heart to resist. It breaks down in front of the force of love and the force of total desperation, leaving two panting Ankas leaning against the hammer's handle, staring into the shadows of Roger's flat.

'Hello,' says Roger.

'All right?' say both Ankas in unison.

Roger looks through the remains of his door at Anka Kudolski. The two Anka Kudolskis look through the shadows of the flat at Roger, leant, tense, against his desk.

'So anyway,' says Roger, nervously, 'I've got all this stuff in my stomach, like I told you. Wires and everything. And my legs are like, you know, black plastic. But . . .' Roger remembers all the lonely, loveless years that preceded this moment. He gets the urge to sing. He thinks maybe he could sing a love aria from *Les Misérables* but he loses his confidence. It wouldn't make Anka happy. 'So . . .' he continues. 'I can't have sex . . . because I've got this numerical keypad where my thingy should be. And also, Anka, I find existing a little bit tricky. I can't just *be* . . . I have to –' Roger's body jolts so extremely he's convinced he's going to fall flat on his face and not be able to get up for absolutely ages. He shouts, his voice like a drill sergeant: 'I'm standing up! I'm leaning against my desk! I'm staring at the girl! I've been thinking about you so much!'

Both Ankas smile. 'Wow, that could get really irritating.'

'I'm nodding,' says Roger loudly. 'I'm nodding at you in agreement.'

'You sure are,' say the Ankas, through deliberately weary smiles. 'So how do you feel about going outside, about going to London for this Wild World thing?'

Roger bleeps: 'To be honest, I'm shit-scared. Did you manage to get a wheelchair?'

'We did, yes. And that reminds us, before we go to the

train station all three of us are gonna go to the EDC. There's one near Piccadilly.'

Both Ankas are still out in the corridor and Roger is still propped up against his desk. Everyone feels a little ashamed. Roger because of all the funny noises he's making and because he's having to try so hard not to describe the situation in minute detail. And the Ankas because despite another night of discussion, neither can decide which of them is starved to the brink of liver failure and which is the genuine, authentic Anka, the one that got born, grew up and wanted to be an artist. But they do have a plan. They return to their flat to fetch the wheelchair that Roger had insisted was necessary if they are to travel to London. They push it together slowly into Roger's flat. They are getting closer to him. They can both hear him muttering.

'I'm standing. I'm waiting. I'm full of technology. She's coming at me with a wheelchair.'

'Jesus, Roger, is there no way you can not do that?'

'What, the describing?'

'Yes, the describing,' shout the Ankas, each grabbing one of Roger's arms. 'Of course that's what we meant,' they shout, needlessly, or rather to drown out the feelings triggered by lifting someone, touching someone. They lower Roger into the wheelchair, their faces straining, imitating the stressed and impatient expressions pulled by mothers at their children. All three people are breathing loudly. They're flustered.

'What's an EDC?' asks Roger.

'Eating disorder clinic,' say the Ankas. 'There's something we need to do. By the way, is that the TV that, you know?'

'That you were on and that I wanked over? Yes, it is. Are you still doing the show?'

'No,' say the Ankas, firmly. 'We quit. We refuse to work as a double act.'

'Right,' whispers Roger and, in so doing, he announces the first official silence of his and Anka's relationship. The first silence of any relationship is crucial. In it, the participants have the first opportunity for evaluation. Firstly, they can judge how awkward the silence is. Secondly, they can decide how likely it is that the other participant in the silence is thinking thoughts so negative as to prevent the relationship even sharing another silence. In this instance, however, all Roger is thinking about is how he can prevent himself saying, 'I'm sitting in silence, in a wheelchair, looking at the only person who can save me. I'm sitting in silence, full of technology etc.' And all the Ankas are thinking is: When, inevitably, lunchtime arrives, what the fuck are we going to do?

The silence is broken by an irritating buzzing coming from Roger's head. He holds it and feigns a painful expression in the hope of getting some sympathy. He doesn't get any. The Ankas simply begin wheeling him towards the door, saying, 'Come on, El Rogerio. It's time.'

When Roger and the two Ankas leave their building, the place where all their solitudes have been played out so forcefully, they are instantly aware of being followed. Or, at least, the Ankas are. They've only pushed Roger as far as Miller Street when, while waiting for the green man, they notice that six or seven teenagers in black drainpipe jeans, painfully straight fringes and neon-pink headbands are standing only a few metres behind them, all staring with expressions of genuine awe. 'For fuck's sake!' say the Ankas, each of them flicking emphatic Vs at the group. 'Who is it?' says Roger, struggling to turn and see. 'Nobody, sweetie,' bleat the Ankas, in funny American accents. The green man appears and the three of them cross the road.

When they get to the eating disorder clinic on Ducie Street, behind Piccadilly Station, the two Ankas crouch down in front of Roger's chair.

'You wait here,' they say. 'This shouldn't take long.'

Roger nods. 'I'm sitting, I'm waiting, I'm full of technol –' The Ankas push all four of their hands over Roger's mouth.

'Just wait here, Roger. We'll be five minutes. Be careful.'

For the first time in almost a year Roger is outside. He sniffs the air. It smells just like the air used to smell in the past, when he would walk for miles each day, selling personal websites door to door. Or rather, not selling them. The sky is still the same. Manchester is crumbling and being rebuilt in all the same ways. Nothing has changed. When he's confident that Anka is safe inside the clinic, Roger expels air as if he's been holding his breath for a year.

'Allow me. Allow me,' he gasps. 'I'm stuck in a fucking wheelchair in central Manchester. I'm wearing baggy jeans and a T-shirt. Definitely, I am. I'm gonna catch a train to London with Anka, we're going to some Wild World party. Fucking bullshit. I'm outside. The air is salt and the sky is pepper. The kind of bullshit you flavour food with. I'm cold. Fucking cold. I can't stop talking. I'm in a wheelchair. I can't stop talking. I wish I had a keyboard. A computer.'

Roger puts a finger in his mouth and bites hard on it. His face glows red. It's no good. He could eat his way through his whole hand if it meant being able to talk. A car drives down Ducie Street at speed. Roger winces, spitting his finger out of his mouth. Now his hand is down his trousers, tapping away on the numerical keypad inside his boxer shorts.

'Allow me. Allow me. The buildings around me are rubbish. Don't you just hate those losers who cry for help. They spend months fucking themselves up and then right at the last minute have second thoughts. Second thoughts are bad thoughts. I'm sitting in a wheelchair. A car just drove past. The car was probably driven by some glistening, silver tit-wrench, probably listening to Snow Patrol, en route to the fanny factory to pick up his wife. Fucking. Can't stop talking.'

Roger is breathing like a punctured tyre. As if he only exhales, never inhales. He's no longer tapping at his cockpad. He's pulling hard on the thick black wires that sprout from both his ears. If I pull hard enough, he thinks, I'll split my head in two.

'Allow me. Allow me. I was born. When I grew up and once I'd left home and learnt to talk, I said shit down the phone to my mum like –' Roger affects a blasé voice – '"Yeah, Mum, everything's fine. I got a job designing a website for Selfridges. Yeah, I'm going to save the cash cos I wanna buy a house. Yeah, of course I wanna have kids. No, I'm not seeing anyone at the moment. How's Dad? Oh, that's good. Yeah, I do know that *Miss Saigon* is coming to Manchester. I'm definitely going to go, probably more than once. Yeah, I'm still doing that constantly, Mum. I breathe in, I breathe out, I breathe in, I breathe out. I'm getting dead good at it. Yes, I'm happy. Tonight? Not sure. I'll probably eat a cheese-and-tomato pizza." Now look at me!' shouts Roger, returning to his own slightly nerdish tones. 'I'm in a bloody wheelchair. I'm trying to pull my head apart so my brain will topple into my lap and I can cuddle it for a few seconds like a teddy bear.'

Suddenly, from behind his wheelchair, Roger hears applause. He turns the chair round with difficulty. The group of teenagers, larger now, are clapping ecstatically, down on their knees. 'Carry on,' they're crying. 'Carry on, El Rogerio.'

It's starting to rain. A sky-sized dirty bedsheet has been pulled over the roofs of central Manchester. Roger feels the raindrops on his face. 'You again,' he shouts, almost rising out of the chair. He senses that blue electrical sparks are coming out of his nose. 'Carry on!' the teenagers cry.

'Allow me. Allow me,' yells Roger with wet hair and reddening cheeks, hands still pulling at his ear wires. 'Life is hugely difficult! If you're like me, a failure, full of crap, then life is hugely difficult. It's a lot like getting shot, life is. Not that I've ever been shot, I'm unshootable, full of the kind of bulletproof bullshit you can buy at PC World. But definitely, life is a lot like being shot. I can explain.' Roger clears his throat, making a very deep whirring sound. 'In the early days,' he continues, 'ages zero to eighteen, you live with a pistol pointed right at you and you're thinking, fuck me, this life thing is a very serious business, I better be careful while I'm alive. Then when you hit about eighteen, the trigger gets pulled and, for a while, you feel even more worthwhile. Even more convinced that life is a crucial activity and that you should do your best to take it very seriously. Next the bullet enters your body, this is your twenties. With the bullet in your body, you're happier than ever, everything is very dramatic, you're stumbling around and, if you're lucky, you find a long-term lover, maybe move in together, or, maybe, you get an audition for a local production of *The Pirates of Penzance*. Maybe stuff goes so well you have to call up your parents and be like, "I'm a massive success, Daddy!" But, even though things are more exciting and dramatic than ever, it's difficult to forget that you've got a bullet swimming through your vital organs like sperm towards an egg. "I'm a massive success, Daddy, but, I should also say, I've been shot." By the time you hit thirty, you're dead. You become a chubby ghost. You float around showing off all your cool ghost accessories; your fast ghost cars, your ghost job, your designer ghost shoes, your ghost bed where you conceive the babies that you quickly point a pistol at. You show off, too, about your direct debits to various ghost charities, your ghost homes, your ghost holiday homes and, the proudest thing of all, you show off the gruesome exit wound left behind by your youth.' Roger gives up trying to pull his head apart. He rests his hands in his lap. 'I'm thirty,' he says. 'I'm thirty.'

The teenagers are rolling around the wet pavement in raptures. 'So cool,' they scream. 'So fucking cool.' Roger grins. He's sort of happy. He takes a wire that grows from his appendix and plugs it into a USB port near his collar-bone. He can't resist trying to impress the teenagers. How did they track me down? he wonders. How clever the young are, he thinks, watching as they roll around in the rain.

Across the street, the door of the eating disorder clinic opens with a crash.

'What the hell do you think you're doing?'

One of the Ankas comes storming across the road and begins beating the teenagers round their heads with a rolled-up self-help manual entitled 'Starving Yourself to Death: The Drawbacks'.

'Leave. Roger. Alone,' Anka shouts, enunciating each word with a swipe of the manual. 'Piss off. Go on. Go and find your own messiah.'

The teenagers run off together, still laughing and quoting bits of what Roger had said. Roger, meanwhile, is mumbling again: 'I'm watching teenagers get beaten up. They're running away. I'm sitting in a wheelchair. She's very angry.'

Anka walks up to Roger and hits him so hard with 'Starving Yourself to Death: The Drawbacks' that for the second that follows she's worried she might have knocked him clean out.

'Ouch,' says Roger.

'Stop talking crap,' snaps Anka, kneeling down to button up Roger's jacket against the rain. 'There's something you need to know.'

'What?'

'I've just discovered that I'm the real me. Just now, in there. They ran some tests on us both. They checked our body mass indexes. Mine was healthy, whereas the other me was diagnosed as "practically dead". Seriously.'

'Seriously?' says Roger.

'Yeah, so when we were in the bogs I knocked the other me out. I told her she was a skinny bitch and then I smashed her head against the tiled walls and locked her in a cubicle.'

'Is she dead?'

'I'm not sure, but she'll definitely miss the train.'

Anka and Roger laugh. Once they've finished laughing they find themselves knee-deep in the second silence of their relationship. The second silence is the most exciting of every relationship. It's during the second silence that both parties can really begin to imagine the happy things they're going to do together in the future. The second silence normally ends when both participants become tacitly aware that they are both thinking about the same thing. Normally, it's sex, but it could be something like having a kid, meeting each other's parents or dancing together in a place not intended for dancing. On this occasion though, it's sex. Anka and Roger are both thinking deeply about the practicalities of lovemaking.

'So,' says Roger softly, 'I suppose this means we're not having a threesome.'

'I'm afraid not.'

'Don't kiss me, Anka. You'll be electrocuted.'

'Shh. I won't.'

She isn't. Their lips are wet with rain. Their cheeks are cold and rough. The tips of their tongues touch and both realise they have forgotten so much about being alive. Neither has touched the tip of tongue in far too long.

20

IF THEY'RE GOING to get to the party, then Joe, Sally and Beak must find a way into central London by this afternoon. But they've been stuck here for days, in the Travelodge. Joe and Beak eating trout from the bathroom floor while Sally constructs a nest from the bedlinen in the corner of the bedroom.

Meeting Life in Wow-Bang has only strengthened Joe's desire to win her back. He noticed a weariness in her graphic eyes. A weariness towards Janek Freeman and, also, a general weariness towards a world where people put dicks on their heads and talk loudly about how the future's coming and how, when it does, they're gonna have it wrapped around their fucking finger. He thinks he can win her back.

I'm hopeful, thinks Joe. My heart's wrapped in tinfoil, skewered on a spike with a beef tomato and a yellow pepper, but I still have hope for Life.

Joe can hear a whimpering coming from inside the nest of bed sheets. It is unlike Sally to whimper because Sally is not a whimperer. She's a screamer or a laugher. Joe crawls slowly over to the nest, concerned, every finger bent double against the carpet like paws.

'Sally?'

More whimpering. Joe is pulling bed sheets out of the pile with increasing speed, trying to spot Sally, one of her limbs or her little black eyes. Beak is peeking out from under the bed, miaowing in response to the deep and long burp that's suddenly coming from somewhere inside the nest.

'There you are,' says Joe, pulling away one final sheet to reveal little Sally curled up tight with her hands round her throat. You wouldn't have thought it was possible for a baby to make such a deep sound.

'What is it?' says Joe.

Sally is looking up at him with wide, black eyes. For the first time since he became her guardian, Joe notices fear in her strange gaze. This is serious. I've fucked up. I should have kept her in the north of England. Sally's little hands are trying to grip her neck but they are too inflexible, her fingers are too minute and weak. Her burp is getting worse. 'Show me where it hurts,' Joe is saying, trying to unfold her tensed and curled-up limbs. There's a smell coming from Sally's mouth. It smells like dead animal. An abattoir at night. It stinks. Joe holds her in the Heimlich grip. Every time he heaves her little body the burp accelerates louder than ever from her mouth.

'Come on, Sally!' shouts Joe. 'Come on!'

The burp ends. Sally has stopped breathing. Joe lays her out on the tangled mess of white sheets. He places a hand on her tummy and feels that there is air trapped inside his child. She is inflating. Getting bigger and bigger because her mouth is blocked by something. Joe pulls apart her baby lips and peers into the darkness of her throat. The smell is almost unbearable. A family cat dead in a summer dustbin. Joe holds his breath. He can just make out the object that is blocking Sally's windpipe, but he can't quite reach it with his fingers. 'Breathe, Sally,' he pleads. 'Please. Breathe.' But Sally is only silently expanding, getting ready to burst, her black eyes motionless with fright. 'For Christ's sake, Sally, breathe!' She can't. The skin of her stomach is being stretched. There is too much air inside her. A yellow balloon blown up too much. Joe thrusts his fingers inside Sally's mouth and grabs hold of the object lodged deep in her throat.

He yanks it out, releasing a jet of dead air and a significant amount of black vomit. But at least Sally is breathing. She's still alive, gasping slightly, even smiling. Joe is staring down at the object in his fist, his own breathing refusing to steady.

Because it has hair, the object. Long hair sprouts from one end of it. It's heavy, too, perhaps three times as heavy as Beak. It's about six inches long and not very wide. It lies comfortably and unidentified across Joe's two palms. Lowering it onto the floor and, taking one of the bed sheets, he begins to wipe away the black residue that hides the area near to where the hair is sprouting. The object has eyes. Dead, misted-up eyes that, at some point, were surely made to stare at something too terrible for words. The eyes are surrounded by thin, wrinkled and perfectly yellow skin. It's a face. A head no bigger than a bread bun with a crooked nose, no bigger than a walnut, lips, cracked and light purple, ears, twisted shut. Joe rubs away more of the black residue. He finds a neck, the width of a pencil. He finds a torso;

a miniature ribcage wrapped in the same delicate yellow skin as the skull. He finds that the creature has empty breasts; that they fall like the folds that fasten envelopes. He finds a stomach that is empty. Completely barren. He discovers the bones of a miniature pelvis protruding, as snappable as matchsticks, from the object's groin. Finally, the legs of the creature fall, feetless, from its body like yellow stalactites of hardened wax. Joe places a thumb gently on the area of crumpled skin that surely shelters the creature's heart. He feels nothing. The tiny creature is dead. Maybe she was never alive. Just an old and haunted human doll.

'So who is this, Sally?' asks Joe, holding the little creature upright so Sally can see. But Sally is still catching her breath among the stained bed sheets, sometimes crying, sometimes looking around the room with wide, curious eyes like babies often do. Joe strokes the small corpse lovingly with the palm of his hand. I'll call her Dolores. Dolly, for short. She can come with us to London.

Half an hour spent standing on the service-station slip road holding a sign saying 'Central London' results in Joe Aspen sitting nervously on the back seat of a Mitsubishi people carrier. Apart from Joe, the people carrier is carrying people from the south of England, from Wokingham, to be precise, which is somewhere to the west of London. Joe settles nervously into his seat as the car pulls onto the motorway.

The travel seat is right beside him and luckily its occupants, all three of them, are behaving well; they are asleep or they are dead under the seat's canvas roof. Beyond the travel seat, a boy is sleeping. He's wearing a blue vest, despite the fact he's got very scrawny white arms. He's got a fancy blond haircut, shaved on one side, longish on the other and spiked up Mohawk-style on top. The sleeping boy looks about twelve, Joe thinks.

In the driver's seat, in front of the sleeping boy, is the man responsible for picking Joe up, the boy's dad, Alan. Alan looks old enough to be the boy's grandfather. He has a lined brown face, muddy owl eyes and an incongruous red baseball cap on his head. Beside him, in the passenger seat, Alan has shovelled his wife Ann into place. Her body is smothered in multicoloured floral fabric and she does not speak. It might be that she can't speak.

'How old is she?' barks Alan. In the rearview mirror, his eyes blink due to the force of his voice.

'Nearly one year old,' guesses Joe.

'Where's the mother?'

'London,' Joe lies. 'In fact, we're on our way to see her.'

The Mitsubishi speeds along the M1.

'Is the cat sterilised? You shouldn't keep cats near babies, you know?'

'She's fine,' Joe says, calmly.

'What's that other thing?

'This,' says Joe, taking Dolly from the travel seat. 'This belonged to my mother, to Sally's grandma. It was her favourite doll. It's pretty gruesome, I know, but Sally, like my mother, has such affection for it.' Joe can feel the brittle bones and defunct organs underneath Dolly's skin. It's confusing. This whole period of life is confusing.

'It's disgusting,' says Alan, bluntly. 'What do you do for a living?'

'I don't do anything,' says Joe. 'I really don't.'

The ensuing silence wakes up the boy beside Joe. His eyes open and his hand reaches instinctively to his hair which he flattens and spikes where it is appropriate to flatten and spike.

'All right?' says the boy, his voice even more bendy, high-pitched and Southern than his dad's. His muscleless chest grows firm and twists inside his blue vest. 'Has my dad been picking up strangers again?' says the boy, mid-yawn.

'That's right,' says Joe, noticing that the boy looks older with his eyes open, maybe fourteen.

'How old are you?' says the boy.

'Twenty-four,' Joe replies.

'If you're twenty-four,' says the boy, turning his body round so he can address Joe over the travel seat, 'then why is your hair so white? And what's this?' The boy is shaking the travel seat. 'You've already got a kid?'

'When I was twenty-four,' say the eyes in the rear-view mirror, 'I had two kids and I'd bought my first house.'

The boy groans at his dad's remark. 'Whatever,' he says, offering Joe his hand. 'My name's Sean. I was a mistake. Dad thought Mum was infertile.'

'Sean,' say the eyes in the mirror, their voice full of warning.

'I'm seventeen next month,' says Sean, changing the subject. 'What sort of car do you drive?'

'I don't drive,' says Joe. He can't believe that this shiny thing before him is nearly seventeen. He examines Sean. His trendy 'OSAKA' vest. The cheap crucifix round his neck, the twenty-pound haircut that's not quite stylish, the three-quarter-length jeans and the Diesel sandals. This is what people are like, thinks Joe. At the end of the day, at the end of our days, when we die en masse, many of the corpses will resemble Sean.

'So yeah, I'm getting a TT,' says Sean, 'but I won't drive

it fast. If I had a shit car, I'd drive that fast, course I would, but driving a TT fast? No way, blood. I'll drive it like as slow as possible, past my mates, past the birds, you know?'

Joe realises that, in fact, he does not know. He realises that the life that he has led since he was sixteen has been a bizarre one. He has never once cruised past birds in a TT, whatever a TT is. He has been lost in thought. He fell in love with Life. He worked in the theatre a little, visited the Faroe Islands and currently wants to be a puffin nesting in a cliff. He stopped dyeing his hair. It turned white. No worries. Worries.

'I'm also getting like a new stereo because the one the TT comes with is pretty whack. And like, probably gonna buy like drinks holders so, you know? And then going to college'll be cool cos I'll just like go in when I have to, in the TT, right?'

'Sure.'

'And this summer twenty of us are going to Spain so, like, you know. Feel like it's finally happening. Where you from?'

'Manchester.'

'No way. The North? You a United fan? You like fucking Oasis? Cos I don't see what all the fuss is about. I think I like Grime, you know? In the North, do you like get bored? I get so bored in Wokingham. There's nothing to do until like I can get the TT or like the Wild World starts. But then I also heard that Wokingham isn't gonna get the Wild World cos it's not big enough, like, not enough people.'

'Right,' says Joe.

'But the TT'll get me into London, which is cool for the Wild World. And like. Well, I'm sort of looking forward to

227

the change, cos like, I know I've only been here like sixteen years but anyone can see that's it's not that good, earth, I mean, you know, anyone can see that it could be better, and should be better, and like will be better with the Wild World and once I get the TT and I've passed my test, which is fine, cos Dad's been teaching me the basics, you know, ignition, gearbox, and yeah, when they had me Dad assumed Mum was infertile. Can you believe that? He didn't even like check with her that she was definitely infertile, but, then again, Mum doesn't speak because my brother got hit by a Nissan when he was like thirteen, like before I was born, so like if Dad had asked Mum whether she was fertile or not she wouldn't have replied probably, so it's no real surprise I'm here, really, if you think about it, because it's hard to make plans if one person refuses to speak, if you know what I mean, and so I've been here for nearly seventeen years and I can definitely see ways in which it could be better, not just in Wokingham but like the world in general, so, like, well, when I've got the TT, it'll be cool, things'll be much better, I reckon, I'll be able to like go into Reading and shit.'

Sean's expression suddenly changes.

'Shit, man, have you done one? It smells like fucking dead sheep back here. Have you fucking let one off?'

'It will be the baby,' says Alan, from the front. 'That fucked-up baby with the eyes will have shat its pants.'

Sean starts shaking Joe, saying, 'Your fucking baby has shat its pants and it smells like a fucking dead sheep.' Joe is thinking, God, I hate Southerners. Whiny Southerners who don't have a clue. He looks into the rear-view mirror, it's crammed full of angry eyes, shouting, 'Sort your child out. You're a guest in my car. Sort out that fucking smell.'

Joe can't even smell the smell. I'm no longer sixteen, he's thinking.

'Come on, you white-haired freak,' shouts Sean. 'I can't take it. Throw the fucking nappy out the window!' Sean has grabbed Dolly from the travel seat and he's using her to hit some sense into Joe. 'Oh my God! What the fuck is this? This fucking doll's got a fucking skeleton. I can fucking feel it.' The small white flannel becomes untucked and falls off Dolly's body. 'Fuck's sake, Dad. This doll's got a fucking minge!'

'Put the doll down, Sean,' shouts Alan, making the people carrier accelerate. 'We'll sort all this out at the next service station. Please put that disgusting doll down!'

Joe regains some form of consciousness. 'Do you want to see something really disgusting, Sean?'

'What are you on about, mate? I can't get over your fucking hair. When I get the TT I'll never pick no one up.'

Joe pulls down the canvas roof of the travel seat and Beak lets out an ear-splitting scream, all her fur stands on end and her back arches extremely. The smell of death is worse than ever. Someone should seriously consider winding down a window.

'What the fuck is that?' exclaims Sean.

'What is what, Sean? Tell me. What can you see?' says Alan, hyperactive in the front seat.

'The baby's mouth,' shouts Sean. 'There's something coming out the baby's mouth.'

Sally is once again in labour and in pain. Her windpipe has once again been blocked by a small corpse, a doll, a minute and dead human; her face is becoming red and her black eyes are wide and watery. Joe can sense the loud sound that will accompany the passing of this new object building up inside Sally. He begins to twist the little body and try to ease it out of Sally's mouth. Sean looks on, horrified, silent, watched carefully by Beak. Alan is twisting in the front seat, trying to figure out what's happening.

'This one's still alive,' says Joe, noticing that the naked yellow body he's pulling from the baby's mouth is flinching slightly like a caught fish. 'And it's a man.'

This time the birth is painless. Sally groans as the little body is pulled from her throat. She starts crying but quickly loses interest in the idea and instead begins to dribble black residue over her chin and tries to reach out and seize Beak with her outstretched hand.

Joe, meanwhile, has laid the minuscule man out on his lap. The creature is breathing. Though he looks just as old and haggard as Dolly, he is clearly still breathing. The crumpled yellow skin that covers his lungs is moving up and down so quickly. Joe uses his sleeve to clean the creature's face. His eyes are similar to Dolly's – weathered, worn out, full of sadness. The little creature is petrified. His tiny eyes look up at Joe with an expression so full of fear that Joe can barely hold it. The little man watches as the blue sky scrolls in the windows of the people carrier. He looks across to where Sean is shaking, the back of his haircut squashed against the window.

'Can you hear me?' whispers Joe, bringing his lips up close to one of the little creature's ears, which is no bigger than one of Joe's fingernails.

The little man nods his head, his eyes still wide with fear. He's gripping the upholstery of the car seat very tightly. The ancient skin of his face develops more and more lines as his cheeks clench and his jaw locks with white anxiety. He is trying to speak.

230

'What is it?' asks Joe, turning so his ear is above the man's cracked and blackening lips.

'My wife,' mutters the man, his voice barely audible due to the age and weakness of his lungs. 'Have you seen my wife?'

Instinctively, Joe reaches into the travel seat and grabs Dolly. He holds her up for the little man to see, forgetting that Dolly is dead, is not quite the little lady that the little man recalls. The little man stares with ever narrowing eyes at Dolly's fixed, dead expression, at her withered and naked body. Only when the man begins to weep does Joe realise his mistake. He sees the pinprick tears falling from the little man's eyes and realises he should have made up an excuse, a story. He should have said that Dolly was waiting for him somewhere. But he did not think.

'I'm sorry,' Joe whispers.

The little man nods. He's trying to say something through the tears. His lips attempt to make a word but they're quivering too much, they lack the strength and they give in. For a few seconds, the man just nods his little head, his eyes looking into Joe's wearing a sad expression, but an understanding one. His ribcage rises and falls in an ever more laboured way, until, after a short time, Joe notices that it has stopped moving altogether and that the little man's eyes have turned to look through the window at the vast winter sky, and have completely drained of life.

'He's dead,' says Joe, 'We'll call him Sam, as in, Sam the Man.'

'Who's dead?' shouts Alan, his face twisted towards Joe but his eyes fixed painfully on the motorway. 'Sean, could you tell me who's dead?'

Sean doesn't hear his dad's question. He has put

headphones into his ears and he's staring out the window, his head turned away from Joe, from Sally and Beak, from the dead bodies of Dolly and Sam the Man. Sean does not hear his mother speak either. His mother who has never spoken once during his lifetime, who gave birth without making a sound and who, some years ago, failed to alert anyone when Sean fell from Brighton pier while under her supervision. But she speaks now. She brings a sledge-hammer crashing down on nearly twenty years of silence.

'It's quick,' she says, in a voice in need of repair. 'And it doesn't matter.'

A silence follows. A newer, lighter, fresher-smelling silence. Sean stares out the window, oblivious to it all. Cradling the corpses of Dolly and Sam the Man, Joe shakes his head and wonders how he ended up in a car with a baby, with two little corpses, with a kitten. For once a Southerner is right, he decides, as the people carrier joins the A1.

It's quick. And it doesn't matter.

21

BY THE TIME Life was brought on board to organise the launch party, those involved in the Wild World were rapidly losing faith and less willing to tell others what they did for a living. They spoke vaguely of corporate marketing, never mentioning the Wild World by name. They got drunk a lot instead of doing their work. They spent their days exchanging junk email or chatting on Facebook or fucking each other in Wow-Bang. Paper piled up on desks. Plans were left half made. Designs were rushed. Very little, if anything, got organised. In fact, as the date for the launch party grew closer, it became clear that no one was working at all. If ever employees of the Wild World bumped into each other in Soho or Shoreditch or Bethnal Green they would nervously say 'hello' and then, having composed themselves a little they would say, 'Dear me, you look fantastic, you've got genuine guts and your soul's elastic. And Jesus, that can't be an original Roxy Music T-shirt, surely?' And then silence would prevail and the sounds of London streets would amplify in the ears of both people and in the eyes of the other each would suddenly recognise the same questions and thoughts: *What the fuck was Wild World? It was just hype, right? It was literally nothing. It was irony, yeah, I get it, it was pretty cool, pretty funny, pretty clever. But it didn't mean anything, did it?*

Only Life, who had been taught as a child not to give up, continued to make any effort at all. For her, it didn't matter that she didn't know quite what the Wild World was. If she'd been hired and paid to help, then help she would. With a couple of days to go before the scheduled launch of the Wild World, it was Life who picked up the telephone and booked the banqueting suite at Stamford Bridge, home of Chelsea Football Club.

Her efforts didn't end there. She spent whole nights in Wow-Bang, trying desperately but failing miserably to motivate people and gather advice. She spent hours glued to her mobile phone, calling caterers, celebrities, scientists, musicians, sword swallowers, politicians, athletes, billionaires, every latest sensation. Anyone who she thought might conceivably have something to do with the Wild World. She even called Asa Gunn's agent and offered Gunn the chance to quickly relaunch his pop career at the Wild World launch event. He accepted. A small victory. Mostly, though, Life became more and more nervous. She called the people who she had once considered her superiors in the organisation. She called Bossbitch. No answer. She called the bald guy who had asked her if she knew anyone in the North who could be entrusted with a very special child. He answered, he said he was out of the Wild World, 'far too fucking vague'.

So Life Moberg got her wish, she found herself at the forefront of events management, and, as I say, rather than give up, she got cracking. She had hoped to find a better venue than the banqueting suite that overlooks the pitch at Stamford Bridge. But she struggled. So it's all going to take place here. The Wild World will be launched in a football stadium.

It's a large room, as long as the football pitch is wide. It's incredibly beige. The walls are beige and so is the carpet and the tablecloths. Even the chairs are covered in thick beige fabric. When the guests arrive, few will have ever seen such a beige place in all their lives. Only Life breaks up the beigeness. She's walking between the tables in a red silk dress. Her golden hair is tied back with a red ribbon. She looks beautiful. She has made a special effort. She straightens pieces of cutlery and rearranges some of the flowers that decorate each of the large circular tables. She climbs up onto the stage and nervously tests the microphone. 'One two,' she says, flinching as her voice echoes loudly around the room. 'One two, Wild World, testing.' Above her, a large banner reads 'WELCOME TO THE WILD WORLD'. Getting down from the stage, Life checks the place names on the table nearest the front. Everything is in place. 'Janek Freeman' next to 'Joe Aspen' next to 'Anka Kudolski' next to 'Roger Hart' next to 'Life'. Life picks up her own place name and stares at it, reading it in her head, over and over again. 'Life.' 'Life.'

Satisfied that the room is ready, she decides she ought to go and check on the photographers outside. She places her name card back onto the table. She turns towards the door to find ten straight and fashionable faces staring right at her. She recoils in shock. She even gasps. For a second she can't think straight at all and can't make sense of this group of people who must have entered and gathered around her without making a sound. They stand, these people, closed-mouthed and with trendy, blinkless eyes, staring at her. They are dressed, all of them, in crisp and muscularly ironic fluorescent shellsuits. They're in their mid-twenties with dyed and challenging hair but Life doesn't recognise any of them. Eventually she's able to compose herself and construct an ingratiating smile. These people must be here to help. Thank God, thinks Life. She's about to say hello and offer them each her hand when she notices that some of these bright and shellsuited young people have started to smirk. They are eyeing Life's pretty red dress, the ribbon in her hair, the special effort she has made, and they are laughing.

'We'll take it from here, Life Moberg.'

22

ROGER AND ANKA are first to arrive at Stamford Bridge. The
only problem is, they're too nervous to go in. The entrance
is surrounded by photographers. There's a red carpet. Every
now and then, cars pull up and elderly men and women in
formal dress get out, pause to be photographed, then enter
the stadium. Anka and Roger are watching proceedings
from an outdoor stall selling Chelsea FC memorabilia.

On the train down here, Anka had been forced to gag
Roger with a spare pair of her knickers. He wouldn't stop
describing things, banging on about the countryside, the
various stations, the sound of the train, his feelings, his sitting
position, his inability to make love, the technology inside
him. He wouldn't shut up. When two incredibly fat ladies
sat down opposite them at Stoke, Anka thought it best to
gag him. He still mumbled, and tried to move the knickers
with his tongue. But he couldn't really express himself.

'What are we gonna do?' says Anka.

Roger looks up from his wheelchair, his jaw straining on
the knickers, eyes pleading.

'All right,' Anka says, ungagging him, 'but try to keep the bullshit to a minimum, yeah, Roger?'

Roger splutters. A string of saliva clings to the knickers as they're pulled from his mouth. 'Do you really think it's a good idea, this?' he says, pointing at the crowded entrance. 'Maybe you're used to being photographed, Anka, but I'm not. And they'll probably ask loads of embarrassing questions about why my body's plastic and why I've got a mouse lodged in my head and wires in my ears. What if my belly starts beeping? I know what these kinds of people are like, Anka. They're vultures. They can be cruel.'

Anka doesn't reply. Roger watches as she stares over at the photographers, twisting the knickers tightly round an outstretched finger, deep in thought.

'I don't want to be just another anorexic posing in a magazine,' Anka says finally, turning to Roger. 'And what does the Wild World matter anyway? We've found each other. We want to help each other, right? We're sort of above culture, aren't we?'

Roger nods.

'Why do you like me, Roger?' says Anka keenly, kneeling down beside Roger's chair and forcing him to hold her eyes.

Roger's not sure what to say. Why? he wonders. Why Anka? Because she's fit? Thin, but beautiful. Because she's weird? Because she beats herself up in eating disorder clinic toilets? Because she's on TV? Because when a bra pushes her tits together a pleasing shadow falls between them?

'Because I'm desperate,' says Roger. 'I'm desperate not to be alone. And you're the only person I've properly met in years.'

'I hope you realise that's a bad answer.'

Roger tries some other words: 'Whatever humanity I have left,' he says, 'I'm willing to give to you.'

Anka smiles. 'Better. Do you want to go to the cinema with me?'

'What about the launch, the Wild World?'

'Fuck it,' says Anka, standing up and taking hold of Roger's chair. 'Fuck the Wild World. Let's just go. We'll get jobs. We'll get a flat. You can monitor my eating. We can go InterRailing. Let's just be normal. It'll be great.'

'Fine, but what about my body?' says Roger. 'We'll never be able to make love.'

'You can finger me. I'll teach you how to find my clit.'

At the mention of her clit Roger turns round and looks nervously at Anka. She's above him, pushing his chair along, laughing. She is light-hearted. She's saying, 'What do you fancy seeing? I reckon something with Johnny Depp. Once we're settled down, Roger, I'm going to eat food and watch films that have got Johnny Depp in them. I may even start fancying him a little.'

'Personally,' says Roger, turning to regard the street he's being pushed down; a grey, buildinged, peopled, weathered strip. 'Personally, I'd rather we went to a musical, maybe *Chitty Chitty Bang Bang*. Something fun.'

'Fine,' says Anka. 'Whatever you want, Roger.'

From nowhere a figure steps out in front of the wheelchair. Anka tuts and tries to move round.

'Oh no you don't.'

It's a man. He's tall, dressed in a shellsuit. Fluorescent pink. Likeable clumps of facial hair float unevenly around his mouth and cheeks.

'You two,' he says. 'You're both late as it is, and now I find you striding off in the wrong direction. What's going on?'

'We're going to watch a film with Johnny Depp in it,' says Anka, causing Roger to perform a large and deliberate cough. She corrects herself: 'I mean, we're going to see a musical.'

The man starts laughing. He grabs the handles of Roger's wheelchair and then continues to laugh his head off. 'Very funny,' he's saying, pushing Roger back in the direction of the football stadium, the red carpet and the photographers. 'Very, very funny.'

'Get off him,' shouts Anka, trying to stop the guy but succeeding only in trotting alongside the wheelchair. 'You're pushing him too fast.'

The man is still chuckling to himself, muttering, 'Johnny Depp. That's a classic. Imagine. Johnny Depp. That's an absolute classic.'

23

WHERE THE RED carpet meets with the pavement, a cameraman bends down onto one knee. He allows the auto-focus to do its thing and a second later the camera clicks and flashes. You could take the camera off this guy. You could hook it up to a laptop via a USB. You could stare at the photo. You could stare at this split second.

You'd see Anka Kudolski being dragged by one of her thin arms onto the red carpet. You'd see her head bent down in struggle, a swathe of blonde hair shielding her face from the lens. It's the guy in the pink shellsuit dragging her. He's pushing Roger Hart's wheelchair aggressively with his other hand. You'd see Roger's face frozen, his head turned and staring with wide objecting eyes. Roger's large, round head, with the computer mouse stuck in the top of it and the thick black wires coming from his ears. You would see all of this. All of this would be in foreground.

Zooming in a little, beyond Roger and Anka, you'd see cameramen going mental, frantically pointing lenses in the direction of the two of them, shouting at them, gesturing to them with mad hands, faces begging them to stand still and be photographed. Beyond the cameramen, you'd see Janek Freeman. He'd be a little blurred, I expect, but instantly recognisable in his black beanie, pulled down to his defined eyebrows, his navy blue tank top, his handsome face, his ears; red wires pouring from both of them. He's getting out of a black cab and being greeted enthusiastically by a green shellsuited blonde. She'd have one hand on Janek's shoulder, gesturing that he should walk the red carpet and pause to be photographed. You'd notice in the photograph that Janek looks scared, that he's trying desperately to touch fists with the girl but that she is having none of it. Beyond Janek's taxi, at the very back of the photograph, is a Mitsubishi people carrier. The young man you'd see getting out of this people carrier has perfectly white hair. You'd recognise him straight away as Joe Aspen. You'd see he's wearing a billowing white shirt, the cuffs and collar undone. You'd think that his face looked hot, that Joe looked tense. Perhaps he's tired from carrying that travel seat, you might think. You can't make out much of what is inside the seat; just grey fur, dead yellow skin and a pair of shining black eyes. You'd see that Joe, too, is being greeted by a shellsuited twenty-something. You'd see her excruciatingly precise red fringe. You'd see how she tries to snatch the travel seat from Joe and how he prevents this by clenching his fist.

24

ONCE INSIDE THE stadium, Anka, Roger, Janek and Joe are ushered into a cramped, windowless room next to the banqueting suite.

Joe recognised Janek the moment the two of them were dragged from their respective cars. He looks a lot like his Wow-Bang avatar, what with the beanie. The two take seats at opposite sides of the tight, grey-lit room; Joe sees to Sally while Janek covers his eyes with his fingers.

Anka steers Roger's wheelchair next to her seat. She straightens his various wires affectionately, running the back of her hand against his cheek. 'What the fuck –' she says. She was going to say '– are we doing here?' but she can't be bothered. 'What the fuck are we doing here?' is not a question Anka can be arsed asking any more.

The four people sit in silence.

After a while, the door unlocks with a click. A young man is pushed into the room. The door is slammed and locked once more. Joe recognises the young man straight away as former pop star Asa Gunn. He smiles at him, recalling their recent meeting in Manchester, but the celebrity's face contains only anxiety and nerves. No recognition at all.

'Hello,' says Asa Gunn, addressing the floor, or perhaps the briefcase that he holds timidly with both hands.

'All right, mate,' says Joe, placing Sally into the travel seat and rising to shake the ex-pop star's hand.

'Your wrist!' Asa Gunn exclaims as he takes Joe's hand. 'You're not wearing one of my bracelets. In fact,' he quickly scans the room, 'none of you are!'

Asa Gunn drops to the floor and opens his suitcase. Within seconds he's standing up, carefully offering a wet-looking, red-and-yellow bracelet to Joe. It's shining under the strip light, it's glistening.

'I make them out of my veins,' says Gunn, gesturing that Joe take the bracelet from him. 'Since I accidentally retired from the world of pop, this is what I do. I make jewellery out of myself. I sell it on the Internet. But today is my comeback. That's what's so great, I think. We make comebacks.'

Having handed the vein bracelet to Joe, Asa Gunn lifts up his pink T-shirt a little to reveal several large scars, jet black and barely healed, just below his ribs. He turns round to show them to Roger and Anka but he gets distracted. 'You've got wires coming out of your head. Are you like me?'

Roger glances up at Asa Gunn. Roger is desperate not to speak. Words are gathering round his brain like nails round Semtex. He succeeds in saying nothing. He just hunches his shoulders and blinks.

'What do you mean?' says Anka, bluntly. 'What are you on about?'

'You,' replies Asa Gunn solemnly. 'You are so very thin.

When I was a pop star, my friends were very thin like you. And late at night in posh hotels they liked to flash their limbs at me. One time, a girl removed her pretty green dress for me, and she completely disappeared. Or rather, she was just a sad grey face that floated round the room.'

Janek Freeman jumps to his feet and screams in rhyme: 'I was a normal boy with a bass guitar, I played on a stage with American stars. I fell in love with a girl called Life. I stuck it in and it felt so nice. What the fuck are we doing here?'

Everyone ignores Janek's outburst. He has the air of one that should be ignored. Like a drunk tramp, a boring teacher or a total psycho. Also, everyone can hear the tinny music coming from his red MP3 player and assumes it would be futile to address him.

Joe, having tied Asa Gunn's vein around his wrist, drops Beak onto the floor so he can have a wander around. Joe is feeling strong. The more he watches Janek panic, the stronger he feels. Whatever happens, he's thinking, whatever we're doing here, I'm going to be fine. I'm gonna take care of Sally, Dolly, Beak and Sam the Man. I'm going to be fucking fine. He watches calmly as Janek babbles in rhyme about the fun and funky fuck festival of a life he's just dying to lead. He watches as Roger suppresses the pointless words that are desperate to explode from his arsehole, his nostrils, his ears and his mouth. He sees Anka holding her wrist with her finger and thumb, trying to work out how thin she is, and whether she was right to smash the other Anka's head against those toilet tiles.

In the centre of the room, Asa Gunn inspects his jet-black scars. 'I used to be famous,' he whimpers.

The door to the room opens and there is a brief yet fairly collective sense of relief.

'I was wondering when you'd turn up,' says Joe, smiling up at the doorway.

'Thank fuck,' says Anka. 'Thank fuck you're here. What happened to our front-row seats?'

In the doorway, Life has the look of someone who has been let down. She is awkward inside her beautiful red dress, upset beneath her immaculately styled golden hair. She has the look of a bride abandoned at the altar, as if she would like to rip her dress off here and now and pull at her hair till it's ruined.

'I'm sorry,' Life says, her accent more Scandinavian than ever, almost completely stripped of Englishness. 'I didn't understand. I've been fooled. I've been used and so have you.' Life starts to cry. Joe can't believe this. Of all the people he has met, Life is one he could never imagine weeping. In the two years they were lovers, she never cried once. She was always so happy. He puts baby Sally to one side, stands and holds Life by the shoulders.

'It's all right, Lie,' he says, reassuringly. 'Whatever it is, I'm sure it's fine.'

'It's not fine, Joe,' she weeps. 'That's the amazing thing. It's not fine at all. They've made a fool out of me.'

Life is really letting the tears flow. She has tears round her thick red lips.

Janek rips off his beanie and pulls himself to his feet by his curly brown hair.

'Hip to the hop, don't stop the rot,' he cries, his voice shredded with fright. 'I'm so laid-back I'm motherfucking snoozing, I'm born to win, you won't catch me losing . . . What am I saying?' he shouts, staring psychotically at Life

246

as she weeps uncontrollably. 'Promises are panes of glass. Let me love you up the ass. Promises are panes of glass. Let me love you up the ass!'

There is no time to consider replying to Janek. Because Roger's face just explodes with words:

'Allow me. Allow me,' he blurts. 'It's all wank. It's all total bollocks if you think about it. All us young people wandering around, moaning, getting fucked up. It's a snoring waste of time, all of it, a boozing, boring waste of time. We do not eat rats or cats or dogs, this is not the French Revolution, we do not wave flags, we do not stand together, we do not mutter to each other in gutters and we should not be miserable, we should not be the miserable ones –'

With the help of Joe, who holds down his flailing arms, Anka succeeds in regagging Roger with the knickers.

'Perhaps you'd like a bracelet,' says Asa Gunn timidly to Roger once he's fully gagged. Roger growls at the former pop star, biting down hard on the underwear.

'Who?' says Anka, turning to Life angrily. 'Who is using us?'

Sally starts crying now.

'Come on, Life,' shouts Anka. 'Tell us what's going on.'

Sally stops crying the moment Joe puts her over his shoulder. He shakes his whole body gently and the baby is calm. He touches Life on her shoulder.

'Lie, it's OK, I'll look after you.'

Hearing this, Life, too, stops crying. She stops abruptly. She stops because she knows that Joe can't look after her and because, in any case, she doesn't need looking after. Above all, Life Moberg knows that you can't go back, you just can't. Whatever emotions you feel for those held prisoner in your past, you cannot set them free. She sniffs a snotty sniff and wipes her eyes. She exhales. She runs a hand through her golden hair and approaches Asa Gunn with an air of professionalism.

'I'm afraid you won't be performing today after all,' she says. The ex-pop star is instantly upset. 'I wasn't as powerful as I thought,' Life continues. 'I was deceived and I'm afraid I didn't have the authority to hire you. I'm sorry, Asa.'

Asa Gunn looks at his wrist, wrapped in his own veins. 'So no comeback?' he says, quietly. 'No comeback.' Ten seconds pass like knife-wielding teens on stolen bikes until, quite suddenly, Asa bites down hard on his bottom lip before opening the door and charging through the group of ironically shellsuited goons, screaming, 'No comeback! No comeback!' and he is never heard of again.

Life pulls the door shut then turns to Anka and Joe. 'I thought I was in control. I thought I was living the life, you know, the dream.'

'Who?' blurts Anka, as if she's not sure what the word means. 'Who's in charge?'

'You don't get it,' says Life. 'You don't get anything. All this stuff about the Wild World. It's us. I mean literally, you and me, Roger, Joe, Janek. The Wild World is us.'

25

DOWN ON THE pitch, the players are emerging from a tunnel situated in the corner of the stadium just below the banqueting suite. Some of them wave at the cheering fans; others stare down at the scrolling turf, deep in concentration.

Up in the banqueting suite, the atmosphere is hushed and expectant. Relatively little of the cheers and boos of the crowd outside can be heard in here. It's weird to be sat in silence so close to forty thousand screaming people. Weird to see so many fanatics waving flags and shouting insults at a field, while you yourself are sat quietly at a beige table in a long beige room, watching an empty stage, not knowing quite what you're waiting for.

Next to the stage, five or six of the shellsuits are huddled together and talking in excited whispers, smiles bursting across their faces whenever they speak. Turning momentarily from this huddle, one of them addresses the audience. 'It shouldn't be too long now, ladies and gentlemen,' she says. She's just a girl, a girl with a fringe so straight it could draw blood. Having reassured the waiting guests, she returns to the group and rejoins the whispering. A soft murmur travels round the increasingly stuffy room. Shoulders get hunched. Palms are revealed in gestures of not knowing. Some people even yawn.

Not one person from the fabulously unimpressive list of D-grade celebrities that Life invited to the launch of the Wild World has been allowed in. They turned up in terrible clothes and faces rendered foul by fleeting fame. They got told to fuck off. They got told that the young girl, Life, did not have the authority to invite them. They were told that Life, like them, like everyone else, has misunderstood the Wild World.

There are no celebrities in this room. These people who sit silently round these tables are strangers. They are mostly elderly. Judging by their expensive suits and smart, understated dresses, they are rich strangers, strangers from business, strangers from the aristocracy, even strangers from the government. Irritated by the lack of activity on the stage, most have turned to watch the beginnings of the football match through the long window that stretches all the way down the suite. They watch as a fat man is introduced to both teams.

A minute or two later and the referee blows his whistle and the match kicks off. In the banqueting suite, a few of the guests even call out. 'Come on, Chelsea,' says an old man with a wet, white side parting and a highly reflective face. 'Fuck off, Chelsea,' cries a gentleman wearing a monocle. The guests in the banqueting suite seem so old. The men are wearing waistcoats. Their facial hair is cloud-like and ludicrous; their skin is creased and uneven. The women, too, are old except for their make-up, which cakes over their thinning skin and invents curious eyebrows where little hair now grows. On the table at the front, which Life had intended to share with Janek and Joe, Roger and Anka, a typically elderly couple have become captivated by the football match. The two of them stare at the pitch with fixed, glazed eyes. They watch as one of the players in blue begins to run down the wing, attempting to trick the defender with various step-overs and dummies. The elderly woman, her soft white hair tied into a bun, takes a cigarette from a silver case and places it in her mouth; she nudges her husband, requesting that he light it.

'It seems, darling,' says the old man, removing a gold lighter from his waistcoat pocket, 'that football has changed a great deal since our time.'

The woman leans so the tip of her cigarette enters the yellow flame. She inhales on it, exhales and then crosses her legs, reclining at a relaxed and thoughtful angle.

'Perhaps you're right,' she says. 'I'm told these men are all autistic orphans, that they're raised in fields with only footballs and one or two volumes of pornography to entertain them.'

'Is that right?'

'It's what I'm told. They make good money, of course, but . . .' The woman delays exhaling a lungful of smoke while a free kick is taken on the pitch below. The ball sails over the bar. The woman blows smoke into the air. '. . . but most of these men will die very, very young. They won't live to be as old as us. It's sad.'

The two of them watch as three or four players from each team suddenly get into an argument. They start pushing each other, bringing their foreheads very close together and exchanging fierce stares before their respective teammates start pulling them apart and the referee starts issuing yellow cards.

'Yes,' agrees the old man softly, 'it is sad.'

The elderly guests' attention is grabbed so firmly by the minor brawl taking place below them on the pitch that none of them notice when the lights of the banqueting suite slowly begin to dim. 'Send the tosspot off,' shouts a grumpy-eyed man with a dragged-down face and a top hat, thumping the thick glass window with a white and weakly clenched fist. No one notices when a spotlight ignites and shoots a bright beam across the half-light of the room. Only the shellsuits by the stage turn to stare at the spotlit doorway. They're more excited than ever.

'Look, everyone,' shouts the girl with the dangerous fringe, appealing to the guests, trying to drag their attention from the game with frantic flaps of her arms. 'Everyone, look. Please. Ladies and gentlemen. If we could have your attention.'

Music begins to play. The sound of an orchestra swelling to crescendo is played through large speakers. The elderly guests begin to struggle round in their seats, opening their mouths slightly and craning to look over their shoulders at the door beside the stage. The timpanis join the orchestra, hit firmly, tribally; the music is getting louder and louder. The fluorescent young at the front are clutching each other's shoulders, stooping slightly and peering into the bright light of the doorway. 'Get ready,' shouts the girl with the murderous hair, satisfied now that the elderly guests are no longer watching the match but have turned to view the event. 'This is it,' she shouts. A shadow appears in the doorway, silhouetted by the spotlight's beam. The elderly guests begin to nudge each other, forgetting about the match. 'Look,' they say, shouting to be heard above the now deafening music. 'Look at that. What on earth could that be?' Answers are not heard. The music can get louder. Trumpets, bassoons, trombones and always the rageful dum-dum-dum of the drums. The figure is on the move. It's a man. A man dressed in a spotless white suit. He steps out of the doorway and up onto the stage, tracked always by the spotlight.

When they see him properly, the gasp given off by the elderly guests could suck the features from your face. Their eyes open too wide in horror. Each of them suddenly resembles the gingerbread dead: shocked and simple. The lady with the drawn-on eyebrows and the caked face lets out a scream, tossing her cigarette into the air. There is chaos. On the table near the front a man removes his top hat and he and his wife take turns vomiting into it. Some of the men even struggle to their feet and begin waving ivory-tipped walking sticks at the stage in protest. They're made to sit back down by the shellsuits who can't help but smile and applaud even while forcing guests to return to their seats. The man, meanwhile, has made it to the podium at the centre of the stage. The orchestral crescendo seems intent on going on forever. How long can a group of people go on getting louder and louder? It's unclear. The man straightens the cuffs of his white suit and sends a smile spinning round the room like a boomerang before catching it in his teeth and winking at his horrified audience. Next he feigns a grimace that seems to acknowledge the absurdity of the music and the fact that a football match is taking place in a packed stadium outside the window. To the shellsuits, the man nods, acknowledging their generous applause and their crowd-controlling skills. But not even his evident good grasp of facial expressions can strip the shock from the faces that stare back at him. A woman has removed a red silk glove from her hand and is attempting to blindfold herself. Men bite into their own fists. Women weep. When the recording of the orchestra finally comes to an end, it is replaced by a discordant arrangement of sobbing, loud breathing and human groans.

'Please,' says the man, gesturing for quiet with both hands. 'Please, ladies and gentlemen, please settle down.'

For a second it works, the crowd quietens and the elderly people stare at the floor, eyes wet with concentration. But the moment they raise their heads cautiously to look at the man, they begin to shriek with disgust even louder than before. The man shrugs. He's annoyed. 'Yes,' he starts saying. 'Yes, it's true. Yes.' The crowd gets no quieter. The sickly couple at the front are in need of a second top hat. 'Yes,' says the man, stepping down from the stage and deciding to shout. 'Yes, ladies and gentlemen, you're all correct!' He brings a fist slamming down onto the table nearest to him and finally the elderly people regain a degree of composure. The man smiles sympathetically, nodding a little. 'There,' he says. 'Thank you.' He returns to the podium while the last sobs subside.

'Ladies and gentlemen, let me reassure you. What you see here is just a trick. There really is no need for you to react like this. Please, take a moment to become accustomed to it. I shan't be offended.' The man smiles and leans forward with both hands on the podium. 'What you see here is the result of plastic surgery, I assure you,' he says. 'See this as simply an arrow pointing in the direction of your future. Surely you must have anticipated this. Surely you have heard.' The man deepens the pitch of his voice to lend it gravitas and says, 'A Wild World will come. And with it the end of our days. Then finally, armed with our future, a dickhead will rise from among us.'

The elderly crowd erupts once more, taking immediate offence at the idea that this . . . this dickhead at the podium is some sort of prophet, some sort of Jesus, a messiah or a seer with a penis on his head. How dare he? They fire questions at him and in response the dickhead, that is to say the rather genuine dickhead from whose forehead a dick definitely droops, begins to try and restore calm once more, saying, 'It's Marlon Brando's, if you must know. Jesus! If you must know, it belonged to Marlon, yes, a real star, my God, would you all calm down?'

Under his penis, the dickhead is a man of about thirty-five. He has eyes and a short back and sides. He's handsome. The football match seems like a distant memory to the elderly audience who look up at him. It is only the dickhead's persistent shouts of 'Would you like to know your future?' that finally causes silence to fill the room, preceded by some angry, elderly cries of 'Who are you? Who are you?'

'My name,' says the dickhead, 'is Ian. And that's about as much as I'm prepared to say about myself. My past, like the past, is not relevant. Sure, I was a schoolboy, somewhere, once, I was a student even, but not in this country. My calling was a higher one, you see. I have no past. My name is Ian.' The dickhead is almost chanting. 'I have no past. My name is Ian. I am he that will rise, as it was foretold, he that will rise, armed with our future, forehead thus adorned. I'm here to talk to you about the Wild World. I have no past. My name is Ian. I like sport, music and film.'

There is a modest round of applause that seems to signal

that the audience has come to terms with the contents of Ian's forehead.

'And so the Wild World,' Ian says, his voice calm and authoritative, vaguely light-hearted. 'Yes, the Wild World. I must start by saying that a lot of rubbish has been spoken in recent months about the precise nature of it. In actual fact, the Wild World is . . .' He trails off and begins lightly tickling the tip of the dick with his index finger. 'You people,' he begins again, his hands returning to the podium, 'some of you people must remember the interwar years, yes, you're about that age, aren't you? Most of you, I'm sure, recall the aftermath of the Second World War. Do you? Yes, I'm sure you do, judging by your white hair and your old skin, I'm sure you do. Of course, I'm quite young and I might be wrong, but I dare say the best way to describe the Wild World to you is to go back to the twentieth century and . . .' Ian feigns a slanted and puzzled expression. 'Maybe not,' he continues, tickling his penis once more, perplexed. 'Yes, maybe not. Because I dare say, judging by some of the very grey complexions in this room, some of you remember the nineteenth century, am I right?'

A murmur of agreement grumbles in certain sections of the room. A man at the back says, 'I do.'

'Yes,' says Ian, his excitement growing, 'you remember the nineteenth century! Super. You do, no doubt, recall the cotton mills of Oldham and Manchester, hundreds of chimneys on the skyline, the birth of the modern world, the behemoth of industry, the long working days? Tell me,' shouts Ian towards the man who remembers the nineteenth century, 'what was it like?'

'Crap!' cries the man, immediately. 'It stank. I was a weaver.'

256

'Good, good,' cries Ian from the stage. 'It was crap, his whole life stank, says our friend from the nineteenth century. But tell me, did you not enjoy a seaside holiday from time to time?'

'We went to Morecambe once,' shouts the man immediately. 'It was crap! It was boring.'

'Was it?' says Ian. 'I see. It was boring. And then, what next? The nineteenth century became the twentieth, didn't it? I'm sure that some of you must have fought in and survived the First World War. Tell me, how did you feel when you came back to England after fighting so hard?'

The elderly crowd shuffle in their seats, guests on adjacent tables exchange questioning glances, as if to say, well, how did we feel?

'Bloody awful,' shouts a bloke near the front, before folding his arms tightly and sinking into his seat.

'Extremely angry,' shouts another.

'No, no,' says an incredibly old man on the middle table, rising to his feet. He has eyes like accidents, skin like the pages of a Bible, no hair, just a stained scalp. 'No, it wasn't quite like that. We felt . . . angry, yes . . . but mostly, we felt worthy of a great reward. Yes. And we felt no morality at all, that's right, no morality, not compared to those who stayed behind. We felt like we deserved to do what on earth we felt like doing. We were owed.'

'There it is,' cries Ian, his cock helicoptering. 'We were owed, says our friend from the First World War. And, in 1933, while Hitler came to power in Germany, in England, we were building large hotels, hosting seaside beauty competitions, building large piers out into the sea. Who remembers holidaying in 1933?'

The crowd are much more at ease. They are animated.

'It was a bit better,' says the old man from the nineteenth century. 'Depressions aside, my interwar holidays were much more like it, you know, nearer the money.'

'Great,' cries Ian, 'then came the Second World War. Who survived that?'

'We did!' shout the guests in unison. 'We did!'

'And how did you feel?'

'Pissed off,' cries the woman who earlier had spewed into a hat.

'No,' says her husband, turning on her, 'don't you remember, darling, we were just bored. Really bored.'

'I was still angry,' says the man with accidental eyes. 'I felt I was owed again. I'd seen enough shit. I was owed.'

'And here in England,' says Ian from the podium, 'the Welfare State was founded. And by the 1950s, the consumer society was up and running. Dare I ask about your holidays?'

'They were dirtier,' cries a skinny man maniacally. 'My sex got dirtier. I got a blow job in 1953, in Rhyl.'

'Brilliant,' says Ian. 'Now answer me these questions: Who, during the nineteenth century, used to hold their noses because it stank so bad?'

'We did!' shout the guests.

'Who was angry and in need of fun after the First World War?'

'We were!'

'Who was angry and in need of fun after the Second World War?'

'We were!'

'Who used to work like a fucker in a factory?'

'We did!'

258

'Who used to go to church?'

'We did!'

'Now tell me,' cries the dickhead, 'who enjoyed the final decades of the twentieth century?'

The guests inhale, they're about to cry 'WE DID!' in unison but then their brains engage, their eyes blink and they all start babbling in quieter, less certain tones. It's impossible to tell what each of them is saying. They sound like a rabble. Each guest has turned to the person next to them and is regaling them with what seem like anecdotes. Occasionally, some of them rub their thumb against their fingers to suggest 'cash' or 'I earned a lot of cash'. Sometimes they point at themselves and shrug in a rather self-satisfied manner. Others in the crowd appear to hold regrets or to have experienced despair during those decades. They lean on the table with their heads in their hands. They shake their sad, elderly faces as if to say, 'It didn't quite happen for me.' Some seem to be talking about computers and other pieces of technology, they can be seen tapping on invisible keyboards or switching on invisible appliances and then shrugging, as if to say, 'It's as easy as that.'

From the stage, Ian the Dickhead brings the crowd to quiet with broad gestures of his arms.

'Yes,' he says. 'It's been a complex period for many of us, I dare say. But culture brought us together, to some extent at least. I mean, who could fail to enjoy the music of the Beatles or the many images of Madonna? Who could be anything but very aroused by the body of Marilyn Monroe or Pamela Anderson, and who couldn't be made to laugh by the comedy of Laurel and Hardy? Who wasn't scared by the literature of Stephen King, or excited by the football of Diego Maradona or moved by the great acting of Robert De Niro, or, dare I say it, Marlon Brando himself?

'But in the Wild World, and this is crucial, we will not be united in our admiration for such great men and women, no, no. In the Wild World there will be no entertainment as we understand it today. Instead, there will be personalities so wild and crazy and imaginative that, to feel happy and overjoyed, those that succeed us here on earth will simply have to close their eyes and think of themselves.

'Ladies and gentlemen, so much nonsense has been spoken about the Wild World. Let me put all the rumours to bed. The Wild World is the end of evolution. The Wild World is a revolution of species. The time is almost upon us. Soon we will cease to lament that the humans are behaving like robots. We will celebrate the fact that robots are behaving like humans. And, inevitably, after the celebrations are over, it will then be time for the human being to take its bow and retreat from the stage. It's simple really. When robots become cool and totally convincing, how and why will we humans motivate ourselves to go on living? We won't, will we? No, of course we won't. Why would we?'

The elderly guests nod understanding. They all look a little tired on account of all the shouting and excitement of a few minutes ago.

'The Wild World is inevitable,' Ian the Dickhead continues. 'I see signs that the revolution is coming in the behaviour of our young. Their human instinct to survive is causing them to try everything they possibly can to appear interesting. They are feverishly buying clothes, piercing their tongues and nipples, acquiring sharp knives, going for teenage boob jobs, painting their faces, scouring the

Internet for a rare band or two. They do all this in the hope that they might be able to blend in when the Wild World comes. This process has been accelerating since the 1950s. Youth culture is, broadly speaking, our final attempt to justify our species, to keep it from extinction. But it's getting out of control, such is our desperation to survive. I dare say many of you have marvelled at the sophisticated appearances of young people in recent years. There is, I'm sure you'll agree, barely a child over the age of ten whose haircut and hair colour doesn't contain a great deal of charisma and meaning. Be the children shaved or dyed, they are discovering the importance of having a wild personality. Talk to anyone in the teaching profession here in England and you'll find that most kids are incapable of concentration. Many don't understand the concept of *general* knowledge or the relevance of sitting in large groups and all receiving the same information. It seems weird to them. They don't get it. They wonder what the point is. The past is boring, they say. Their sense of themselves goes even further. Look at television. Even given the numerous new channels, to most young people television programmes seem too broad, too boring, too tame and irrelevant. They are more happy when at home, talking online. Many children are finding happiness in talking about themselves for hours on the Internet, often to strangers. They are so full of themselves, it breaks my heart. They are brimming. They talk with such enthusiasm about themselves, about what they're really like, deep down, about what they think, how they shag, how they laugh, how they kill, how they feel and about how fascinating they are. But all this effort is futile. It is, as I say, simply the final murmur of human evolution, the last flex of the survival muscle and, sadly, it will not be enough. Let me assure you, when the revolution comes, we will not last long, even a man like me with a film star's penis on my forehead, or the babes with beach-ball breasts, or the kids with neon-lined eyes and highly complex musical tastes. No, no amount of tattoos can save us. No amount of new shoes, plastic surgery or gang affiliations. The fact is, none of us will seem insane enough when the revolution comes.' Ian bats the penis with the tips of his fingers and smiles as it swings like a pendulum above his eyes. His smile dies young: 'No,' he says. 'I'm afraid that when the world becomes wild, there's not a human on earth that will seem interesting enough to survive.'

Ian placed unnatural emphasis on the word 'survive'. It was clearly a cue; the moment he said it the sound of the orchestra came again from the speakers. Another slow, foreboding crescendo.

'Today's special guests, the people you're about to meet, ladies and gentlemen, were all recently built in buildings. And, my God, I must say, we had a good time building them, let me tell you. The atmosphere was incredibly funny, very creative. The banter between us all was brilliant as we filled each of them to the brim with jet-black blood. These people are, in effect, archetypes of the Wild World. They represent precisely the kind of creatures we can expect to see in the future. In the future, ladies and gentlemen, these crazy people will stride around the world. They will replace us. Why? you might ask. Well, they will replace us because in this way –' Ian the Dickhead is having to raise his voice to be heard over the orchestra – 'in this way, with personalities like these, the future will be peaceful, it will be harmless, finally, it will be happy. Please, ladies and gentlemen, welcome them to the stage!'

The door to the back room is opened; the sound of applause and the orchestra bursts in causing Roger to squirm in his wheelchair, chewing on the knickers. Baby Sally starts crying. Joe grabs Life by the hand and Anka jumps angrily to her feet. She is the first to be taken by the arm and led from the room by a purple-shellsuited girl. The others follow. One by one they are led out onto the stage.

'Introducing,' cries Ian the Dickhead, 'Anka Kudolski!'

The applause intensifies after each name is called. Anka is attempting to struggle with her minder but it's no good.

'Roger Hart!'

Ian is slightly surprised when Roger emerges gagged and in a wheelchair. But he continues nevertheless.

'Introducing . . . Janek Freeman!'

Janek appears. He has the eyes of a drunk. He stares at the audience with no understanding at all.

'Finally,' cries the Dickhead. Please welcome Life Moberg and, holding her hand, Joe Aspen and, in the travel seat, Sally! Come on, ladies and gentlemen, welcome them all to the stage. Give them a generous round of applause.'

The shellsuited young with this season's eyes position everyone in a line at the front of the stage, either side of Ian's podium. When everyone's where they should be, the helpers leave the stage and for a moment, the banqueting suite is awash with applause. Some of the elderly guests even rise from their seats, clapping and turning and smiling at their fellow guests in amazement.

'I'm sure,' says Ian, carefully pushing Marlon Brando's penis off his nose, 'I'm sure you'll all want a chance to meet these people face to face. You'll get that chance, I assure you. Soon we will serve you food on trays. All these people will mingle with you and you'll get a chance to have a little chat with each of them. But first, I'd like to just give you a little background information, if I may.'

Joe is staring across at Life. He's thinking, whatever all this is, I'm going to sort it out, I'm going to fucking save the day, I'm going to stand on the harbour in the Faroe Islands, waiting for the fishermen, for the trawlers with the catch. Beside him, Life is deflated. Things have twirled and twisted so far out of control. She's tired.

Anka Kudolski isn't tired. She's pissed off. She is staring at dear little Roger, next to her, squirming in his chair. I'll save him, she's thinking. I'll shag him. I'll teach him where my clitoris is. We will help each other live. I'll get back into art, back into food. Life will be good again.

Roger is flustered and staring around the banqueting suite at the elderly guests, then at the football match taking place beneath the window. At the far end of the stage, Janek is dead to the world.

'I'll begin, ladies and gentlemen, with Anka Kudolski.' Ian turns to Anka and lifts one of her arms by its wrist.

'Some of you, no doubt, will already be familiar with Anka Kudolski. She's something of a late-night TV star in Manchester. Let me explain her appearance. Though traditionally a rather depressing mental illness, in the future most of what we now know as women will stride around looking as skeletal as Anka here. Characterised by a sense of duality and a desire for control, the anorexic is not just an exciting and entertaining mentally ill young woman, but increasingly she has become a person to look up to, aspire to and find attractive. Again, this is a sign that evolution is ending, that the humans are trying to survive, that women are trying to blend in with the wild future by rarely eating.

'Anka here is a vivacious masturbator. Do you get it?

264

Anka as in wanker. I must say, we were all pissing ourselves in the lab when we came up with that idea. We gave Anka the desire to masturbate over the image of herself. She is designed to delight in the idea of others masturbating over her. She is designed to never eat. In the Wild World, such desires will be widespread. Our successors here on earth will sexually fantasise over themselves. When wanked over by others, they will feel extremely proud. They will enjoy the feeling of starving to death. How have you found it, Anka?'

Anka is seething. She is staring at Ian the Dickhead with a red face. She speaks through gritted teeth.

'I've killed her. I have. I've killed her. I've killed the Anka you made. I smashed her head against a tiled wall. I met Roger. I'm getting better. Soon I'll be able to eat. You think I'm incapable of putting on weight, but you're wrong. I'm an artist. I'm Jackson fucking Pollock. I'll eat till I'm a fat bitch.'

Ian turns and grins at the audience. 'Imagine that, ladies and gentlemen. A young woman who believes she's killed herself. A mentally ill young woman, starving to death, who wants to be an artist. We can rest assured that in the future, as I'm sure you're beginning to realise, those that succeed us will be fascinating. So entertaining.'

The audience applauds. Anka bows her head with rage.

'And so to Roger Hart,' cries Ian, 'who Anka here seems to have developed some affection for.' The dickhead sniggers. 'Roger is another crazy guy. He is what we at the Wild World call a loudmouth. We designed Roger so he would be . . . how can I explain?' The dickhead kneads the tip of his dick with his eyes closed. 'We designed Roger to be addicted to expressing himself. Yes. That's probably the

265

best way of putting it. In the Wild World, many individuals will become little more than descriptions of individuals. They will become so familiar with talking and writing about themselves that they will be unable to stop. But, and this is the important thing, they will describe themselves magnificently. They will spend hours on the Internet, for example; expressing wild opinions about themselves, describing the events of their days in exciting ways, coming up with all sorts of emotions that they believe themselves to be feeling. They will express shocking and hilarious opinions on every subject imaginable. Let me show you.'

The dickhead bends down and removes the knickers from Roger's mouth.

'Allow me. Allow me. I'm in a wheelchair!' gasps Roger. 'There's an audience. I haven't wanked in ages cos my cock has disappeared. A dickhead's saying I was made in a lab. I love Anka, I really love Anka. I wasn't made in a lab. I want to be a West End star. I've got a past. I remember my past. I wasn't made in a lab . . . Anka!'

'Very entertaining, I'm sure you'll agree,' says Ian, carefully regagging Roger. 'We also planted technology into Roger. This was just a bit of a joke really, but we also thought it might help explain his personality a little. The past that Roger claims to remember is, I assure you, complete fiction. All these individuals got to know themselves by reading websites we designed for each of them. They read long lists of their "Interests", "Musical Tastes", "Favourite Books", "Favourite Food", "Family History", "Blog History", "Romantic Status" and so on. They believed what they read, as we knew they would. But all their memories are entirely fabricated. It's wonderful. In reality, they're just wild creatures, built in buildings!'

Ian moves along the line to Joe. He is clutching his travel seat tightly by the handle. He bites on his gums. He's trying to look hard. He's trying to intimidate the dickhead. Trying to make it clear that he can save this day.

'Joe Aspen here is convinced he had a glorious relationship with the beautiful girl beside him, Life Moberg. I assure you, Joe, it never happened. You're programmed to be a lover of others, that's all, a carer, a rescuer, if you will. Even in the Wild World, our successors will need to talk about love and to be reminded that, unbelievable as it may seem, planet earth is a natural place. That's where individuals like Joe will come in to play. They will remind everyone of love, nature and all that stuff. Joe is even capable of caring for this little mutant baby we invented for a joke. He even cares for the little corpses we programmed for the baby to regurgitate. He even appears to have acquired a kitten. Marvellous! Above all, Joe has a desire to return to nature, and this will bring a pleasant poetry to life after the humans, indeed, such characters will be a polite nod to the deceased poetic of humanity.

'Joe's former girlfriend, meanwhile,' says the dickhead, turning from Joe to Life, 'is little more than something we invented because we were feeling really horny in the lab. And of course, in the Wild World, to give it variety, some females who aren't anorexic will devote a huge amount of time to looking beautiful. All worlds, even wild ones, need sexy females. That's sort of why we go on, isn't it? In addition to eating, females like Life here will be very open-minded towards sex. We called her "Life" as a joke. We made her Faroese because I holidayed there once and greatly enjoyed the food and the wildlife. Ladies and gentlemen, please, give both these people a generous round of applause.'

Joe and Life are staring at each other and shaking their heads, the sound of clapping in their ears.

'Life,' says Joe quietly, 'don't listen to him. He's a dick-head. What we shared was real. I love you. I can say it so easily. You left me, yes. You took a shit in my toilet, that was insensitive, but we can go back. We can be together. Listen to me, Life.'

Ian the Dickhead turns to the audience and raises both his arms in a shrugging gesture of genuine pride. The audience respond with even more rapturous applause, shaking their heads in disbelief, amazed at how real these people seem.

'Finally,' he says, gesturing for silence, 'many people in the Wild World will resemble this fellow.' The dickhead points at Janek. 'They will live with earplugs in their ears. Exciting music of various styles will be pumped into their heads until, well, until everything around them becomes affected by that music, everything conforms to the merry beats and melodies that they hear. To people like Janek, life will seem like a lovely, upbeat dream. Janek here is incapable of seeing sadness. Everything he sees, however awful, is made sense of by the very cool beats and melodies we gave him to listen to. In fact, ladies and gentlemen, I could brutally sacrifice any of these individuals onstage and Janek wouldn't care. For example, I could slit the throat of Life here and drain every drop of black blood from her body, and Janek, though he's rather fond of her, would be utterly incapable of giving a shit.'

26

EVEN IAN SEEMS surprised when the elderly audience begin baying for black blood.

'Really?' he says, sweeping the cock over his head. 'You'd really like me to kill one?'

The smartly dressed guests, even the guy who recalls the nineteenth century, are smiling, nodding and clenching their fists, shouting, 'Yes. Yes. We'd like to see one bleed.'

A commotion is developing. 'Really?' the dickhead keeps saying, 'I can't believe you'd like to watch one die.' He's genuinely moved by the excitement of the crowd. He had, no doubt, expected a little more decorum from such elderly people.

Behind him, Joe has gathered everyone, even Janek, around Roger's wheelchair.

'Let's make this quick,' says Joe. 'Does this make sense to any of you?'

Life shakes her head. 'It's bollocks.' She leans across and starts trying to get the earplugs of the N-Prang out of Janek's ears. It's difficult. It's like they're glued in.

'Roger,' says Anka, 'if I ungag you, you have to promise not to start talking crap. I'm serious. Can you do that?'

Roger nods. He relaxes his grip on the knickers and looks at Anka with honest, loving eyes. A second later she's ungagged him and he's taking deep breaths, trying to stay calm.

Life, meanwhile, has succeeded in pulling the N-Prang's earplugs out of Janek's ears.

'Life,' gasps Janek. 'It's. I . . .' Janek has tears in his eyes. 'What's happening?'

'It seems that you've been listening to the Beatles.'

Everyone can hear the familiar sound of the Beatles coming from the N-Prang earplugs. It's a famous song. 'All You Need is Love'.

'We're real,' says Joe. 'Does everyone agree that we're real?'

Apart from Life, everyone seems unsure. Anka looks at Roger.

'Was there two of me, Roger? Tell me honestly. Did you ever see two of me?'

Roger stares into his lap. He can feel the technology cranking inside him.

'I'm not sure,' he says. 'I'm sick. I'm confused. I'm not sure. I'm full of –'

Roger is interrupted by a loud and sudden bang.

Even though everyone is looking at Anka, waiting for her to decide whether she's real or not, it still takes them a second or two to realise that a bullet has just travelled through her head. To Life and Joe, it just looked as if her expression had changed a little. To them, when the bullet went through her head, it just looked as if she had all of a sudden remembered something extremely important. It was

270

only when the black blood started pouring from where her ear once was that they noticed she was dying. Anka Kudolski collapses lifeless beneath Roger's wheelchair. The others look towards the door at the side of the stage, to where another Anka Kudolski stands with a smoking gun in her hand and a bandage wrapped around her head.

'It's me, Roger,' cries the new, still-living Anka. 'She lied.' Anka points at Anka's corpse. 'I'm the real me. Look.'

The new Anka is, in fact, just as thin as the one she just killed. But to Roger, she does seem slightly different. It's hard to explain why. But we have senses, us lot, weird ones. We're freaks. We are intuitive and wild.

'Anka!' Roger cries.

'Come with me, Roger. Now!'

Having been silenced by the gunshot, the elderly guests and Ian the Dickhead are now all staring in astonishment at Anka. They watch as she reaches into her rucksack and produces a ham sandwich. Holding it in the same hand as the gun, she brings it to her lips and takes a large bite.

'I'm the real me,' she says again, her voice obscured a little by the food. 'I can eat. I can get better. You're not full of technology, Roger. I swear you're not. Let's just go.'

Roger looks down at his body. It does seem so heavy. So full of crap. He fingers the black cords that come from both his ears. He looks at the corpse of Anka beneath him, the black blood leaking from her head, then at the living one eating the ham sandwich in the doorway. Around him, the young shellsuits with this season's arseholes are closing in. Fuck this, Roger decides, life is just too much fun. He leaps from his wheelchair and dashes for the door.

'Let him go,' says Ian, calmly. 'Let him go.'

Up on the stage, Janek, Life and Joe are being held by

their shoulders while the corpse of Anka Kudolski is cleared away.

'Get those earplugs back in his ears,' whispers Ian to the girl holding Janek. 'For fuck's sake,' he murmurs, adding, as an unsteady afterthought, 'for Christ's sake.'

Though Janek tries to prevent her from doing this, deep down his struggle is all for show. He's glad. Better to live with music in your ears, he's thinking, than to actually listen to and understand the bullshit that goes on around you. Seconds later his head is swimming in happy sounds. The Beatles, or some other many-legged and musical group of men. In Janek's eyes, the elderly crowd are all suddenly sexy-dancing with each other, having a really cool time. In his eyes, Joe Aspen is not grimacing or trying to shake off his guardian and reach the travel seat. Life is not wiping tears from her eyes. To Janek, both seem fine. To him, they're both watching in amusement as Ian the Dickhead dances centre stage, swinging his head round, helicoptering his knob to the beat of the song.

In reality, however, Ian has regained his composure and is returning to the podium. 'Ladies and gentlemen,' he's saying, 'I can only apologise for that little interruption. Naturally, with such a complicated and groundbreaking project, there is still a little room for improvement. There are still things we can't fully control. After all, when we made these people, we were all pissing about so much that it's possible we weren't as thorough as we ought to have been. Yes, we were joking around so much that we often lost sight of the fact that we were building humans. But I'm sure we can still have some fun with these remaining specimens. Of course we can.'

Behind the dickhead, Joe finally succeeds in pushing his

minder to the ground. He runs to the travel seat, lifts Sally from it, places her over his shoulder and then turns to confront the dickhead.

'I don't believe a word you say,' says Joe, bouncing on the spot in order to calm Sally down. 'It's bollocks. All this. I've met dickheads like you before. I used to work in a theatre. I've known knobs who prance around making everything seem weird and dramatic, you're simply –'

'I should say, ladies and gentlemen,' interrupts Ian with a smile, 'that I think we made Joe's love for Life, that is to say, his love for this beautiful girl beside him, a little intense. I should make it clear because it might help us to understand his rather dramatic behaviour. We were drunk when we did it, the scientists and I, we were drunk and it's possible we made his love for this girl a little too intense. I'm sure you're familiar with how melancholy men can get when they've been drinking too much beer and wine. It's possible, in our drunken state, that we made his love for her far too strong. But don't be fooled. This boy bleeds black blood like the rest of them.'

'I don't,' snaps Joe. 'I bleed red blood and I love her because she's real. Aren't you, Life? Tell this dickhead. Tell him how real you are. Tell him about that shit you took before you left me.'

Life inhales anxiously inside her pretty red dress. Her lungs fill with air, causing her large and perfect breasts to protrude. 'I don't know, Joe. I just don't know.'

You do, thinks Joe. You do know. We all know we're fucking real. It's just that sometimes we're afraid to admit it. In his frustration, Joe turns baby Sally round so she's facing Ian and, knowing full well that Sally will grab anything placed in front of her, he thrusts her forwards till her fingers are inches from his forehead.

'Aaaaaaaagggghhhhh,' cries Ian. He's having his dick pulled extremely hard. Sally has a firm grip. Joe's pulling too. He's holding Sally by both feet, leaning back with all his weight. A shellsuited twat is up like a shot, trying to unpick the baby's grip. But the baby, naturally, is far too strong.

'Keep hold, Sally,' shouts Joe, keen to tear the silly penis from the man's head and restore some normality. But as hard as they pull, it isn't coming off. How good the surgeons of plastic are these days. What absolute experts we are. What a gifted bunch of total fucking losers.

'You are real, Life!' Joe's shouting, pushing away the tosspots who are trying to detach himself and Sally from the dickhead's dick. 'I'm telling you. Listen to me. Remember, I kissed your arse. I cared for your crap. You are real, Life! We ate puffins together. You are real, Life. We ate puffins together.'

The whole occasion is chaotic. The guests don't know what to do. They hide their faces with their gloved hands. They cry out in shock. They groan. Heart attacks concealed in their ancient eyes. Ian the Dickhead has lost control. He's furious. His forehead is bruising under the strain of Sally's pulling. 'A knife,' he keeps shouting. 'Bring me a sharp knife!'

27

HOLDING TIGHTLY TO each other, Anka and Roger run down the cold white corridors of the stadium. Neither of them knows where they're going. They turn corners at random, breathless, desperate to maintain the enthusiasm caused by their escape. The sound of the nearby crowd echoes down each corridor. Large undulations of human misery and human hope and joy. Men in orange coats stand at intervals staring at the floor. Anka and Roger turn down yet another corridor and come to a halt, panting and leaning against each other.

'Should we kiss?' says Roger eventually. 'I'm guessing we should kiss on account of you just shooting someone. Well, you sort of shot yourself, didn't you? And I leapt from the wheelchair having previously been barely able to move. And so . . . She gagged me, the other you, do you know that? You're not going to gag me, are you? Should we kiss?'

Anka has removed the remains of the ham sandwich from her rucksack. She's finishing it with small bites, chewing each one meticulously. 'I could never have done this without you, Roger. Eat, I mean.' She takes another bite.

Roger leans against the wall, staring briefly at a selection of corporate logos. 'But, Anka,' he says, 'how do I know you're the real you? I mean, that's exactly what the other you claimed to be.'

'I can prove it,' Anka replies. 'I can. I promise.' She has finished the sandwich. She swallows emphatically: 'You're such a little nerd, Roger. It's so strange. You and me, like this. You're such a little nerd.'

Roger grins. 'When I'm with you, Anka, in fact, even when I was with the other you, I had such a desire to be seen. That's so weird for me. I mean, recently, as you know, I barely left my flat. But even when I was gagged in that wheelchair with this mouse stuck in the back of my head, I wanted to be looked at by other people. I didn't feel ashamed. Is that what love is? Just some sort of pride?'

'Look down there.'

Anka is pointing down the corridor to where a canvas tunnel curls away from the exit. A small section of green grass can be seen where the tunnel ends.

'That's the pitch,' says Anka. 'How strong are you feeling?'

'Stronger than before, definitely, but I've still got a lot of heavy equipment inside me.'

'Turn round then. Come on, Roger, turn round and be thankful I weigh next to nothing.'

The moment Roger has turned away from her, Anka leaps onto his back, throwing her arms round his neck and allowing him to grab her legs. 'Now, run, Roger,' she cries, grabbing the wires that fall from his ears and tugging them like reins. 'Come on, El Rogerio, run!'

Roger does run. He begins to gallop down the corridor at quite a pace. 'I'm thirty,' he cries, his voice echoing harshly in the narrow space. 'Thirty years on planet earth. Ha ha!' Anka, as she has at last acknowledged, is very light. Roger finds he can run as fast as if a child were hoisted on his back. He enjoys the feeling of her kicking his backside with her heels as a jockey might a horse. Oh yes, pretending to be a horse, being kicked on the backside by a girl, even an ill one, it's so much better than crapping a motherboard into a toilet, so much more fun than bullshitting teenagers on the Internet. At the end of the tunnel, two bright orange men are attempting to form a human barrier to prevent Roger and Anka from reaching the pitch. They look terrified. Terrified by the blonde, beautiful and sickly thin girl riding the big-headed boy as if he were a horse. The orange men hold hands and spread themselves out. They say shit, shit like 'Stop', shit like 'You can't go through 'ere'. They say shit in angry cockney accents. 'You can't go through 'ere.' But Roger can. He just knows he can. He's running faster than he's ever run before.

If we were one of the guests up in the banqueting suite, like, say, if we were that old guy who remembers the nineteenth century, then we could turn from where Joe Aspen and Sally are trying to pull the dick from off Ian's forehead and stare down at the pitch. We'd see two people burst from the tunnel in the corner of the pitch – a girl on a boy's back. We'd see the girl waving happily at the crowd, pulling hard on reins that come from the boy's ears. We'd see the two of them go charging off down the touchline, galloping over lush green grass, past the stupid Chelsea mascot, who to us, through our nineteenth-century eyes, would look like a massive blue lion. Dumb Southerners. We'd see many a bright orange steward chasing these two, arms outstretched, attempting to run in a calm manner that befits a chubby bunch of crowd controllers. We'd see the crowd waving their fists and opening their mouths wide, passionately willing that the two heroes avoid capture.

If, by chance, we grew tired of watching the chase and our attention turned briefly to the action taking place on the pitch, we'd see the huge Chelsea midfielder, Michael Essien, whose face, I could add, seems forever electrified with delight. We'd see him hoof the ball from his own penalty area up into the sky. Following the flight of the ball, we'd see the much loved and much maligned midfielder Frank Lampard turn his marker on the halfway line, spring the offside trap and suddenly find himself running alone towards the goal, monitoring the ball's progress with occasional glances over his shoulder. Fuck me, we'd think. Fuck me. Even though we recall holidaying in the nineteenth century and even though our head contains every single year the twentieth century had to offer, we'd still think, fuck me, this is entertaining.

Down on the touchline, suddenly aware that certain activities on the pitch have drawn the attention of the crowd away from themselves, Roger and Anka are considering running onto the pitch.

'You wanted us to be seen together, Roger,' shouts Anka, pulling hard on the wire that comes from Roger's left ear in an attempt to make him turn onto the pitch. 'This is your chance. Run onto the pitch. It's our only option!' Anka's laughing. She's laughing at the alarmed tone she heard in her own voice. Roger's laughing, too. He's laughing so much that Anka's slipping down his back. His grip is shot to shit by his sense of joy. He has to pause and shunt Anka higher up his back and strengthen his grip on her legs. Glancing up, he notices that more orange stewards are coming towards them. We're trapped. Anka's right. It has to be the pitch.

Once again, if we were that nineteenth-century guy staring down at the pitch from up in the banqueting suite, then we'd have a cracking view. Jesus, we'd be thinking, I once shared a world with the likes of Oscar Wilde and Otto von Bismarck, and now, over a century later, I'm sat watching the England international Frank Lampard running through on goal pursued by a big-headed guy with wires in his ears and an anorexic on his back, who, in turn, are being pursued by several men in weatherproof jackets and bobble hats and several athletic men in football kits who, presumably, are keen to stop Frank scoring. Superb, we'd think. This is superb entertainment. Because even when you've lived as long as we have and you've holidayed in 1870s Morecambe, witnessed the advent of the computer age and watched men stick flags in the moon, you still can't shake the feeling that life is too short, that we just cling to the porcelain with all the other shit, staring up, praying that a well-aimed jet of piss doesn't spray us away. Thank God, we'd think, thank God for these light-hearted moments. And what's this? we'd wonder, rubbing our eyes in disbelief. What's this? Suddenly we can see dozens of teenagers leaping over the advertising hoardings near to the dugout. These, I believe, we would no doubt say, aren't these the latest batch of sceptical young life fearers? They're piling onto the pitch in black T-shirts. Purple drainpipe jeans. Hooded heads. False red hair. And even though we remember Teddy boys, mods, rockers, the jitterbug and the Nazis and the time before Teenagers, we would, to our credit, ask, are these not those who are fond of loud music, guitars and heartbroken American men with high voices? Are these not those who have invented new dances? Is it true, we might ask, regarding these young people piling onto the pitch, is it true that these are the latest generation of young people, scared like we were of every single second, past or future, every single second except for that one dry, nutlike second that lies split in their palms, protected by their fingers, fingernails painted black? Life is short, we would say, every year of the twentieth century rattling round our heads. They should relax. Life is short.

'Tackle him!' Anka's shouting. 'You can catch him, Roger. He's overrated. Tackle him and boot the ball in the net yourself!'

Roger has no idea who the footballer they're chasing is. He does not follow the game. Famously, he enjoys musicals. Staring up at the crowd, he can't help but fantasise about singing and performing for such a large audience. To sing a song sincerely in front of such a crowd. That'd be nice. As it is, he's happy to just be seen by them, happy to be seen in public with Anka riding on his back. Because as much as we pace quietly around our skulls as if we were the librarians of our brains, what we really need is to be seen, occasionally touched, occasionally cheered up, occasionally kissed, occasionally ridden like a horse. Roger realises this now.

In front of Roger, Lampard has allowed the ball to drop over his shoulder. He has controlled it well and begun to dribble at pace towards the goal. Further up the field, Roger can see the goalkeeper, dressed in yellow, bouncing out towards the edge of his area, spreading his gloved hands out wide, making himself big, watching Lampard's every touch of the ball. The goalkeeper seems calm. Lampard, too. The moment of truth is coming. The moment of truth is knock knock. Scratch.

Anka has turned round to flick immaculate Vs at the chasing stewards, the desperate defenders and the obsessive teens. The air is unbreathably loud. Thick with noise. Thousands here are desperate for a goal. Thousands are desperate for a save or a miss or a total fuck-up. Even so, Roger can hear Anka's shrieks. 'Piss off,' she cries at the orange men and the trendy little kids. 'We're artists,' she cries. 'We're eaters. We're lovers. Piss off!'

All this throwing of insults is, in fact, quite unnecessary. Because despite the fact that Roger is apparently full of heavy technology and finds it difficult to get about, on this occasion he is proving to be an excellent runner. Not only is he easily maintaining his lead on the stewards, the kids and the defenders, but he's gaining on Lampard. So much so that Anka starts whipping Roger's shoulders with his wire reins, kicking his backside firmly with her heels and actually stretching her arm out beyond Roger's large head in an attempt to grab the midfielder by the shirt and bring him down.

The moment of truth is seconds away. Lampard, pro that he is, can't even hear the crowd, only the sound of his own quick breathing and the thudding of his feet on the turf. He glances up and examines the position of the goalkeeper. Lampard's thinking maybe he should try and chip the ball over the keeper's head. That would be nice for the crowd, he thinks. But the chip is always a risk. If I miss, he thinks, I'll look like a bit of a tit. Maybe I should just take it round him and slide it into the net, Yeah, that's probably easier. But less spectacular! Oh, thinks Frank, it's a worry, life, I mean, football, scoring, it's a worry, I'm always worrying nowadays. It's age. Age.

'We've got you, Lampard!' cries Anka. She and Roger are within inches of being able to bring him down. 'Better be scared. We are sick! We are eaters of food! We are lovers!'

Lampard glances over his shoulder to see the galloping Roger bearing down on him, his large bespectacled face perspiring madly, and, on his back, Anka, shouting, reaching out with her fingers splayed. Naturally, Frank's a little alarmed to find that he's being pursued by a strange couple, several stewards, three or four defenders and a gang of EMO kids, puffing and panting, calling out all sorts of crap: 'El Rogerio, slow down. El Rogerio, you're so cool. So cool!' Naturally, Frank's confused. But he's also a professional footballer halfway through a difficult season. He needs to score. I need to score. He calculates he's got little more than a second before Anka drags him down. I'm gonna have to try and chip the keeper. There isn't time to go round him. If I fuck up, he thinks, I fuck up. It's as simple as that. It's been a difficult year.

It's time. The England international straightens his back and tightens his shoulders. He spreads his arms out wide for balance. He takes one last look at the keeper to check his position before bowing his head and staring straight at the ball. His right leg starts bending at the knee. He's going to stab the bottom of the ball with his boot, causing it to sail over the keeper's head and bounce calmly into the goal. It's time.

It is certainly time. Anka, for the sheer humane and humorous hell of it, is going to pull Frank to the ground and then instruct Roger to dribble the ball past the keeper and into the net. She sees that he's about to shoot and decides to go for it, reaching with both arms for the footballer's shoulders. That's when it happens. (The simple thing.)

It is fashionable to crave the simple life. I myself crave the simple life.

There is a

There is an extremely loud thud.

The crowd, all forty thousand of them, look on, amazed and suddenly silent. Rubbing their eyes with fists, saying, 'Good heavens,' and 'Good grief.'

It is simple. Something *very* simple has happened.

A large blue rock, clearly a section of the sky, has fallen from the heavens and crushed Frank Lampard. It has flattened him like a pancake. Just one Adidas football boot and a bit of blue sock poke out from underneath the rock. The ball must have been burst. The footballer must be dead.

Anka's fingertips had just brushed Frank's shirt when it suddenly felt like he'd disappeared. Roger noticed the fallen object and was able to alter his path and stumble out of the way, causing Anka to fall off his back. Now the two of them are stood staring at the blue rock. It's as big as a small car. It's shiny. It smokes like ice. Every inch of it looks sharp. The sun has gone in. The stands are darker; you can't quite make out the faces of the crowd.

Anka grins at Roger. 'It's good this, isn't it?'

Roger nods. 'Yeah, it's ace.'

'It beats the past,' says Anka. 'My past, I mean, and I'm guessing yours.'

Roger nods again. 'My past, Anka. Jesus. You should have been there . . . awful. Absolutely awful.'

The stewards arrive, followed by the other players and then the teenagers. No one's bothered about capturing Roger and Anka any more because they've been totally over-shadowed by the fallen rock. The stewards are looking with amazement at the thing, thinking, Wow, so unlucky, he looked all set to score, all set to make the crowd roar.

Some players are trying to figure out whether they could lift it. They're plunging their fingers into the soil to see if they can get a grip on the rock's bottom. After all, Lampard's worth a fortune, he gets given a lot of shit but he does score a lot.

'It's not meant to happen, is it, like?' says one player, a stocky, mid-twenties man with long, wet hair. 'They'll reckon it's total bollocks and we'll get fuck-all cash, do you know what I mean? No compensation.'

'I know what you mean,' says a teenager, a gaunt one in a baseball cap with the word 'Hatebreed' written across his T-shirt. 'What you mean is, the sky's not meant to fall on our heads, and I totally agree. It isn't. And I think it's just typical. I really do. I mean, take a look around you. Look at us all. You guys, for example.' The teenager points to the players who are trying hopelessly to pull Frank Lampard out from under the rock, causing them to look up, perplexed. 'You guys have been practising your football for many years, I expect. Since you were pretty young, I dare say. And now, and I congratulate you for this even though I'm not a fan of the game, now you've reached the height of your profession. I mean, you're not all megastars, but you're clearly on the right track. These many thousands of people have come to watch you play, to cheer you on and be amazed by your high level of skill. You've got into these lovely bright kits, each with your different names written on the back. But still, in spite of everything, this happens, this catastrophe!' The teenager points at the blue rock. 'And let me introduce you to someone who you're probably not familiar with. That man over there standing with the thin girl with the bandaged head is El Rogerio, a legend, a man who at this moment is dying, yes, dying, I don't exaggerate. He's full of technology. Look at his head. Full of wires. He's fascinating. He's so cool. He's a man of genuine wit and angst. You only have to read his blogs. And yet even he is shown up by this miracle, this terrible miracle.' The teenager punches the rock and instantly regrets having done so. His hand kills. He shakes it and breathes in air through his teeth. 'And look at us,' he says, still squinting with pain. 'Look at all the effort myself and my friends here have gone to in order to appear exciting. Look at our piercings, some of them were very painful. Look at our clothes, our retro sports tops, these T-shirts. We have tried hard to be interesting people. People worth watching. We have made choices. We have swum around God's silence. We have interpreted that silence as a clear hint that us lot, the humans, should have dominion over the world and over nature. We did this with good humour. I myself have learnt to hate God and to play the guitar. I'm really into new music. What I'm saying is, and I can't stress this enough, what I'm saying is that we have, as individuals, tried to make ourselves alive and exciting. Haven't we? We have. And now this!' The teenager nods at the rock. 'And now,' he splutters. 'And now this not insubstantial section of the sky has fallen on top of one of us. It has undermined all our effort. The Wild World . . . I don't know. I can only hope. I can only . . . I suppose, I guess.' The teenager is exasperated and angry. 'I can only hope that we are the kind of people who it might be nice to go for a drink with. Are we? In spite of this?' Again he points at the rock. 'Are we still the kind of people it might be nice to go for a drink with?'

Oh, Frank Lampard is crushed. The other players have accepted this and stepped away from the blue rock. The teenager walks backwards into his crowd. He is patted on the back. There is a general sense of anger towards the fallen section of the sky. A young midfielder with stylishly bleached hair mutters, 'Fucking bollocks.' The referee arrives. A stocky little man with a basic head. He points at the protruding foot of Lampard and then blows hard on his whistle. 'Foul,' he says, calmly, one arm pointing in the direction of the banqueting suite. 'The sky has fouled Lampard. Free kick to Chelsea.'

The Chelsea players clench their fists in delight and start jogging towards the penalty area on the under-standing that a well-taken free kick could lead to a headed goal. The stewards jog obediently to the touchline, each of them holding a teenager by the wrist. The crowd re-animates. Shouting complaints and encouragement. The players from the opposing team gather around the referee to complain angrily about his decision. 'You lying, balding, cocksucking cunt. It's only a fucking meteor, you bent bastard,' says one. Then his teammate joins in: 'He dived. He did. You dick. He dived. You're taking the piss. It's a meteor!'

* * *

Roger and Anka leave the scene as soon as the teenager draws attention to them. Anka touches Roger's shoulder and gestures that they should make a quiet exit. Good idea, Roger thinks, nowadays these teenagers only get me down.

The two of them hold hands and walk quite slowly away from the fallen rock. The crowd in the stands do not notice them. They don't cheer or whistle. In the dugouts, the managers of both teams mutter to themselves anxiously, wondering, I suppose, how many more expensive humans might be crushed by the sky today. How can we win the league if the sky keeps falling on our heads? We must avoid more of these terrible injuries. Anka and Roger walk quietly by. It feels like a walk in the countryside, it's so quiet and peaceful in the seconds that follow the rock's descent. The stands look like mountains. The fans like an intricate rock formation. Anka and Roger walk back down the tunnel in the corner of the pitch under the banqueting suite. They locate a changing room in the warren of white, silent corridors. The changing room is square with wooden benches round the walls, all covered in the players' tracksuits, spare boots, sports bags overflowing with towels. In the corner stands a blackboard, haunted by a chalk sentence, still legible despite having been erased. *No tactics. No point to this. Run wild.* They pass through the changing room to a starkly lit, white-tiled shower room where the floor slopes inwards towards a large silver plughole. At head height around the walls, rusting silver showerheads drip. Roger and Anka understand that the fate of their relationship will be determined in this wet, dripping room. The air stinks of nervous men. They sit down against a wall and Roger is immediately hit by a drop of water.

'If I sit here, Anka, I'll be electrocuted. Of course, my body, I'm full of –'

'Roger!' Anka snaps. 'You're not. For Christ's sake. You're not. You're full of normal organs. Don't you get it?' Anka begins to unwind the bandage on her head. With each turn a bloodstain begins to appear until finally, with some discomfort, Anka pulls the last of the bandage away from a long, moist scar just below her hairline.

'Red,' says Roger.

'Exactly,' Anka replies, softly. 'We're real.'

Anka leans in towards Roger, causing him to panic. He's not sure what she wants. A kiss? A hug? A whisper? Several minutes of spooning on this cold wet floor? He puckers his lips in desperation, eyes shut, forehead creased. But Anka is not ready to kiss. She must, she knows, take small steps. Ham sandwiches. Gun disposal. Therapy. But no kissing, not yet. Instead, she grips the wire that runs from Roger's left ear and begins to pull on it firmly. At first Roger winces and starts moaning, muttering, 'My brain, Anka, you'll pull out my brain.' Anka just ignores him, sticks to her task. It doesn't take long. She pulls the wire from his ear and examines the end.

'Glue,' she says, showing it to Roger.

'Really?'

'Yeah, it's just glue.'

The mouse lodged at the back of Roger's head comes away easily, taking a clump of curly brown hairs with it.

'I glued a mouse to my head?'

'You did. Just like I didn't put any food in my mouth.'

'It's just that we're alive.'

'Yeah.'

'And we were nervous about it.'

'Yeah.'

Anka undoes Roger's belt and takes down his fly. Roger lifts himself off the floor on the heels of his hands and feet allowing Anka to pull down his trousers and his underpants. Roger lowers his chubby buttocks onto the wet floor. I should have changed my underwear more often. I should have gone outside to buy things. I should have joined a choir and sang with other people. Instead, he thinks, staring down at the numerical keypad where his penis should be, instead this. Anka has paused to stare. She starts tapping on the keys, deep in thought. 7-8-1-3-5-0. Her childhood phone number. Before mobiles. Back when she was bright and full of fresh brain. Before her age began to rise and rise and food became a non-event.

'From now on,' says Anka. 'From now on we'll just have to be together. The fact is, I didn't realise that life was going to be like this. I thought, when I was growing up, that it would be easier. That things would keep happening in nice, year-shaped ways, like they do at school.'

Anka begins to pull at the sides of the numerical keypad. Lifting the glued plastic off the delicate skin of Roger's groin.

'We'll go back to Manchester. I like Manchester. Either I'll move into your flat or you can move into mine.'

She's almost there. Roger's petrified. I was born with a penis. I remember playing with it when I was young. But lately. Lately. I've spent a decade watching porn. I've spent years writing lies about my penis on the Internet. Saying I've done such-and-such with it. Put it here and put it there. All bollocks. I glued a piece of plastic over it. I must have done. Perhaps it has given up on me. Felt betrayed. Perhaps it's disappeared. Or perhaps it's retreated into my body to be consoled by my other organs. My shallow lungs. My harmed, faithful heart. Allow me. Allow me.

'There we are,' says Anka, as if she's talking to a smiling baby. 'There we are.'

Roger does have a penis. It is warm and curled and clinging to his two testicles. The three of them have the look of startled children, those that have spent a war hiding in a cupboard, holding tightly to each other. Anka takes the penis tip gently in her fingers. She pulls it away from the testicles. She's reminded of peeling stickers off her school folder. Old heart-throbs. Given up. Replaced. Roger's is a good penis. A normal scared one. Not the kind that could ever adorn a forehead or spit swear words at women's bits. Gently, only half thinking, Anka begins to move the foreskin up and down. I am Anka as in wanker. We all are. Humans as in. Cute people. True-hearted wankers.

'The other you,' Roger murmurs, his cheeks raised in nervous hope. 'The other you talked about teaching me . . . to find her clitoris.'

Anka's hand stops. The penis grows noticeably in her hand, like a recluse finally answering the front door. Don't bring her into it, Anka thinks. The other me. The black-blooded one. The starving one. The dead one. Again she begins to massage Roger's penis, saying . . .

'One day, Roger, I will teach you to find my clit. Soon, that's exactly the kind of thing I'll do. You and me are young people. We're going to become a couple. We're going to be lovers. We're going to decorate two or three rooms in styles that appeal to us both. We're going to get jobs, good ones hopefully. We're going to leave our home each morning, work hard and then return to each other. We're going to ask each other questions. Ones like, how was today for you? How are you feeling? We'll even take interest in specific issues that arise in our respective workplaces, you know, certain inter-personal difficulties or certain crucial, make-or-break situations. We'll ask each other very relevant questions at around seven o'clock each weekday evening. Maybe over a glass of wine. We'll discuss things seriously. And inevitably, when I'm ready, when I've put on some weight, when my bracelets can no longer be threaded the whole way up my arm to my shoulder, I will, I promise, teach you to find my clitoris with your finger or your tongue.'

Roger has an erection. He can't believe it. He stares at it in Anka's hand. It's as if a second head has grown suddenly from his groin and started laughing and gasping for air. Anka handles him so gently. It's strange. She seems committed to causing him joy.

'One night we'll go to bed early,' she continues, still wanking him carefully. 'Yes. One day, I'll decide not to read a book or spend time painting. You'll decide not to prac-tise your singing or to listen to one of your favourite musical soundtracks. We'll turn the lights off. We'll get into bed. We'll kiss each other softly and whisper the details of our love to each other. We'll spoon. I'll turn from you and snuggle backwards into your body. I'll take your hand and guide it into my knickers like it's all just a game, a friendly skill. Meanwhile, between my buttocks, I'll feel your erec-tion, but we won't deal with that immediately. Instead, I'll hold your index finger and place it right on my clit. You'll feel it. So that's it, you'll think. You'll be so happy, Roger. And I'll be aroused. I'll start making you massage me at the pace and force that I find lovely. Instinctively, you'll start rubbing your erection against my bottom. You will, Roger. I promise you will. And when I'm satisfied that you've got the rhythm and force just right, I'll leave you to it. Maybe I'll start rubbing my nipples. I enjoy that. I'll be thrilled. For minutes on end, we'll do this. Lying in silence, you rubbing my clit. And then, when I'm close to orgasm, I might say something like, "I want your cock." Honestly. I'll be so lost in pleasure that I might just say that. Then I'll pull down my knickers and help guide your cock inside me, from behind, we're still spooning. You'll be so aroused that you'll be close to orgasm pretty quickly. You'll be rubbing my clit frantically, but also enjoying the sensation of making love. I'll be biting my bottom lip. Then I'll be craning my neck to place kisses on your face. I will. I promise. We will. We'll do this one day, Roger. I'll be making noises. You'll be making noises, too.'

Anka has stopped wanking Roger. She has simply made a circle with her thumb and her forefinger. She's holding this circle down by her side and Roger is thrusting his penis in and out of it.

'You've had a tough time, Roger.'

Anka is having to raise her voice over Roger's grunts. 'You've been talking so much crap online. You won't do that any more. You'll be asking me questions. Relevant ones about my day. We'll cook. We'll sleep. We'll eat!'

Roger's penis is already weeping colourless fluid. The little circle that Anka's made with her thumb and forefinger is glistening. Roger is having a brilliant time. 'This little circle,' he's saying, through the moans and inhalations of his pleasure, 'I love this little circle that you've made with your thumb and your forefinger!'

'This little circle, Roger, is only the beginning. There'll be more. Once my body is healthy. There will be so much more. Remember the sex we had in Wow-Bang? I imagine it'll be more like that. We'll be athletic in bed. Moonlight coming through the bedroom window. We're just normal people. Humans. It's just that we've been so nervous. So ill. But, yes, this little circle is just the beginning!'

Roger is pushing in and out of the little circle at top speed. This is it. He's clinging onto Anka's sides and shoulder, his fingers hold her bones like handlebars.

'I'm going to come,' cries Roger.

'Come,' says Anka. 'Come, Roger.'

A rhythmic rattling sound can suddenly be heard. The sound of football studs tap-tapping across hard floor. It's the players. The professional footballers. It's half-time. Anka listens as the door to the changing room is pushed open with force, giving way to a cacophony of groans and complaints. 'That was bullshit.' 'Bent cunts.' 'Fucking sky.' 'Meteor!' 'They're shit anyway.' Roger doesn't register any of this noise. He has not felt this real in years. He doubts whether he has ever felt so real and full of pleasure.

Some of the footballers have come into the shower room and have begun watching in polite silence but with evident amusement as Roger thrusts into the little circle that Anka has made. Roger doesn't notice. His eyes are squeezed shut. Anka looks up at the players with stern eyes, warning them to keep quiet, to let Roger enjoy the little circle she's made with her thumb and forefinger. The footballers obey, though some hide smiles with sideways hands.

'I'm gonna come!'

He means it this time. Roger's entire body spasms and he lets out some very real noises, jolting his penis into the circle with short, random, staccato movements, his whole body relaxing blissfully onto the floor. The first spurt of liquid is projectile. It flies a good metre. The second lands on Anka's jeans, just above her knee. The third coats the little circle and the rest of Anka's hand. I'm tired. These people have come to an end.

The footballers watch in sentimental silence. They smile and they even weep. They suddenly regret all the gang bangs and the call girls and spit roasts. They realise life is simple.

Roger says nothing. He's just floating. His body buzzing. Eyes shut. A smile, blindly drawn, coating his lips.

The footballers begin to back slowly out of the shower room. In the dressing room, the manager has arrived and is shouting for silence. 'It's no excuse,' he's saying. 'We were hopeless before the sky fell. It's no excuse.'

Anka has sat right up. She's holding her hand up into the light, fingers crooked, dripping with human semen, lines of it running down her arm towards her elbow.

Roger comes round. He has broadened his smile and sat up cheerfully on his elbows before he, too, catches sight of Anka's dripping hand. He regrets the bullshit, the porn, the words, the glue and the wires of his lonely years. He and Anka watch as the liquid drips from her elbow and onto the cold floor. A future grips them. A wire looped around a neck, pulled from either end. A future grips them. It's Saturday afternoon.

28

HAVING BEEN HANDED the sharp knife, the dickhead does not hesitate in cutting the penis off his forehead, causing Joe and Sally to fall backwards onto the stage floor.

'Get them back in line,' he shouts, now with just the balls and the stump bunched above his eyes. There's no blood. He's clearly in no pain. 'Get them back in line!'

Janek, Life and Joe are held in position next to the podium. In front of them, the elderly audience are still very much entertained. Many have stood up from their tables and come forward to linger at the foot of the stage. They regard the three individuals with intrigued but cautious expressions. Perhaps the same expressions these same people used to regard the freak shows of the late-Victorian era. 'Let's see some,' shouts a woman whose scraped silver hair is failing to hide her baldness. 'Let's see some of this black blood.' The crowd make noises of agreement. 'Show us how he can't care!'

The dickhead gestures for Janek to be brought forward. The audience roar with approval. Outside on the football pitch, Anka and Roger are yet to emerge from the tunnel. Lampard is yet to run one on one with the keeper. The sky is yet to fall.

Janek is aware of being gripped by the shoulders. His brain is boiled, seared, served in his skull, topped with a sprig of mint. To him, the greying crowd that bay for his blood seem perfectly normal and happy; just another gang of geriatrics who bounce and gyrate to the beats and melodies of the N-Prang. He's held in front of Ian the Dickhead and can't help but stare up at the bloodless penis stump on his forehead.

'Janek,' says Ian, 'have a flick through these.'

Janek takes a stack of postcards from Ian and begins to look through them. He smiles at the first image, then, looking up, he notices that Ian is holding his nose in amusement, using a frantically pointing finger to inform the audience to watch Janek carefully. The first image shows a little boy, crying and naked in a dark cage. The little boy is sitting in a circle of his own blood. A small piece of timber attached to one of the bars has nine lines carved into it. Tears are falling from the little boy's granite stare. Janek looks at it carefully. Smiling. Listening to the very cool, high-spirited music. The driving music. The walking-to-work music. The sex music. The posing music. The just-let-go music. The second image depicts the aftermath of a car bomb in a desert state. An Arab has been blown limbless. A woman no longer has a head. Listen to this perfect party music. Listen carefully. It's so perfect for a party. So perfect for the bus, for the club, for the tube. The third image shows an old lady begging for cash on a British street. She's had the crap kicked out of her. She should have been listening to this well-wicked sex music. Totally she should. The fourth image is gang rape. Happy hardcore. The fourth is a child soldier, black skin, sunshine on his forehead, clinging to a Kalashnikov. Chill out. 100 per cent chill out. The fifth image is a mass grave. Hundreds of dirty dead scribbled together. Jazz. The blues. Dead bodies everywhere. Hip hop. Murder. Indie. Rape. Classical. War. Reggae. Genocide. Pop rock. Robbery. Janek stares down smiling at the mass grave, noticing, with amusement, that some of the dead are wearing football shirts dating back to England in the early 1990s. He glances up at Ian and at the members of the audience. In some part of Janek's brain a little man with claws, backache and a beanie hat whispers, soberly, 'What a joke. What a complete joke.' Out of the window, in the outside world, Anka emerges from the tunnel riding on Roger's back. Again, Janek smiles, listening to the good songs, staring at the mass murder, thinking of his unfair life.

'I get it,' he says, pulling the earphones from his ears and handing back the postcards. 'Yep. I accept all this completely.'

The dickhead places the cards into the inside pocket of his white blazer and looks a little confused. His back bends. He's leaning towards Janek with a rising face, saying, 'What do you mean?'

'I just mean,' says Janek, 'I'm not a great guy. Am I? I won't be the one to save anything. I'm not a great guy. Because I thought . . . No. No. Forget it. I understand.' Everyone is staring at him. 'But when we realise,' says Janek, 'when we finally realise what our little story is about. It's painful. Because . . . Because. I thought I was going to be all right. I really did. Even when I was dancing with my dead mum, I was thinking to myself, it's OK, Janek, don't worry, this is a low point, a strange point, clearly, but you're a good sort deep down, this is just a blip, you'll be fine in the end. But I'm not, am I? This is the end. And I'm some guy a dickhead made for a laugh in a laboratory and . . . well, that doesn't bother me at all. Not really. Whether I was made in a womb or a white room doesn't matter at all. What bothers me, what I regret, is not speaking up sooner. For example, when my world was changing, when everything I saw became so sexy and rhythmic, I should have said something. I should have said that I didn't believe. Not fully. But instead, I was telling myself to bear with it. I was thinking, sure, my life's like a sexy video, I'm losing the plot, but in the end I'll be fine. In the end I'll find, you know . . . In the end I'll find my way to the Fuck Festival. I was really serious about that. I genuinely wanted to be happy . . . but . . .' Janek holds out his hands in despair, pointing at the audience, at Ian the Dickhead, at Joe and Life. 'Now all this. And I'm just the guy with headphones in his ears, the guy who can't tell right from wrong, the guy who smiles at murder and giggles at gang rape . . . I'm a seriously good bassist. I am a seriously good bassist. There's a part of me that still loves Life, too. There's a part of me that still wants to make love to her, to crane my neck and watch it go in and out but . . . but when you're alive, while we're alive . . .' Janek pauses and stares fiercely at the ceiling and says, 'We are weighted down. We truly are, all of us. Life is what you make it? Is it fuck. We end up in rooms like this one, just thinking, how? How has this happened? And what you realise is that you barely had a choice. And the only real option is to obey. To nod my head. I can't tell right from wrong. Whatever. Sure, I can only sway along the streets, lost in my own shit. Talking bollocks. Misinterpreting pain. I'm a twat. I get it. Very clever. I'm an arsehole.' Janek pauses to put the headphones back into his ears. He points at Life. 'So,' he says, stuttering slightly, before clearing his throat and seemingly finding his rhythm and singing: 'So let's go, yo, I have spoken, take that ho and slice her open. I've shagged her, I have sucked her tits, so stab her, I won't give a shit.'

There is a round of generous applause. A few old couples turn to each other and nod with enthusiastic smiles. Good, they think. Good speech and a good rap to finish. Next to Janek on the stage, Ian looks a little worried. As if he too has been dragged here and had little choice in the matter. He thinks carefully about his dickhead past for a moment and then, apparently reassured, turns to the audience with renewed vigour. 'Yes, yes,' he shouts, clapping his hands. 'That was good. I enjoyed it, too. We did, I must admit, make these people extremely well. It will be nice, I'm sure, in the Wild World, to hear such heartfelt speeches concerning the nature of life and suchlike, as well as such lovely rap songs. It will, no doubt, be comforting, sweet and surely quite profound. Yes. Don't be shy. Give him a good clap.'

Janek nods hopelessly as old people applaud his effort. It's over. In the remains of his brain, he's thinking things, things like, life could be good, sure, I could have craned my neck each morning and each night and been a happy festival goer. Just in and out, in and out, in and out. I could have. I could. It would've been good.

'Now, ladies and gentlemen, like the young man said. Let's cut the stomach of this beautiful girl here. Step forward, Life.' Life is pushed forward by her guardian, causing Ian to smile broadly, saying, 'Oh, when I see you like this I'm reminded of how horny we all were when we made you. How we fought like schoolboys to sculpt your nipples and violate your once brainless body. Could you pull up your dress for me, Life?'

On the floor at Life's feet, Joe Aspen is crouched, staring down, both his fists full of perfectly white hair. He looks up when he hears Ian addressing her. Their eyes meet. His and Life's. Eyes. Both blue. I am not desperate to remember. But I can.

Life obediently pulls her red dress up over her knickers and holds it just below her breasts. Ian gulps and his stump twitches. He mutters, 'Yes, we were so horny.' Then he stares down at the knife in his hand.

'Lie, what are you doing?' says Joe, scrambling to his feet. 'Don't just let him.'

Ian, the former dickhead, holds the tip of the blade against Life's belly. The crowd are hushed. None of them notice when, outside, a piece of the sky falls and crushes a talented footballer. They're staring at Life's stomach, licking their lips, waiting for a moment of colour and revelation.

'Not too deep,' says Life. 'I want to survive. I just want to see.'

Joe is staring at her. Joe is dying to catch her eye. Those torn unwillingly from love will often die to catch their former lover's eye. Just for a second. Just long enough to stare like you could stare through flesh. To show them, with a desperate intensifying of your expression that you are still very much in love with them. To stare in such a way as to remind your former lover of the times, the good times and the quiet moments. The brilliant bits. When you whispered I love you. When the wind blew and you grabbed each other. When you behaved outrageously in tricksy bars. When you spoke sincerely of the future. Promised it to each other.

Without doubt. Promised it. Promised it in the day, holding hands in Manchester. Then, stirring in some rare hour of the night, forcefully re-entwining your bodies and promising it again.

'No,' says Life, turning to look at Joe. 'Whatever happens. You and I are over.'

Ian is weeping. Quite unexpectedly, he has started to cry.

'Now I just want proof,' Life mutters.

'We made you,' weeps the dickhead. 'We did. We were trying to be cool. We were horny. We made you.'

The tip of the knife is pressing hard against Life's stomach.

'No,' says Joe, shrugging and sweeping his white hair backwards off his face. 'That's just it. That's the amazing thing. You didn't. We are real. That's what's so sad.'

Joe grabs Ian by the wrist. He does not flinch. He yanks the former dickhead's hand towards him, pulling every inch of the knife inside him. Ian immediately lets go of the handle and begins to back away from Joe's pierced stomach. Not daring to look down at the wound, Joe reaches out and grabs Ian by the collar of his shirt and stares into his eyes and then at the stump. The remains. The delicate testicles. Joe grits his teeth and he smiles. 'It's red,' he hisses, still not looking down. 'It's red, isn't it? Isn't it? It's red.'

Releasing Ian, Joe sways round like a skittle preparing to fall. He looks at Life. She's watching quite calmly. In her eyes, Joe can see the future. Life's future, without him. She will, he can tell, mourn him for a while, be sad for a bit, then go on. Quietly continue. This is how it will be. He wants to say he loves her. He can't. She wouldn't reply. He would die in the middle of an awkward silence. Those terrible seconds that wait for love. For a verdict.

Joe just falls to the floor, breathing some shallow, closing breaths. On the other side of the stage, near to where Janek is tapping his foot and nodding his head, Joe can see little Sally. He smiles. She's playing with the severed penis of Marlon Brando. Pushing it in front of her and then crawling after it eagerly. Beak is playing too and it looks like fun. Joe's happy because they're happy.

Rolling onto his stomach he pulls himself in the direction of the travel seat and, reaching in, succeeds in removing the yellow corpses of Dolly and Sam the Man. It's then that he feels Life's hands on his shoulder and happiness for the last time. She helps to pull him back round onto his back and they stare at each other. Joe holds up the two corpses to show her. He hasn't got the strength to tell Life their names. He just shakes them at her, hopefully, trying to mime some meaning with their weak little bodies. Life just shakes her head. She'd like to speak but fears what she'd say. Instead, she watches as Joe turns onto his side and stands the two corpses up on the floor, holding each of them under their arms. She watches as he begins to bounce them in the direction of each other, like children do with dolls or action figures to make them walk. She watches as Joe makes the two corpses meet and then presses their faces together gently. Joe turns to her and smiles. His smile is real normal. Life watches as the corpses kiss.

I AM JOE Aspen. I might have told you so at the beginning but it didn't feel right. Keeping pointless secrets is a popular reason to live. Although, I should say, I did not live. I did not survive. I pulled that knife into my stomach. And I died.

It was a silly thing to do, kill myself. It was also pretty pointless. You see, I couldn't bring myself to stare at my wound to see what colour I was bleeding. If my blood had been black I would've been so disappointed. I would have been stumbling round that banqueting suite, dying, unloved and so pissed off. I'm a wet really. I couldn't have handled it. So instead I kept my eyes averted from the truth and made Dolly's dead body kiss Sam the Man's. After a minute or so I found I couldn't move any part of me. I stopped breathing. I'm dead, I thought to myself, I'm a corpse.

Death is not what you might think. Death is like the ultimate form of politeness. Something happens to you, like you have a heart attack, crash a car, jump off a high building or pull a knife into your stomach and it's as if your whole body gets stage fright. You freeze. You shit

303

yourself. You stop breathing. You worry a little bit. And then above you people start crying and talking to each other like you can't hear. But you can. You can see them too. It's quite embarrassing. Because they're talking to each other, saying stuff about how you were a good guy, an honest guy, a sweet guy, a confused guy who died too young, who loved life too much, who loved Life too much, who would have been more suited to earlier times when we, the humans, were closer to the natural world. I tried to speak but I couldn't. I just had to lie there and listen. I couldn't even blush.

Luckily, they put me into a coffin quite quickly. Nail me in, I was thinking, nail me in so I don't have to listen to this any more. But they didn't. They left me in a room in an open-top coffin. People came in to chat to my corpse. Life came in. Janek. Roger and Anka came by and kissed as if I wasn't there. Even Ian came, wearing Janek's beanie to cover up his stump. He seemed upset. He seemed insane. Each of them banged on about their problems. They banged on about the colour of human blood, the beauty of human semen, the problem with leading lives, the pain involved in love. If I wasn't dead already, this would've killed me, or at least sent me to sleep. But I listened. I did. I listened carefully as they dribbled the plot of this story onto me. Dribbled it into my coffin. And it was as I was staring up at Life, listening as she moaned about living, that I suddenly became aware that my ability to move was coming back to me. I could feel it in my fingers. I became sure that if I wished, I could reach up and touch her. I was sure I'd be able to speak, too. I could have told her to shut up, to drop it, to face it – life's painful. But I didn't. I just lay there like a corpse in a school play, only one that wouldn't be getting up to take a bow and smile at the clapping. Fuck it, I thought. It would be impolite. Dead as I am, it would be impolite. That's what clinched it. If people go to the trouble of dressing you in fresh clothes and laying you in a coffin, of weeping over you and gripping your cold hands with theirs, then the least you can do is pretend to be dead. It is only polite, I thought to myself, as I watched the wooden lid move over me. It is only polite, I thought, as the lights went out, as the sound of weeping quietened and the hammer began to bang.

I have written this story in my own blood. For paper, I have used the calendar that Life placed beside me shortly before the lid was closed. I have written over images of wildlife. Let me say that again. Imagine I'm shouting. I am. I have written over images of wildlife. Photographs of puffins, crocodiles and great white sharks. I have written blind, not knowing the colour of my ink. Red or black. Dead or alive. Dogged, even in death, by these are old-fashioned concerns.

It wasn't long after I was buried that I experimented with moving for the first time. I thought about trying it during my funeral, which I could hear only faintly as it took place beyond these wooden walls. But I figured that would have been as impolite as it gets. That would have been a total piss-take. So I lay quietly and tried to decipher the speeches and enjoy the hymns. It wasn't until afterwards when I could feel the silent soil packed tightly around me that I dared to knock-knock on the lid above my face. I suppose I was shocked. I knock-knocked. Still living. I scratch. I have two, maybe three more things to say.

Why am I still alive?

Why?

I don't know. Not for sure. But during these dark, tight-fitting days I have thought a lot. An image keeps recurring in the black. A human being, all four of its limbs knotted together like ribbons. A firm tug on a foot or a hand and the human unravels. It unties. It lies inert on the floor. *The last thing they gave us, as a present, I mean, was ourselves.*

I know what you're thinking. You're thinking that the ink is black, that my blood is black, that I was made in a laboratory by ironic arseholes with no sense of grace. That's why I'm still alive. I was sculpted by a tit-wrench with no sense of honour. That's why the dickhead's knife didn't finish me off. Why I continue to talk.

Maybe, maybe.

Knock. Scratch.

But I think back on those days and I wonder whether something different wasn't happening. Is it possible to love yourself too much? If every fat inch of your proud brain was bent in that way, enchanted by itself, could an individual learn to cheat the ancient hobby of death? I think they could. I think I have. I think that's what this is. I bet I'm not the only talking corpse down here. I bet if I lay still I could hear others, tapping sentimentally on the lids of their coffins, muttering about themselves, their shit-shifting personality, their life, about how their time on earth was too short-lived, about how that's a shame, a real shame. We think too highly of ourselves, our self-love outlasts our condemned bodies. While alive, we make ourselves so real. Too real. Unkillable. Unlikeable. The dickhead was right. Whether we're robots or humans, I don't reckon it matters. We're a wacky bunch. Too wild for death. Roger Hart was right, too: we'll talk ourselves stupid, write ourselves pointless, staring at screens, ripping new arseholes for ourselves, describing them, marvelling. We're bullshitters, nowadays. Expert at describing but not at living. I guess it's no big deal. Just passing thoughts. The only thing that matters is the journey of our heart.

I'm glad I died so full of frustration and young love. I feel it draining out of me down here. It fertilises the soil. It cannot be recaptured. Pain fades like a pop song. To silence. To this.

I like to imagine my gravestone above me. I hope it says: 'Here lies Joe Aspen. He was only joking.' But I bet it doesn't. It's probably just my dates. Jesus, I died young. Dickhead!

Let the Wild World burn. Let the rest of them burn. Roger, Anka, Janek. Let them go on and on with you and the others. You can enjoy the world. I know you can. Make it fun. It is not mine. Me, I'm wondering what became of baby Sally. I'm wondering what became of Beak. I hope he grows up to be a good cat. A cool cat. Did Dolly and Sam the Man get decent burials? They should have been cremated or buried together. I should have seen to it. And then of course, there's her. I wonder what became of her. She broke what chews and spits my blood. My red blood. My black blood. She broke my blah-blah. I am lifeless. In every sense. I am without Life.

And this story. It's over. What colour is the text? Tell me it's red. Go on, don't be mean, tell me it's red. I can dip fingers into my wound and hold them an inch from my eyes. But there's not even a speck of light down here. I can't see. So fuck it.

Let me shut my eyes softly like a good corpse should. Let me cross my arms and flatten my hands across my chest.

Yes, this is how it should be, perfectly polite and convincing. I was a fool to pull that knife inside me. I was in love. We are. We are in love. I was a dickhead. We are!

I died. I did. For life. For *it*. For *her*. And now I'm alone. I'm off. I'm going off. I'm fucking off. Because I stink. I stink of memory. And the pop song is all but sunk in silence. I have nothing but my memories of wildlife. Nothing but this grave, this description and this joke. Yes, that is it; this joke.

www.vintage-books.co.uk